HOW TO OVERCOME APOCALYPTIC EVENTS

BRANDON LEMAR BASS

COPYRIGHT & PERMISSION

BLB Productions
An imprint of DoubleB Publishing, LLC
161 Senator Street.
Springfield, Massachusetts 01129

Copyright © 2022 by DoubleB Publishing, LLC

All rights are reserved. No part of this book may be reproduced, stored, or transmitted by any means whatsoever—whether auditory, graphic, mechanical, or electronic—without the written permission or consent of the author, except in the case of brief excerpts used in critical articles and reviews. The unauthorized reproduction of any part of this work is illegal and is punishable by law.
Copyright laws are different around the world. If you're not located in the U.S., check with your local laws before using this book.
Fictitious disclaimer – This is just our advice; you do your own research.

Library of Congress Cataloging-in-Publication Data
Bass, Brandon LeMar, author.
How to Overcome Apocalyptic Events / Brandon LeMar Bass
Includes Index.
LCCN: 2022911209
ISBN: 979-8-9864444-0-6 (Hardback) 979-8-9864444-1-3 (Paperback) 979-8-9864444-2-0 (Audio) 979-8-9864444-3-7 (Digital) 979-8-9864444-4-4 (Ebook)

Non-authorship activities performed on public domain items—so-called "sweat of the brow" work—don't create a new copyright. That means nobody can claim new copyright on a public domain item for, among other things, work like digitization, markup, or typography. Regardless, to dispel any possible doubt on the copyright status of this book. The contributors release this book under the terms in the CC0 1.0 Universal Public Domain Dedication, thus dedicating it to the worldwide public domain all of the work they've done on this book, including but not limited to metadata, the title page, imprint, colophon, this Uncopyrighted, and any changes or enhancements to, or markup on, the original text and artwork. This dedication doesn't change the copyright status of the underlying works, which, though believed to already be in the U.S. public domain, may not yet be in other countries' public domain.

Website: https://linktr.ee/smoothdoubleb

MESSAGE FROM SPIRIT

"It's your time. You know it is, so why are you doubting me and especially yourself? I know it might look terrifying out in the world. I know you may not have a true connection with your inner world. No matter what, we'll always be there for you. Through all your highs and lows. Through your ups and downs. Guess what? We're still here and we have your back. Don't focus on the outer world and start focusing on what truly matters; yourself. Know more about yourself, your likes, your dislikes, your talents, skills, etc. Your light shines brighter than your shadows. Show the world your light. What are you so afraid of? Sure, people may judge, may have their opinions about you, or will criticize you; but there's no measure in the amount of abundance you'll receive from being your authentic self. I know most of you have hidden talents, skills, and creations you dream about, think about, and talk to me about. Well, luckily for you, this is your confirmation. It's time for you to express yourself wholeheartedly. The only person who's stopping you is yourself. Don't let other people's views, opinions, and judgment hinder you from expressing your true self. If you let people do these things to you, then you'll run further away from your true mission and purpose here on earth. That's why I placed you down here right? To make you express yourself while doing your missions and purposes. So why aren't you doing it? You have to trust yourself. You'll never accomplish your goals and dreams by being scared and playing it safe. It's your time.

— Spirit

IMPRINTS

This book is intended for anyone who's in a collapsing system because of their government officials. Anyone who's looking for answers, questioning reality, and/or having a spiritual awakening; this book is for you. This will help your ascension process and give you the necessary tools to help create your reality. You're the co-creator of your reality, and it's time to reclaim your power. These characters in this book are relatable, so, it'll help your progression. What these characters go through and the issues they face are what people are going through right now. You're not in solitude, and you're enough. You're more than superfluous, and you have to feel that in your soul, spirit, heart, and mind to generate that energy from yourself. It's okay to be solivagant because that time alone is necessary.

This book is about a group of real people, real feelings, real emotions, going through multiple apocalyptic events that are occurring. We go through each character's past lives, childhood traumas, and what they experience before the events occur. You'll see that based on their childhood, karmic debt, and traumatic experiences affect their life decisions. Their decision-making is crucial during apocalyptic events because it's life or death. This book is more than apocalyptic events on a physical plane, but also from an internal plane as well. This book tells real stories and real problems of what people go through on a day-to-day basis. Connect deeply with the characters since most people have convergence dilemmas. This will make you feel for the characters and what they must go through internally and externally. On top of that, the characters must go through their disarray to survive. The main characters will have to team up because of what takes place throughout the story. Will jealousy and envy get in the way? Find out and see in How to Overcome Apocalyptic Events!

DEDICATION AND SPECIAL THANKS

I want to thank Smooth Doubleb for illustrating and hosting this book.

I want to thank the people that helped me create this book.

I want to thank God within that gave me the strength to make this dream come into reality.

I want to thank my Higher Self for giving me this download through deep meditation.

I want to thank the Universe for guiding me in the right direction.

I want to thank my Spirit Guides who gave me different ideas throughout this process.

I want to thank my spiritual team for saving this project and not allowing dark entities to get ahold of it.

I want to thank my supporters; I deeply appreciate your support.

I want to thank the reader who's reading this; thank you so much!

I want to thank the listener who's listening to this; thank you so much!

I want to thank my family/friends for allowing me to take the time out in creating this book.

I want to thank myself for executing this goal of mine.

I want to thank all the people who gave me guidance in publishing my first official book.

I want to thank all the companies, narrators, designers, and editors who helped me along this journey in publishing this book.

If I missed anyone, whoever's reading or listening, thank you for everything you do.

TABLE OF CONTENTS

MESSAGE FROM SPIRIT 3
IMPRINTS 4
DEDICATION AND SPECIAL THANKS 5
CHAPTER ONE: Lucky 7's 1
    Character 1: Indigo 1
    Character 2: Apollo 25
    Character 3: Aleemic 40
    Character 4: Joey 57
    Character 5: Indiniya 70
    Character 6: Bastet 84
    Character 7: Aqua 101

CHAPTER TWO: The Beginning 114
CHAPTER THREE: Time to Play the Game 152
CHAPTER FOUR: Apocalyptic Events 201
CHAPTER FIVE: Disaster & Turmoil 218
CHAPTER SIX: The Awakening 235
CHAPTER SEVEN: The Chosen One 245
APPENDIX/ENDNOTES 255
BRIEF OVERVIEW OF MY OTHER BOOKS: 258
    Raising Energy by Meditation, Frequency, and Vibration: 259
    Grandma Got Ran Over by Santa: 268
    Winning With Women: 272
    My Autobiography 278

ABOUT THE AUTHOR 280
QUOTE FROM A CLIENT 282
END COVER PAGE 284

Chapter One

LUCKY 7'S

Character 1: Indigo

Welcome to "How to Overcome Apocalyptic Events" with your host and illustrator, Smooth Doubleb. I want to give my introduction in the beginning before we dive deep into these various rabbit holes and characters. How about we get started. Before we start with our first character, I'll give my poem from Smooth Doubleb: how does that sound? *Audience cheers.* Yes, I have my live studio audience right here.

Love. Where do I start, where do I begin? Is it real? Is it fake? Is it even true now? It's up to you to decide. Just like life, love is, what it is. If it's all of a sudden, then that person is weighing two options: you and someone else. Then when you take that mentality, just to protect yourself, now there's going to be an innocent person who you might get with and do them the same way because of naïve. Then the cycle continues and that's why it never stops. I like how people change, but memories don't. You could be with someone and feel like it's the closest you've ever been with a person. Or they can feel a million miles away, as we lay wide awake. Now you drive by like a car with a strap in it. Every time I think of you, you bring ice to my veins just like D'Angelo Russell. Every time I see you, you bring heat to the brain, call it a fever. I have now taken my focus and care about people off and put my focus and care on people who are going to help me in my future. If you want to take something out of this poem, take it and leave with this: You don't even need a gun, you don't even need a pill, if you ever want to die, fall in enamoring and you'll get kilt, pow.

I'm not choosing death, it's just if I don't go, I wouldn't know what it's like to be alive.

It's not hard to convince someone that you love them if you know what they want to hear. How can I judge anything you've done when it's not so different from the things I've done? If I let myself forgive and just be happy with you, with all the light and good that comes with your bad, what kind of boyfriend would that make me?

Real love doesn't evaporate when things get hard. Sometimes a man gets exactly what he wishes for and that can be the perfect punishment of all. Some men say they pick up women but let them walk past without saying a word. Talk a lot of game in your head but won't say it out loud. Then have the nerve to look back at it and stare when they walk by.

Some women spend all this time in the mirror getting dressed just to go out and curve men all night. Then go back home lonely and complain about men again.

Isn't it crazy how the ones that don't want us, we want them? Then the ones that want us, we don't give them any look. The craziest thing is that looks can only go so far. Looks and this glob of meat fades out, so make that time to get to know the ones who want to get to know you. Hey, maybe they'll change your life. After all, the most beautiful gift can come in the plainest box. Thank you. So, let's dive into one of the main characters named Indigo.

What a beautiful divine soul Indigo truly is. At the beginning of his life, he had to go through a lot of hardship and pain to be here today. Let's start from the beginning, right out of his mother's womb.

While his mother (named Sherly) was pregnant with Indigo, she already knew what it'll be like to have a newborn. His mom gave birth to his future sister named Sandy. Indigo's father (named Jerry) is used to being a dad since he already had a son named Barry. Barry had a different mother because Jerry had a kid when he was only 16 years old. We'll get to all these characters eventually.

It was a long nine months for Indigo's mother and the whole family was excited about the big reveal. At this moment in time, his parents were already married for three years now, and Sandy was currently four years old.

His parents were preparing to have another daughter because of all the stuff they already had for Sandy. Sherly was manifesting to have a son because she never had a son before. It's always a 50/50 chance of having a son or daughter. At the baby shower, his future aunt got it right. They were going to have a baby boy.

In the external world, it was a special time as people were rebelling because they thought the world was going to end that year. Sherly didn't pay attention to it because she was waiting for her child to be born. As any woman knows while being pregnant, there are things you can and cannot do. You can keep exercising, eat healthier, and speak to your future baby. Things you shouldn't execute are doing drugs, alcohol, and negative actions that'll affect the child as a whole. Caffeine, alcohol, sugar, and nicotine are all proven, pain killers. By sedating your pain, instead of dealing with it, people continue to go down a negative path on their journey.

People use drugs, pills from the big pharma, drink alcohol (which are dark spirits entering your body), and smoke just to cope. You can tell when someone's mad or doesn't want to talk about something when they drink from a glass and pour up some more shots.

People tend to pop a pill, snort, and do different types of drugs because it seems "cool" and everyone famous does it. Most of these rappers and celebrities aren't killing, robbing, and doing drugs like how they say they are. They want to push the narrative of your auspicious celebrities doing them, so you can do them too. That's why all these so-called celebrities call themselves "influencers" because they influence their viewers. You never really see these celebrities getting in trouble while you're the one who goes to jail. Celebrities go to celebrity jails which are underground caves to perform different rituals, sacrifices, and cloning.

Keep robbing, stealing, and killing people and see what happens. When you're in court, you can't say a rapper made you do it. It doesn't work like that because you're in control over your mind and body. I didn't add the word soul because people have sold their souls.

People tend to listen to everything their doctors tell them to do just like how the mainstream media tells sheep what to believe. They tell them what to do, feel, or act. A lot of people are just sheep in wolf's clothing. They use regular hardworking people as their pets, test dummies, and robots. If you keep taking these artificial, useless, and poisonous big pharma pills, then you'll never heal from your rooted problem. That's why people use various amounts of pills as they grow older. They need so much because none of them work. The more they take, the more temporary feeling they receive. They say to take two every four-six hours (for example) because you need to keep taking them to be in a state of comfortability.

Pharmaceutical drugs are witchcraft. The word pharmacy comes from the Greek work pharmika, which means magic, sorcery, and enchantment. Your doctor got through medical school not because they were smart, but because they could memorize and repeat huge amounts of raw data. Memorizing that much info left little time for actual critical thought. It created the perfect credible drone army to regurgitate corporate pharmaceutical propaganda with zero critical thinking. Doctors are big pharma sales reps. People are reluctant to bear the pain, to suffer the discomfort, to wait patiently upon the processes of life, while these correct the situation. Instead, people reach for a pain killer, a tranquilizer, a cathartic, an antipyretic, or some other poison to smother the discomforts and add to their troubles.

Hence people drink, smoke, and take pills every day. It's just a way to hide and pull down their true problems, so they won't deal with them at that moment. Drinking spirits will allow these dark entities to have control over your body. That's why most people black out, faint, can't remember what they did last night or have a massive crash in the morning. This can lead to putting your health and life in jeopardy. This could cause you to drink while driving which can cause an accident. Or this can mean someone bringing a male or female back home and forcing sexual assault or rape. This can lead to passing aids and STDs (which stand for sexually transmitted demons). The demons can be the spirits after drinking or the person's demons.

If a person is still healing from something, still has major issues, and their DNA and RNA aren't divine, then you'll have to watch out for those people as well. Watch who you have sex with because those demons can be passed on to you.

People are slowly turning into zombies as they keep taking these toxic big pharma items into their system. They're losing brain cells and lowering their consciousness level.

As melanated beings, we have the strongest, most powerful, and divine DNA and RNA out there. That's why they do all their main tactics on the black community because they view them as being the devil or evil. They see us as satanic and a disgrace in this world. That's why people talk about white privilege because some people still think we're in slavery.

That's why people sag their pants. Sagging started in slavery when the homosexual slave master would rape young black slaves. It's called buck breaking. You were forced to wear your pants below your waist so other homosexual slave owners would know you were already buck broken. They did this by actively and sexually abusing black slaves publicly and in front of other slaves to assert dominance.

Most African American or "black" people are afraid of water or don't know how to swim because of our history. Slave masters dumped our ancestors in water, drowned them, and traveled to newer slave trades across the sea.

When slavery is mentioned, too many people automatically think of whites enslaving blacks. That's not even one-tenth of the story of slavery (which existed on every inhabited continent). The very word 'slave' derives from the word for some white people who were enslaved on a mass scale. The Slavs had slaves for more centuries than moors who were enslaved in the Western Hemisphere.

Every other earthly race is just collateral damage for them. Even though the race agenda is an illusion; DNA and RNA are different. You couldn't teach them how to connect with the stars because their skin isn't made out of stardust. You cannot teach them how to connect with the solar system because they don't have a soul. You cannot teach them how to connect with nature because they're not natural. Only purebloods will survive because of the radiation that's being unleashed right at this moment. People are becoming sick due to the high UV radiation, gamma rays, and not having a connection with the sun.

Melanin is worth more than gold. Melatonin is the fundamental unit of the Universe and exists in four forms: cosmic, planetary, plant kingdom (chlorophyll), and animal kingdom melanin. Melatonin is made out of the triple layers of darkness which is based on the laws of physics and metaphysical anatomy. Once we let go of the programs, we'll become chaotic beings that generate electricity that the sovereign draconians are scared of since that'll unlock our powers. Melanin is black because its chemical structure allows no energy to escape making black melanin the super absorber of energy and light. Melanin is ubiquitous in almost every organ of the body and is necessary for the brain and nerves to operate, the eyes to see, and cells to reproduce. Melanin can rearrange its chemical structure to absorb all energy across the radiant energy spectrum (i.e., sunlight, x-rays, music, sound, radar, radio waves, etc.). The "black" human can charge up his or her melanin just by being in the sun, around the right type of musical sounds, or other energy sources. Melanin itself (on a philosophical plane), is a black biological door that the life force of African spirituality passes through in moving from the spirit to the material realm. Even though some melanin people can easily change their divine DNA and RNA as well. You're only limited by your philosophies.

Only the black African woman has all the genetic DNA variations to produce every skin tone, different eye colors, and different hair texture. No other race can do that except duplicate their kind. Every scientist has admitted that all of us come from Africa, so that means the black woman is the mother of the human race. That's why they speak negatively about black women in general because they know their true beauty. They want to lower their self-esteem and view other people as the beauty standard. That's why for many years, it's been other races being publicized while black people were condemned.

The Gods are electrical beings composed of six protons, six neutrons, and six electrons at our core. The Gods are made up of dark matter energy which manifests in this material realm as carbon. Carbon used to vibrate green, blue, or red in the ancient days of the planet Klin. In current times, God's pigmentations now vibrate brown or copper due to the electromagnetic field PF. The planet beings were knocked out of balance ever since the great invasion of 1492. Being electrical, the Gods require electricity to properly function. The avatars of the Gods are highly advanced, being able to perform things that completely defy the laws of physics. The avatars of the Gods can still operate without electricity but will have access to only 10% of their body. The avatar they're leading will perform in a zombie-like state. The other 90% is being disconnected from the God race and hidden in hue which is known as junk DNA.

Sherly felt this tug and pull, then her water broke, and it was finally time for Indigo to come out of his mother's womb. Jerry rushed to bring

Sherly to the hospital, and he got pulled over by the police. His speed was 75 miles per hour and when cars got in the way or someone cuts Jerry off, he'll have road rage. He would start talking under his breath at first and if the driver looks at him wrong, he'll flip them off. If the driver talks back to Jerry, he'll roll down the window and start cussing at the person. Luckily for Jerry, no one was furious enough to pull out a gun or fight him.

So, Jerry told the officer that his wife was pregnant and had to rush to the hospital. The police officer understood the hindrance and gave them a police escort. I feel like people are the kindest when someone's about to give birth, when someone's about to die, and when someone wants something from someone.

So, they made it to the hospital and Sherly was checked in. After a few days of being in the hospital, Sherly was getting nervous because of all the what-ifs caused by overthinking. Not knowing those what-ifs could enter her reality and cause a negative manifestation. This is a perfect example of regular human tendencies of not living in the now. People tend to be in their heads and let their minds take over their bodies. That's why logic and emotions are different.

Have you ever seen a Ying Yan symbol? Ask someone who wears it, do they know the meaning of it? Most people would either say it's for fashion or balance. It's more than just balance. As you notice that on the white side, it has a black dot, and on the black side, it has a white dot. In this representation, without one side, you still have to notice the other side. You can't be or stay on one side or the other. Doing that will make you unbalanced and unaligned with life. Nikola Tesla 369 shows proof of it Let me give you an example; there must be a balance between the two. Do you focus on pleasing other people's feelings instead of your true feelings? That's putting other people above you and making yourself second. Then your ego would say, "Oh I love myself, I already know this," but your Higher Self knows something's wrong. Even though your ego likes to stay stagnant and act like everything's okay when in reality, you're burying your true self. You don't want to grieve or hold onto anything as we keep ascending. This will hinder your spiritual growth and you won't learn your lesson until you properly do your inner work. You must dethrone the issue at hand to step back into your truest power to become decisive.

The doctors knew it was time for Indigo to come out. The doctors thought it was just a regular baby popping out of the womb, but this situation was devastating. The doctors were ready to pull Indigo out, but they noticed every time they tried to pull him out, it wasn't working. They looked at the X-Ray and saw that his umbilical cord was wrapped around Indigo's neck. For anyone that doesn't know, the umbilical cord provides oxygen and is connected to the placenta. Also, the umbilical cord connects the newborn child to their past lives, spiritual roots, and the highest of realms. See why doctors cut the umbilical cords of newborn babies?

Having a water birth for a child is much more sustainable and efficient. Since these doctors get paid basically to inject you with poisonous toxins throughout your body. They do this because when you're born, you're closest to the Divine Spirit and fully awakened. That's why kids have imaginary friends who are their Task Guides. Say if a child sees or hears something under their bed or in their closet. It's because their senses are heightened, and their first eye is completely opened. They're tapping into those frequencies where they can hear, see, and experience other lifeforms around them. Inner experiences show them a side of reality others are oblivious to. Each step of their journey is made by following the heart instead of the crowd. By choosing knowledge over the veils of ignorance.

That's why they want you to eat fast food, baby food, and other measures that'll make you unaware of your awakening. Dairy products are the most mucus-forming foods and refined sugar is the second most. Both of these products and ingredients will cause excessive congestion build-up through your tissues. Yeast, fungi, and worms love to feed and thrive in these congestions without decay.

How to decalcify the pineal gland? Eliminate certain foods and environmental factors that are causing additional calcification. Ditch your nonstick cookware and other PFCs. Most non-stick coatings are fluoride-based substances that are both toxic and calcifying just like fluoride toothpaste and tap water. Don't trust all these so-called vegan items because some brands aren't who they say they are. It's there to differentiate people into thinking they're eating vegan when they aren't. Avoid chemicals in processed foods, especially synthetic calcium phosphate.

Everyone's awakened, but a lot of people haven't recognized or realized it yet. When you're born, they offer you something called vitamin k, which isn't a vitamin at all. It's presumed to stop immerging. You don't give blood tests for respiratory issues. Most people nowadays need vitamin d because they no longer have a connection with the sun. Fortunately, some babies are born with spiritual immune systems that sooner or later give rejection to the illusory worldview grafted upon them from birth through social conditioning. They begin to sense something is amiss and will start looking for answers. In reality, there's no "immune" system.

Rather, there's a continuous concerted effort on the part of all systems to maintain the body in a state of health.

Whatever you focus on grows. Whatever you allow into your senses will enter your reality. Some people work on alchemy which can turn something negative into a positive. It's all about setting intentions, being pure, and finding what brings you the most joy. The alchemist is the one who transforms all energies into higher frequencies of light and love. They're the bringers of a new dawn, transmuting the old paradigms into higher intelligence and order. Love is the only master they answer to. To love who you are, you cannot hate the experiences that shaped you. You may encounter many defeats, but you must not be defeated. Everything's happening for you, not to you. Everything happens for a reason and a season. The greatest challenge in life is being yourself in a world trying to make you like everyone else. Love the people who saw you when you were invisible to everyone else. There's no giving up; you'll always come out on the other side.

If you believe something's happening to you and you're affected by that, then that's being a victim with a slave mentality. Don't ask why this is happening but ask what lessons you're learning. Stop playing the victim card and take ownership and accountability for yourself. Don't play the blame game either. Stop allowing your old self to creep in and don't allow people to bring you back to that mindset. Don't let other people's words affect you while you're trying to kill your old self to renew your true self. You can only achieve what you put your mind to. Now decide whether you want to be a loser or you want to conquer the world.

Your sensitivity is an asset. You're not isolated from this world, and your soul tribe said they'll meet you on earth. It's better to walk alone than with a crowd going in the wrong direction. Walk your path and align with the right people. If you expect the world to be fair with you because you're fair, you're fooling yourself. That's like expecting the lion not to eat you because you didn't eat him. We didn't come here with anything, so leave here with nothing.

Owning your feelings, rather than blaming them on someone else is the mark of a person who has moved from contracted to expanded awareness. Your mind is a magnet and what you think, you become. What you feel, you attract. What you imagine, you create. If you think of blessings in your life, you'll attract blessings. If you think of problems, you'll attract problems.

What comes, let it come. What goes, let it go. What stays, let it stay. Always cultivate good thoughts and always remain positive, hopeful, and optimistic. Keep your thoughts positive because your thoughts become your words. Keep your words positive because your words become your behavior. Keep your behavior positive because your behavior becomes your habit. Keep your habits positive because your habits become your values. Keep your values positive because your values become your destiny.

You'll lose a lot of friends when you get serious about your life. That's why the Bugatti has two seats, and a bus has 30. Stay focused with no distractions to achieve your goals. Even though goals are seemingly endpoints, there are never endpoints. So instead of setting goals, set achievements and keep working towards greatness.

Desiderata go placidly amid the noise and the haste but remember what placid there is in being silent. It's better to be silent than to dispute with the ignorant. As much as possible, without surrender, be on good terms with all persons. Speak your truth quietly and clearly. Listen to others, even to the dull and the ignorant since they too have their own story. Avoid loud and aggressive people; they are vexatious to the spirit. If you compare yourself to others, you may become vain or bitter, for always there'll be a greater and lesser person than yourself. You have no right to compare yourself to anyone for you don't know their whole story.

Enjoy your achievements as well as your plans. Keep yourself interested in your career, however, humbleness is a real possession in the changing fortunes of time. Exercise caution in your business affairs, for the world is full of trickery. Let this not blind you to how much virtue there is. Many people strive for high ideals, and everywhere in life, there's heroism. Be yourself and don't feign affection. Create your path and live your life unapologetically. Neither be cynical about love in the face of all aridity and disenchantment, it's as perennial as the grass. Take kindly the counsel of the years, gracefully surrendering the things of youth.

Nurture strength of spirit to shield you in sudden misfortune, but don't distress yourself with dark imaginings. Many fears are born of fatigue and loneliness. Beyond a wholesome discipline, be gentle with yourself. You're a child of the Universe no less than the trees and the stars. You have a right to be here. Whether or not it's clear to you, no doubt the Universe is unfolding as it should. Therefore, be at serenity with God, whatever you conceive them to be. Whatever your labors and aspirations in the noisy confusion of life, keep peace in your soul. With all its sham, drudgery, and broken dreams, it's still a beautiful world. Be cheerful and strive to be happy. You're growing in a direction that makes you thrive.

When you die don't go to the light because that would be reincarnation. They promote and exploit it to people for them to translucent when they either die or are about to die. They want to place that program inside your mind to have everyone go to the light.

In this case, Indigo's cord was wrapped around his neck, so every time they pulled, he loses oxygen. The doctors needed to get him out because Indigo could die if he stayed in his mother's womb. It was a lose-lose situation, but desperate times equal desperate measures. As the doctors contemplated what to do next, Jerry proceeded to go to an empty closet within the hospital and started to pray. Miracles happen when you're at the lowest moments of your life as you call out for help.

Indigo didn't want to come down to this earth even though he had to for humanity, face his karma, and learn his lessons. God kicked Indigo down upon the earth. Everyone who comes down to this earth plane has karma and certain lessons you'll have to face while experiencing this earth realm. In this case, the dark entities tried to stop Indigo from entering this earth dome because of what he'll achieve. Everything in your life is already preplanned before birth. There was a contract between your guides and yourself in seeing what you'll experience. Even through hardship and trouble, you shall prevail because the Universe wouldn't put you through a situation that you cannot overcome. Since everything's preplanned, you'll have to comprehend why you made those decisions before birth and how it impacts your life. You know the truth and the truth will set you free.

Don't dwell on the past and don't worry about the future because what Zen has taught me is to be in the here and now. Be at one with your past, accept it, but don't run away from it. The here and now vs. the present moment is two different ideologies. The biggest difference between the two is that in the here and now you'll become one with the activity you're doing. For the present moment, you're just presently there, but your mind and soul could be elsewhere. Whereas your mind, body, and soul are focused on the activities you're doing in the here and now.

Earth is an experience and we as spiritual beings have to come down here to have a temporary human experience. We're the volunteers who have to help those who are still trapped in this chaotic system. On earth, we wouldn't be able to remember anything from before. It was designed that way in such ignorance and darkness. Remembering who you truly are takes real mastery.

Earth has its own set of laws that everyone agreed to experience. For example, gravity; whatever goes up must come down, nuclear time, and days followed by night. If gravity cannot sink an egg in salt water, then it's not gravity that makes things fall, but density does. Proving that gravity is a lie.

For manifesting we could instantly manifest in the spiritual realm, but here on earth, it was a delay. The delay made the earth so difficult

Before going to earth, you would choose your family, whether you wanted to be male or female, what race you wanted to be, your location on the planet, and things of that nature. It's like choosing your character or creating an avatar in a videogame. You would enter the earth as a baby and be solely dependent on others to teach you the moral code. Since no one could remember the rules, they made up their own rules by instilling fear to give up our power. It wasn't fun for most people. Gatekeepers get to watch people on earth go about this life wrong and it was funny for them. Here are these magnificent beings playing the most unique cutting-edge experience the Universe had to offer, and they were clueless. Atavism Gods and Goddesses would try to guide people in the right direction as much as they can. We're more than just Gods and Goddesses because we were the ones that created everything; even them. Hence, they made us come down to earth to help ascend the planet.

Your spiritual team can communicate with you, but sometimes you cannot hear them. They would impulsively pose synchronicities to help guide you, but some people don't recognize the signs. People didn't trust themselves and that's why we sent out a call for help.

The first volunteers who came down had it worst because they killed them. Those on earth cannot comprehend what the volunteers were telling them. The idea of them being equal scared them. Everything the volunteers were telling them was commonsense. All the answers you seek are within you and everything they can do, you can do, plus more. Once they killed them, they would twist the volunteer's message and create an even more fearful state in humanity. For example, the saying, "God is inside you" got twisted into "You're separate from God." The message, "All the answers you seek is within you" got twisted into "You cannot trust yourself." People believed that they were the only intelligent species in the Universe. It was out of control because people bought into that narrative without realizing the real truth.

God is consciousness…not a creator. God is the source of creation itself. It (not he or she) isn't independent of you. It's the totality of everything. So, when someone calls themselves a God, they're not talking about the expression of the God itself, but the God that rests inside them. The verb, the energy, but not the noun. Once you think God is a noun (person, place, thing, or animal), you separate yourself from it and immediately become a limited being. That's what separates the believers (religious) from the knowers (spiritual).

The designers knew the earth was going to enter a new section of the galaxy that humans have never experienced before. This section is filled with a frequency that might be able to reconnect human DNA. Our DNA didn't work anymore, and that's how we connected with our Higher Self. That's why the incarnations couldn't hear their spiritual team rhetorically speaking to them. To pull this off, they would need millions of volunteers in the physical form wired and ready to tune into these frequencies. These are the 21st-century humans that all the stories were about.

They volunteered from every corner of the Universe to help humanity to wake up. Once they appeared on earth, they had to wake themselves up, attune to these frequencies and spread them throughout the rest of the planet. Most people thought we couldn't pull it off. Once they got to earth, they were taught the same fear-based beliefs that have been handed down for eons. They lived like everyone else (totally clueless about who they were and what was going to happen). As soon as the earth entered these clouds of higher frequencies, the volunteers started to question everything. There are things we were taught to accept without question. Those are the things that need to be questioned the most. One by one they started to wake up. The plan was working by trusting themselves more, the quicker we reconnected and the faster we remembered what was taking place. Since they were spread out evenly all around the planet, the planet frequency began to rise quickly.

Once the planet frequency arose, the human's experience of time began to speed up. They started to manifest their beliefs swiftly. Those consumed with fear created even more trepidation and eventually, the earth just spun out of control. These low-frequency beliefs that had controlled the human experience for eons no longer exist. So, they began to self-destruct, and the world fell into complete chaos and anarchy. It was terrifying for those who were in fear, but for the volunteers, they all knew it was the end of the old energy and the beginning of the new.

A tipping point was then reached in their awakening, and they created new earth without dread. The old earth continued for those who couldn't let go of their frightfulness and they had to play out their lessons. For the volunteers, they created new earth that matched their higher frequencies and all the fear-based beliefs simply fell apart. In an instant, we remembered who we were, and how connected we are. We stopped hurting each other, started respecting each other, and started to love one another.

Just because you care for someone doesn't mean you have to be attached to them. Being attached is an earthly thing and we shouldn't be of this world. Don't conform to this world but be transformed by the renewal of your mind. They'll test you and it may bring discernment but bring that discern within yourself to know truly what's right and wrong in any given situation.

So, in this case, these dark entities didn't want Indigo to come into this realm because of his light, soul, and the impact he'll bring upon humanity. Remember everything's already scripted out in your life, you just haven't realized it yet. The evil deities will try to attack you at your highest moments. Will this be the highest moment for Indigo, or will it be his lowest insignificance?

As Jerry came back into the room, the doctors tried to pull Indigo one last time before Indigo gave his last breath. He finally came out and the doctors took him right to NICU. Indigo couldn't be in his mother's arms or even in an incubator. After some tests, cutting of the umbilical cord, and injections; the doctors went back to the room and stated that Indigo couldn't go home. That crushed the spirits of the family who came to see their little man. Everyone went home sad, crushed, and in a dark mood. Most families hold the baby right after it comes out of the womb, name them, and so on. This wasn't the case for this family. With grief, anxiety, depressed feelings, and raised emotions, time felt like it stood still.

Three days passed by, and the phone ranged. It was the hospital informing them that Indigo is all set to come home. With excitement, Sherly and Jerry went to check in on him. Indigo wasn't little though, because he was 14 pounds. Regular male babies are on average seven pounds, but indigo was a massive 14 pounds. Now audience, I can work out holding this baby and that's some facts, *audience laughs and claps!*

Indigo had to wear some protective gear to make him safe and healthy. Sherly and Jerry finally got to hold their little boy. They finally took him home and introduced them to the family. Since Indigo had to go through so much pain and complications at birth, he developed a disability through the process. Not only that, but he had to wear glasses as well.

Growing up for Indigo was tough for him because he was shy, had learning problems, and needed someone to speak for him due to his disability. His parents had to get him an advocate for extra support throughout the school.

Schools, universities, colleges, churches, prisons, and courts are government indoctrination camps to program our minds. The similarities between school and prison are the school buses, the food, uniforms, walking in straight lines, teaching you about western societies and a false history, and much more. Children don't learn in school; they're babysat. It takes maybe 50 hours to teach reading, writing, and arithmetic. After that, students can teach themselves. Once you sign your birth certificate, you're signing your children to the corporation, and they'll become government property. In consequence, they give you a social security number to be a number within the system. They psychoanalyze us like animals, and they see us below animals. That's why they want robots to take over the world and wipe out humanity. That's why having children in this polarized civilization we call western society patronize will be bad.

A society whose citizens refuse to see and investigate the facts, who refuse to believe that their government and their media will routinely lie to them and fabricate a reality contrary to verifiable facts, is a society that chooses and deserves the police state dictatorship it's going to get. Nothing in this world operates the way you think it does.

Banks don't loan money, governments aren't empowered to protect you, the police department isn't there to serve you, and institutions of higher learning (colleges and educational institutions), aren't there to educate you. The entire superstructure of civilization in the Western world was brilliantly well-planned and put together. Scheming the direction of people's minds in such a way to serve their masters. Western cultures believe we must be alive for a purpose, to work, and to make money. Some indigenous cultures believe we're alive just like how nature is alive. We don't need to achieve anything to be valid in our humanness.

Church tries to send you to hell and the court tries to send you to jail. Don't think hell is a place, it's a mental mindset of constantly giving up your power. Living in a state of suffering internally plays out externally as well. Your body is the house of God. The temple is the architecture of men, but inside you're the craftmanship of the Most High God. Never violate the house of God by eating improper or uncleaned foods that clog up your system.

In this case, schools didn't care for Indigo and just looked at him as another kid with a disability. Luckily for Indigo, he had an advocate and his mother to demand what he deserved.

Indigo was innocent, so most people took advantage of him and didn't care for him as much. Fast forward a few years, Indigo had problems expressing himself to connect with people. He used to doubt himself and overthink how he'll be perceived by others. This made Indigo even shyer, so he never raised his hand at school. This was the start of Indigo burying his true self. Sandy could tell that Indigo was going through something because of all the impediments that were constantly occurring in his life.

Barry wasn't always there because he was out on the road doing shows. His other family members barely checked in on him. He started to notice and feel that most of his family members didn't truly care for him. As people tend to gravitate toward Sandy more, he knew Sandy was their favorite child, and all the other family members would always feel happy connecting with her. This was the opposite of Indigo. He knew people would only connect with him because he was "the other child." He started to gain a competitive lifestyle, was ambitious, and tried his hardest to succeed and show his potential. Even though he kept trying and trying, still Sandy's achievements ranked higher than his.

People can do stuff for you, buy things for you, and all these other materialistic items, but do they truly have a deep relationship with you? Do you feel comfortable enough in telling them what you're going through? Do they really care, or do they just act like a roommate? As Indigo grew older, he noticed that and started to realize that most people don't care for him truthfully. Through people's actions and words that are spells and the English language is fake. You can say anything to anyone, but the body language, the tone of voice, and everything's taken into par. Once he figured that out, Indigo was going through dark depressing times. That's why his love language is acts of service to see if anyone truly deeply cares for him or if it's all a fluke.

Indigo didn't realize that his parents and family were just trying their best. They were taught by their family, and they passed on what they've learned to their kids. There's no manual on how to be a great parent or family member. Even though it was his physical family (the Bloodkin), Indigo learned and knew how to treat and connect to his future kids when he was craving it all from his family.

Middle school is tough for anyone. Nowadays, it seems like elementary schoolers act like middle schoolers, middle schoolers act like high schoolers, and high schoolers act like typically high schoolers. You have some elementary schoolers who are already above 5'8", middle schoolers are already on social media platforms, and high schools look older than some older people. Now audience, what type of genes do these young folk have? Like geez *the crowd laughs.*

Middle school is full of puberty, acting wild, and bullies. Indigo had his fair share of bullies and people who like to pick on him. They knew he wouldn't say anything because he wouldn't stand up for himself. This lowered his confidence level, and it impacted his life.

During middle school his parents brought him into this military school and just like any other kid, he didn't want to go. He wouldn't know how much that program will elevate him to the next level. He ranked up, received ribbons, went on trips, learned the 14 leadership traits, and learned a lot about himself.

As the years went by, he learned a lot about himself, became a leader, and he gained more confidence through the various programs he was in. He had all this built-up pain within himself for years, but could he overcome them? He keeps burying his pain inside him. Will it get in the way of his success? We'll see how it'll play out throughout this book.

Chapter One

LUCKY 7'S

Character 2: Apollo

Apollo, what a savage I shall say. I mean this guy was really a savage. I feel like he's in his savage ways to cope with what happened throughout his life. It seems like he doesn't care for anyone's feelings. Even though this may seem like a bad thing, he doesn't get attached to anyone or anything. He is fully detached and disconnected from people. He tries his hardest to show that he cares, but it never seems good enough for anyone. Apollo was insecure about himself because he would find a gem and think she was cheating on him or something of that nature based on his past. Even though they showed him that they cared a few times, he didn't believe it. He didn't express self-love enough, which made him insecure when he was with a beautiful woman. He felt unworthy, not enough, always having to prove himself, and was being used by people. They take his kindness for his weakness because he always said yes to people. He put others above himself, so in turn he was giving up on love, didn't feel worthy of love, and there wasn't anyone out there for him. Maybe he was just there to be a beacon of light for people.

Apollo loves the chase of wanting something, but he knew his worth, so he never chased after women. He liked pursuing them because he felt like he wanted to have them. Once, he has them, it felt like it was game over for him. He was already preparing to go after his next target. He would blame others instead of blaming himself. People would care for Apollo, but won't express it to him, so he would think they didn't care as much. That's why he struggled with not feeling good enough for people, so in turn, he wouldn't open up because he knew they'll run away eventually. Hurt people, hurt people. No one stays just like his parents…

Apollo was a single child, his dad was Zeus, and his mom was Leto. Since his bloodline was aristocracy and such powerful beings, he got everything he wanted. He was a prince and a king. Even though he was a savage, he had class, had sovereignty, and knew his powers and how to use them. This was till the day that his parents got divorced.

He still had his powers, but his viewpoint changed. Once Zeus and Leto got divorced, he kept seeing his parents always fight, argue, and become abusive toward one another. Zeus cheated on Leto, and it went downhill from there. They tried to stay together for the family's sake, but it turned out to be a toxic relationship.

Everything stems from childhood trauma and past life karma, so Apollo seeing this instance of his family made him think that was normal. This conditioned his mind, and he took it wherever he went.

In middle school, Apollo was the class clown, most popular, and everyone gravitated toward him. It might've been his powerful energy, his savage ways, or his knowledge. He used to pick on people for their lunch money.

Apollo liked the finer things in life and was pretty bougie but hustled a lot. He doesn't care about what he has to do as long as he succeeds and wins in life. This can come off as being manipulative, narcissistic, and standoffish, but that's not the case. People call him narcissistic and stubborn, but he calls it persistence. A lot of people like to bring him down and try to lower his vibration for him to stoop to their level. Apollo knows their tactics and he has the confidence and self-love to see right through the bs. When someone's confident within themselves a lot of people try to bring them down. It's a constant battle between he said she said.

We're not just fighting the psychopathic reptilians, we're also fighting the narcissistic, brain-dead sheep. It's an uphill climb because they have weaponized the human race against itself.

Is there a more radical idea in the history of mankind than turning your children over to total strangers whom you know nothing about, and having those strangers work on your child's mind, out of your sight, for 12 years?

People cannot see the truth anymore because exposure to true information doesn't matter anymore. The truth can be placed in plain sight, in a book, on the TV screen, in a movie, or someone telling them with evidence; but that still doesn't cut it. Do you know what's absurd though? These people would read a book or watch a movie about the truth and then speak on some of the truth after. Then they'll go back to their everyday lives like it doesn't affect them, applies to them, or it's not happening right now.

A person who's demoralized is unable to assess true information. The facts tell them nothing, even if you shower them with information, authentic proof, documents, and pictures; they'll refuse to believe it. That's the tragedy of the situation of demoralization. Once people's morals have been debased, education becomes scientific indoctrination, entertainment becomes hypnotism, criminals become "leaders," and refusal becomes the truth. This confusion is based and designed on the idea of giving up trying to figure something out yourself because it's too complicated. You then have to trust someone "more educated" to explain it to you. At that point, they can make up any story, and you'll believe it.

Never argue with someone whose TV is bigger than their bookshelf. Consciousness is the new sexy. Inner peace is the new success. Kindness is the new beautiful.

Success isn't about being perfect; it's about being authentic. Strive for greatness because you can't rush perfection. No matter the situation, never let your emotions overpower your intelligence. The strongest factor for success is self-esteem. Believing you can do it, believing you deserve it and believing you'll get it. A satisfied life is better than a successful life because our success is measured by others. Our satisfaction is measured by our soul, mind, and heart.

No longer look for the good in people, search for the real. While good is often dressed in fake clothing, real is naked and proud no matter the scare. You're far too smart to be the only thing standing in your way. Self-control is strength. Right thought is mastery. Calmness is power. You have to get to a point where your mood doesn't shift based on the insignificant actions of someone else. Don't allow others to control the direction of your life. When writing the story of your life, don't let anyone else hold the pen.

Someone will always question your judgment and doubt you. No matter what you do, people will always talk about you. Forget people. Buy the red car, people will say you should've gotten blue. Start a business, people will say you should've gotten a job. Get married, people will say you picked the wrong partner. Learn a trade, people will say you should've gone to college. Everyone has an opinion about everything. At the end of the day, personally know who you are, believe in your work, and make sure it brings you happiness when you put it out. Everything else is noise, so don't care. You'll go crazy trying to please everyone, so don't even try. Smile, agree and then do whatever you were going to do anyway.

When life gives you a hundred reasons to break down and cry, show life that you have a million reasons to smile and laugh. Never let your terrors decide your future. Nothing in life is to be feared, it's only to be understood. Now's the time to understand more, so we may panic less. The mass media is a translation into the actuality of Plato's celebrated figure of the cave. The defect of the prisoners is that they cannot perceive the truth. The wall before them, on which the shadows play, is the screen on which the press, motion picture, and radio project their account of life.

How can you not love yourself enough and put yourself first? Do it in such a way, you'll never lose yourself in any instance. When you're overflown with abundance in your life, that's how you can pour into other people's glasses. If your cup isn't filled yet, how can you love yourself and others at the same time? Sometimes you have to be selfish to love yourself the most. Stop putting other people's feelings and emotions above yourself. You should be your main focus. Don't worry about if someone texted you back, being on social media, or trying to please everyone. This isn't the way to go about life. Who cares if someone doesn't text you back? You're focused on your growth and grind. Who cares about your social media presence? People on social media only present their highlights. Just because they only show their glamorous lifestyle publicly, doesn't mean they're living that same lifestyle internally. The reason why we struggle with insecurities is that we compare our behind-the-scenes with everyone else's highlight reel. There's a difference between their inner world and their outer world. They don't express what goes on behind closed doors; the anxiety, the depression, and the whole nine. The pain will leave once it's done teaching you.

You see anxiety, you see jealousy, or you see that negativity inside you, but let's sit with it for a minute. Let's observe these feelings and not instantly react to them. Don't automatically assume it's any of these things. Question it to help you understand more. Once you bring love, oneness, and peace, you'll be able to see that distortion and begin to heal it. Look at it and assess it for what it is, instead of letting it control how you think.

Whoever can scare people enough (produce bio-survival anxiety) can sell them quickly on any verbal map which seems to give them relief. By frightening people with hell and then offering them salvation, the most ignorant or crooked individuals can 'sell' a whole system of thought that cannot bear two minutes of rational analysis. Beware all is distortion and if you're not careful it'll draw you into a fickle embrace, blind you with its dazzling distractions, and tempt you with their fleeting games of chance. Whatever you do, don't be led astray, don't lose focus, and don't forget why you're doing it. Remember the courage you seek is inside you and it'll come to you in the hour you need it most.

When you focus on the future, you're not meditating. The future is a concept, and it doesn't exist. This whole world is a holographic Universe full of illusions. Tomorrow never comes, and the only time that exists is in the present moment. Don't grieve a past that doesn't exist anymore. The reason why you're stressed, depressed, and have anxiety is because you keep thinking about the past, future, and all the mistakes that you've made. Tomorrow is a mystery, but our thoughts help create our reality. Today's the present moment which is a gift; that's why they call it a present. Your spaceship doesn't come equipped with rearview mirrors we dip. You should be living here; live at the finish line constantly. So, when someone tells you no, do you think you should be worried? You should already know what the future is. Don't care if they said no, say, "It's already done, time hasn't caught up yet." Accept your past with no regrets, handle your present with confidence, and face your future with no fear.

People forget that social media is a tool, but they're a tool for social media. That's the difference between people who constantly post captions of, "I need a break on social media" or tell people publicly what they go through. People spend too much time on captions and not enough time on action. Say if you're in a relationship with a person, and they post a caption saying, "I deserve better" or "Why stay when I can leave without being played or hurt." This fear-based tactic is based on not presenting the information at hand to you, but instead, running to social media to make it known publicly. Social media can be toxic if you allow yourself to be taken over by it.

Many people are attached to the likes, followers, subscribers, comments, views, and attention. Even if people say they don't care about it, you know who cares by their conversations. Feeling sad because people don't show you "love" on social media or someone didn't view your story is a sign of attachment to people and social media. It's a sign of validation for them and if they don't receive that validation, then they'll doubt themselves and be in a petty mood. Be at a place in mind where all you have to do is express who you are. If you get this many views then I suck, that's not the case. It doesn't matter how many people will see it, you did it by expressing yourself, and you put it out there in the world and that's all that matters.

Apollo doesn't need validation or praise for something he's done because the Universe will send him true abundance throughout his entire life. Don't feel pressured or try to please anyone by doing something you don't want to do. Apollo only wants to express himself in a real authentic way. People tend to say he's mysterious, or people are confused by the way he operates. Just because people say they know you, doesn't mean they truly know you. Sure, they know your favorite color, food, or TV show. The difference is that they don't know how to treat you because people tend to only look at it from their point of view.

People tend to mix pleasure with pain because they're addicted to it. People will tend to say their love language, but in clairvoyance, they're afraid to receive it. Once you provide that for them, they start switching up because they're not accustomed to it. They're customary to people hurting them, so now when they're in a solid relationship, they let their minds wander and hinder the relationship over the fear or doubt of the past. That's why people are living in the past because they haven't healed their issues. Even though a lot of people say to live in the moment, only some are living in the present.

Don't trust everyone's words because people can lie to you. It's about the actions behind the words for Apollo. If your love language is physical touch and that person doesn't touch you or give you that solace, then what's the point? We missed that sense of touch so much, that we crash into each other just to feel something. Don't set your expectations too high because if they're not meeting that standard, then you'll only focus on the negatives in the relationship instead of the positives. Most people don't express what they want or need. They automatically expect someone to provide their wants, desires, and needs for them by beating around the bush. This might not seem like a big deal at first, but as time goes on, it'll be a recurring cycle.

Once Apollo went to high school, that's when the built-up savagery began. Apollo has some luscious hair; and when he started growing it, that's when all the powers started to kick in.

Hair is your antennas. With long hair, it draws more energy to the brain. The body is like an inverted tree in which the spine is the trunk, the nervous system is the branches, and the hair is the roots. The cabal is aware of the health benefits of long hair, which is why they persuade keeping the hair of the male population short. When men join the military (which is a corporation controlled by the controllers), they're required to cut their hair very short. Most people in the military will often tell the common folk it's due to safety or health reasons. Those claims may be true, but the convert reasons for requiring them to cut their hair very short is to weaken their moral compass and to mark them as slaves of the military-industrial complex. Modern slaves aren't in chains; they're in debt. The bankers will ensure we stay in debt. The pharmaceutical companies will ensure we stay sick. The weapon manufacturers will ensure we keep going to war. The media will ensure we're prevented from knowing the truth. The government will ensure all of this is done legally.

During the day, the hair absorbs solar energy, but at night it absorbs lunar energy. Keeping the hair up during the day and down at night aids this process. Braiding your hair at night will help your electromagnetic field balance out throughout the day. Hair getting frizzy represents the field that has been placed. This will energize the magnetic field (your aura) and your brain cells that stimulate the pineal gland in the center of your brain. Placing chemicals on your hair and scalp isn't only bad for you, but it dulls your receptive abilities. These chemicals have the potential to access the body's bloodstream and will create a chain reaction. It takes 30 seconds for the products to access the bloodstream through your skin. Once there, they can linger for a long time causing possible adverse effects. Fragrances can have up to 4000 unlisted chemical ingredients. The skin is our largest organ, and it's incredibly absorptive. People should take caution with what they allow to enter their system, using only natural, organic substances as often as possible.

In the beginning, Apollo was left alone with only the butler, the maid, and his parents coming in and out from time to time. His only family was the butler, and his only real friends were some people down the street. Even though Apollo was a very popular, famous, and fortunate person who was wealthy; he was still sad inside. He still didn't have a real quote on quote "family" who gave him attention. He was pondering if people messed with him because of who he truly was or because of his fame and fortune. This shows you that money doesn't make your life happier, it'll only bring more comfort. Yes, Apollo technically has friends and family, but they're mostly just acquaintances. Most of those relationships weren't deep and most of them just want something from Apollo. Remember he has powers as well and knows how to heal people through his hands. Even though he helps a lot of people, he barely receives love back. No one checks in on him because people automatically assume that he must be doing good based on his lifestyle. That wasn't the case, and that's why we're all one no matter how notorious, how much money, or success you gain.

Money is a concept that was created to cause division within the people. It's not real. The only thing that makes it real is your belief that it's real. That's why everything's changing, and the currency is going into a quantum financial system. Why do you think it's happening? That paper money that everyone loves so much; has no value.

Eventually, high school came around and Apollo was a bit shy because people tend to use him. At least Apollo had some good friends that lived on the same street as him. They would always ride their bikes, but Apollo didn't know how to ride a bike, so he just ran with them. They loved playing sports, cracking jokes, and listening to music. This sparked some inspiration and Meraki in Apollo's life. He was known for shooting his famous bow and arrow, was magical on the harp, was the God of music, and did content creation. He started to get out of his comfort zone when he started to know his worth. As he realized his new worth and power within, this caused some people to fade out of his life. It was like a release or detox of anything or anyone that no longer serves him.

In high school, people acted like he was doing something bad because of his fame and worth, but he wasn't. This was a major problem for Apollo throughout his relationships. No one wants to be accused of doing something that they didn't do, and that person doesn't believe them. Women tend to think because he's gaining all this attention that he must be doing something behind closed doors. Most women aren't used to people being loyal to them and when they have someone that shows loyalty, they have that voice in the back of their heads to say otherwise. It's a way to guard their hearts and not get hurt. People are always manifesting and are master manifesters. If someone's worried that something's going to happen to them, it's going to happen. Especially if you key in and focus on that scenario for a long time.

Everyone has their problems and hardships they've experienced, but since women are more emotional, they tend to hold on and accuse you of doing something that happened years ago. That's why most women hold grudges against someone who may talk behind their back in high school, for example.

Most men use logic when dealing with their emotions. That's why you always hear men say, "It is what it is" because it's a way to forget about the situation quickly and become distracted by something else. That's why when most relationships are over, they would run to social media and make their private business public. Posting all these quotes which are shots towards their ex, posting pictures trying to act like they've moved on, or post pictures of a new person right after they broke up. They don't want to experience those feeling or deal with them. People diminish others instead of uplifting them and realizing their differences.

In Apollo's eyes, that's a red flag and he started to move carelessly. This can be in a form of talking to or having multiple women, doing sexual activities with more than one woman, and not caring about anyone's feelings. Apollo was acting like a doppelganger because he was living two different lives. If he wasn't receiving love and care from someone, he will easily lose interest. Apollo doesn't want to stay stagnant or be in a repeated loop. He wants something new and exciting, not boring, and dull. It's easy for Apollo to not care because he already made the executive order to not be in the relationship. He didn't want to cut things off because they either haven't fully tried or he wants them to be around. This made him even more powerful, and all this attention was getting to his head. He would say certain things that feel right to the other person. Although this feels good at the moment, he knows deep down that it wasn't going to work. He goes through the motions and the cascade. He's flowing instead of forcing anything that's not meant for him. Create a space for what's truly meant for you in life.

Apollo is sneaky and manipulative in getting what he wants. As a child, he got heartbroken because of certain experiences he had to face. So, now if he's not all in, he's not all in. His mission is to have multiple wives because he deserves it. He stated that it's not for lust or pleasure, it's to build an empire and dynasty. The art of building and coming together as one. This made some relationships with Apollo edgy because he wanted it all. He wanted the best relationships, the best art, and the best of the best in everything. This made Apollo super competitive and try to be perfect. If it wasn't perfect, then he wasn't having it. For example, if one of his relationships isn't operating on a high frequency, then he'll be checked out.

We all have the potential to be spiritually in tune, but people haven't awakened to their true power yet. No one is above or higher than anyone because we're all equal. Yes, people may experience different things, are on different paths, or know more of a subject matter than another person. People should feel comfortable asking for help and those people providing the help should feel the need to help them overcome a subject or issue. It's not about forcing people to wake up or know certain information. Take what resonates with you and don't judge people's specific journeys. People have gone through a lot, so be supportive and uplift people instead of tearing them down. If someone wants to learn more in a subject, help them out and steered them in the right direction. People tend to not ask for help because people constantly use their egos to act like they know everything and try to save humanity. They would brag and boast about it. These types of people would say they're above you and you need to listen to them. If not, then you'll be doomed. These types of people only look at life through their lens and aren't considerate of other people. The body language and tone of voice are important as well. If they feel better about themselves and the topic, then that person is a true teacher. That's why Apollo teaches as well! He loves to teach, uplift, and support people in becoming their greatest versions. That's why Apollo needs a woman who can play different roles. Someone who can be the sports type, the business professional type, and the adventurous fun type as well.

People tend to not have a connection with their inner child. Since you express your inner child, people will bring you down by saying you're childish or immature. Everything in life shouldn't be so serious all the time. It's built on jealousy of where you are and where you're heading comparing their life to yours. People would judge you on everything you do, even people who say they love you. Watch for the people that are closest to you because they're the ones that could easily bring you down. Just like if you start your own business. Strangers would support you more than your friends and family. Then, when they want to support you, they'll ask for it to be free. Focus on how they make you feel in that particular moment. If you feel embarrassed, sad, or feel weird energy, then something's off.

People would rather be comfortable and stagnant instead of going outside the box and trying something new. Hence, there are so many people who still eat meat and seafood. They see people who are on vegan, plant-based, and alkaline diets, but they wouldn't try it. They tell us that we need proteins, fats, calories, etc. but that was all false. They know eating flesh doesn't generate electricity or cleanse the body, but they still do it. Take away seasoning, herbs, and condiments (that mostly came from nature) and you'll be left with that piece of meat that wouldn't taste the same.

Since Apollo always saw his dad cheat, his tendencies were the same. Not treating women right or correctly. Will Apollo ever change his ways? Will he finally get answers about his childhood trauma? We'll see this later on throughout this book.

Chapter One
LUCKY 7'S

Character 3: Aleemic

Aleemic; the old soul himself. Aleemic already had his spiritual awakening and is on the path to enlightenment. He experienced major shifts throughout his life. He just finished college and he's on his way to doing major things in life. Let's talk more about the great one, Aleemic.

Ever since Aleemic received a download of him being the true messiah, the CIA was trying to kill him. These dark entities try their best to wipe Aleemic out of this world. He wears some stones and crystals, but he realized that he's the biggest and most powerful stone and crystal out there. He doesn't need protection because he's always protected. They cannot touch him because of the divine light he gives off. These dark entities are like energy vampires; they hate the sun and want to suck your energy. That's why they live in underground caves and tunnels. When they see your light, they burn alive and melt. They try to make him afraid and paranoid, but that doesn't hinder Aleemic from sharing his light with anyone he encounters.

Stealing people's energy is how you react. So, if someone comes at you talking crazy, smile and don't allow their words to diminish your true light. You'll absorb all that energy they're feeding you and they'll receive zero.

He goes through the struggles of being different, not fitting in, and not having as many soul tribe members (even though your soul tribe is your Master Guides and not physical people). He knows some like-minded people, but behind closed doors, he knows that he's just on a higher wave link than most people. He can connect with people easily, but he doesn't want to because he doesn't see the value in it. If he notices that you're operating on a lower frequency, then he'll just continue his path. Everyone he encounters that can bring him mental stimulation ends up having a boyfriend, ghosting him, leaving him on read, or putting him in the friendzone.

Aleemic was also battling his sexual urges toward women. This was a hardship for Aleemic at the beginning of not feeling good enough or meeting the standards of other people. He eventually didn't care at all about what others thought about him and continued his path. When you come into this world you come by yourself and when you exit, you exit by yourself. This journey is about knowing thyself more and loving thyself fully. Since he had so much power internally, gang stalkers followed his every move. Everywhere he went, every turn he faced, and every road he was on, they followed. This brought a sign of apprehension for his life at first. Once, he stopped caring and giving them his power, the gang stalkers started to watch him from a distance and Aleemic realized that he was untouchable.

Aleemic was a genuine, pure-hearted man who wanted to see everyone succeed in life. Aleemic had one brother named Aleem and one sister named Divine. His dad's name was Alchemy and his mom's name was Esoteric. His whole family was conscious, but Aleemic stuck with his path and shared his knowledge publicly.

You guessed it, his father Alchemy studied psychics throughout his journey and then started to dabble in alchemy later on. His dad had a way with words and knew how to run a family. Alchemy was the divine masculine and Esoteric was the divine feminine. Esoteric studies esoteric knowledge, occult, and magic while being the backbone and the support system for the family. If any of them were going through anything, the first person they'll turn to is Esoteric. Esoteric gave great advice and acted like the Oracle.

The parents mostly keep their information private until someone on the same level of frequency comes into the picture. Once they come into the picture, they would easily share all their knowledge and hidden secrets of life with that person. The Universe responds to your frequency. We're chaotic beings, so anything goes. It doesn't recognize your desires, wants, or needs, it only understands the frequency at which you're vibrating. For example, if you're vibrating in the frequency of fear, guilt, or shame, you're going to attract things of a similar vibration to support that frequency. If you're vibrating in the frequency of love, joy, and abundance, you're going to attract things to support that frequency. It's like tuning into a radio station. You have to be tuned into the radio station you want to listen to just like you have to be tuned into the energy you want to manifest in your life.

Aleem was a basketball and football player. He was the most popular kid in school and getting women was easy for him. Aleem was indecisive in the beginning, so he sent a nude selfie to a woman, and she shared it throughout the entire school. With the world of social media, the picture ran rapid and Aleem's career was in besmirch. He had women trying to seductress him. He had guys trying to philander with him. It was a whole imbroglio of the circumstance.

At first, it was inopportune for him, but he started to savor the moment. He was sneaking out, going to parties, getting high, doing drugs, all of the above. Most importantly, he was having sex with low vibrational people who transferred demons to him. With motherly instinct, Esoteric knew whenever he entered the temple of their house, she knew something was off. He would beat around the bush and not tell the truth, but one day it all changed.

His basketball and football career has desperately changed the course of his direction. From being a star athlete and gaining scholarships to now sitting on the bench and losing his scholarships. He knew something had to change, and he finally came out with the truth to his mother. Since Esoteric was into potions and magic, she already sensed it from the beginning. She already was working on a detox to change his life for the better. She gave it to him, he guzzled it down, then he went to sleep. In his vivid lucid dream, he saw his mother doing witchcraft spells on anyone who disobeyed Aleem.

Aleem saw all of his past scholarships coming back to him and he was gaining his power back. Once he woke up, it was a whole two months beforehand. Esoteric made a potion for him to time travel back in time and the only people who knew were Aleem and Esoteric. Aleem thanked his mother, and he was back on track. Esoteric terror-stricken him so much that he didn't want to fully go into spirituality. He still knew some information but would rather keep it to himself after what Esoteric did to everyone who contravened him in the past. Those people were erased, gone, and no one asked about them or acted like they ever existed.

Divine was a beacon of light for people and her family. Divine brought this glow to her to lighten the mood for anyone who came across her. In this family, they needed Divine to keep them all tranquil. Early on, she had experienced bullying because of her pure kind soul. They love to talk down on you when you're at your highest moments. You're above these beings and don't you ever lower your vibration, frequency, or energy to be a standard for anyone's feelings or emotions. Do you hear me? They don't deserve your presence, they don't deserve your light, and they certainly don't deserve your energy. You're higher and have done the necessary work to be where you are today that you don't need someone who's unhealed to try and make you stoop to their level. Be proud of that. They must do the work for themselves. Know this for yourself or keep interacting with them and watch how you bury yourself. Let lost souls find their true souls while found souls keep attracting what they rightfully deserve. Protect your energy, save that energy, and make that energy flow throughout your body for new innovative ideas. Isn't that right crowd? Give me a hell yeah, "What?" Can you hear me? "What?" GIVE ME A HELL YEAH, "HELL YEAH!" So back to Divine.

Divine had issues internally but would bottle them up and put a smile on her face to cope with the pain. You can numb the pain, but that hasn't erased your problem; it's just given it time to grow. Anyone asks, she replies she's doing good, don't you see the smile on her face? Wrong, and that's what's wrong with the majority of people in this world. They would put a smile on their face and act like everything's blissful. Before judging anyone or just believing in their contradiction, use your intuitive spirit in knowing if this person is okay or not. Even though they say they're fine, that's just a coverup of what they're hiding. Be there for that person. Not only tell them that you care, but show them that you care with active listening, eye contact, comforting, support, no judgments, and body language. Most people don't open up in a therapy session right away because they're afraid of being judged or looked at differently. Society told people that you should be good 24/7 and if not, then you must have problems and issues that you're not facing. It's also based on the way they talk to you as well. Most people aren't exactly like you. Don't expect someone to treat you with respect, have professional manners, or use kindness because they were raised differently. Learn how to take criticism without losing yourself or your temper.

Kill people with kindness. Like everything in life, it's not what happens to you, but how you respond to it that counts. Even after all you've been through, choose kindness, always. The only person who never makes a mistake is someone who does nothing. No one truly likes to hear what their true issues are. Certainly enough, they won't listen to a stranger who they just met, telling them what their problem is. It's a form of trust which is paramount in life for every creature on this earth. For example, do you think a dog is going to run up in your arms if you aren't giving off that loving energy? Body language, setting intentions, and being pure is always crucial in building trust. For a human, do you think someone's just going to spill out all their problems to a person without fully knowing them or having a connection with that person? Very few indeed, but most people are guarded of their hearts because they became vulnerable with a special person and got heartbroken. No matter how much someone says their spiritual, if they've not healed from their past, they'll enter their next relationship guarded, without trust, and setting expectations of the person. This would cause toxic behavior, overly attachment, and unimaginable pain for the people within that set relationship.

Everyone ridicules you when you make a mistake even after all your correctness. Although everyone analyzed all your rights correctly, no one congratulates you. When you do one mistake, everyone starts to judge you. That means even if a person is successful, society will notice the slightest mistake in your life. So, don't let criticism annihilate your dreams. This is what Indigo struggled with. Dream so big you get uncomfortable telling small-minded people.

Do you remember who you were before the world and society told you how you should be? Don't be stubborn because some people are trying to help, so take it as advice. Realize your faults and your flaws to own and improve them. Watch for those who only try to bring you down though. Everyone's the same in their shell operating their bodies. Look at life through their eyes because everyone's their own person. No one's different because we're all just going through life. Their human who drinks, eat, poop, pee, have emotions, etc. just like you!

Exercise:

If you have thought about talking to someone, use the three, two, one, go method. This will help you not overthink the situation, so you won't regret not talking to the person. Have that confidence internally that you express externally and realize you're all the same. Put yourself back out there with no judgment over how people will view you because you know how powerful you are. You go through life with all these problems you hold onto. Then you become spiritual, and all this blissfulness comes to you. You feel so confident, so free, and so connected with your spiritual practices. You then go deeper into various rabbit holes and those problems come back because you're now equipped to face and overcome them.

Challenge:

Day one: I challenge you to go up to two different people and give them a personalized compliment. This could be their eyes, personality, characteristics, etc.

Day two: I challenge you to go up to three different people and give them a physical compliment. This can be their clothing, glasses, or style. This time I want you to generate a conversation with them about that item you complimented. Could be where they bought it, how much it cost, etc.

Day three: I challenge you to generate a conversation with four people without complimenting them.

Day four: I challenge you to talk to five people and if you're single, I want you to try to get two numbers. Remember, a phone number or social media shouldn't be the end goal of why you want to talk to them. So, if you're in a relationship, talk to five different people.

Choose people who choose you, ask how you are, who sees you, let you be you, feel good to your nervous system, breathe easily around, you don't need to perform for, are good for your mental health, want to see you win, and who doesn't try to control you. Being yourself is the greatest gift you can offer yourself and others. Be brave enough to show the world who you are without an apology.

Rumors are carried by haters, spread by fools, and accepted by idiots. Hate without reasoning stems from jealousy, guilt, and fear. When the whole world is running towards a precipice, the one who's running in the opposite direction appears to have lost their mind. It's better to keep your mouth closed and let people think you're a fool than to open it and remove all doubt. It's easier to fool people than to convince them that they have been fooled.

Whenever you find yourself on the side of the majority, it's time to pause and reflect. Some of you are on your way to success and someone wants to come back into your life because they don't want to miss out on their opportunity. You'll be surprised by the number of people who'll come back at your highest moments. When you take a break or go through your darker moments in life, watch them all fade out. When you take a break from social media and then come back; you'll see people who weren't there during your break, come back into your life. Don't go back on social media or message people and forget all you've learned. They don't want to put in the work that you did. They think you got where you are by casting spells, but they don't realize that you're the spell. You're a natural alchemist. You manifest whatever you want because you're highly favored and protected. You're a magnet to abundance, success, and opportunities that they don't understand. Yet, they want to come along and benefit from the fruits of your labor. This person can't get on your team no matter what they do, try, or say. Even if you choose to be "nice" to them and let them back into your life, they're blocked from your success because all of their intentions aren't in the right place.

Exercise:

Give up the habit of criticizing yourself. Delete the programs that you've been taught that limit your way of thinking. Remove what people say about you, remove other people's limitations from your life, and remove other people's experiences that have nothing to do with you from your life. You also have to remove all of the programs that make you think you'll never succeed or obtain anything you wish or choose to obtain in life.

Challenge:

For you to delete the program is by closing your eyes and taking several deep breaths until you get to a state of relaxation. Then visualize all the different things that people had told you and those belief systems that you picked up on by your own will. These programs don't serve a purpose for your greater good anymore. For you to be able to obtain the things you want to obtain, visualize scissors that are coming in and cutting them. Or visualize yourself pressing the delete button and see it be deleted out of your mind. Or you can visualize yourself unplugging your brain from those situations. Be very careful because the television isn't your friend. Even on social media, be careful about the things you tap your energy into because these items are there to program the mind with fear, not to think, and arrest the mind. Be careful what you allow to enter through all your senses. Stay in real life and focus on yourself. Whenever you feel like something or someone trying to distract you and kick you off your course, do and say this: put your hand up and say, "When my hand goes up, your mouths stay shut." This will make these entities quiet and leave you alone.

The conscious mind wishes and desires while the subconscious mind is a program. It's time to escape from the programs in your life. Before you take a devil's bargain, that says in exchange for this shiny object (maybe air travel, maybe venues for concerts, or whatever that thing might be), you'll get it only if you take this industrial chemical intervention. Ask yourself this question. Will you be a fully functional human being at the end of that transaction?

Before you talk, listen. Before you react, think. Before you criticize, wait. Before you pray, forgive. Before you quit, try. It's called emotional intelligence. When you can listen to somebody even if you don't agree with them. We're intellectual anoetic beings. You don't silence someone because they disagree with you. Everyone has the right to say their piece. If you and another person disagree about something, the same genuine person you first connected with is still in there.

Some people are too attached to someone, and they try to control who they are, who they talk to, and who's allowed to see them. It's a program they have about you. They've been living their lives through other people for so long. Who are they? The only real battle in life is between hanging on and letting go. Most people don't want the truth. They just want constant reassurance that what they believe is the truth.

You stop doubting and being so hard on yourself. Stop it. You're doing the very best that you can. You're going to be okay. This too shall pass. It's just a brief moment in time and the juice is worth the squeeze. It can't rain forever, but while it's here, you better start dancing. Whenever you find yourself doubting how far you can go, just remember how far you've come. Reminisce everything you've faced, all the battles you've won, and all the fears you've overcome. Everything always ends up working in your favor. So, stop being so hard on yourself, you got to take things one day at a time. Take things day by day, step-by-step. You cannot expect things to happen overnight but look at you now compared to where you were. When you were at your worst, in the beginning, or when you didn't understand. You're better than that and you made progress.

So, stop beating yourself up thinking you haven't. You have and it'll happen if you keep going, so take it easy on yourself. Everything's going to be alright; no one's going to maliciously harm you. The Universe always watches you, and you're protected. Certain people come around you with that bs, they'll be dealt with in the spiritual realm. You have a force field around you to bounce off those energies, so keep your energy high, keep your faith, and stand tall when you walk around.

Divine was in so much pain over the bullies that she went to her mom and asked her to cast a spell on people. Casting spells on people will come back to the sender since it's the Age of Aquarius (even though these signs were made from the Western societies just like all these other Western-created names). All those spells and magic people put on you are returning to the sender. Instead of casting spells, cast your light outwards. Back then it was the Age of Pisces, which was the age of believing, but now it's the age of knowing. That's why people don't associate with some of these non-profit organizations because dark entity puppets have control over them. We're not woke or a part of the woke community, we're conscious. We're spiritually connecting to the source, but we're not religious.

Esoteric knew all of this, so she didn't make the magical spell for Divine, and she became furious. She went up to the girl who was bullying her and whooped that ass. Even though we may laugh now, it was no laughing matter at that present moment. Divine used all that anger, unintentional aggression, and pain, and placed all that energy on the girl. The girl was named Mariah.

Mariah was leaving cheerleading practice at the top of the staircase because the gym was being used by the women's basketball team. Mariah was waiting for her ride and was the only one that was on the top floor of the school. She was standing next to a flight of stairs and was looking out the window. Now, you probably are saying, "Oh no, watch Divine throw her off the stairwell, right?" Wrong. See with this book, you won't find those easy way-outs or easy answering questions. You'll have to be ready for anything.

Mariah went to the bathroom. Then all of a sudden, as the door was actively closing, there was a shadow that appeared; it was Divine. Divine couldn't enter the bathroom right then and there because it would be no suspense. Divine waited eagerly to attack Mariah.

Divine then entered the bathroom. As the door shut, Divine quickly changed her attire to all-black with a black hoodie to cover her head and a ski mask to cover her face. After she changed, she turned off the lights.

Mariah was anxious because the bathroom wasn't motion censored, it was a regular bathroom light switch. Mariah was freaking out, saying "Hello" and "Who's there?" Now audience, why would people say those types of words when they're scared? It's like someone running away from an opposer in the woods and they keep looking back, then trips over a log and can't get up. If you're in a panic situation, you don't want to give off being scared because that lets the perpetrator know that you're scared. You want to always be two steps ahead and not two steps behind the killer.

Divine saw Mariah's feet on the ground which were the same shoes she was wearing earlier. When Divine was about to slam into the stall, the door opened again, and it was a teacher. The teacher came in and turn on the lights. Divine ran into one of the stalls just in time with her feet up so it would seem like Mariah was the only one there. Mariah indulged in lividness and stormed out without informing the teacher what happened. As Divine was changing, she noticed that Mariah didn't tell the teacher about the situation, so she left afterward. Divine watched as Mariah went inside her family's car and they drove off.

Divine still had gifts like no other. She was so enraged, that she made all of the traffic lights stay red for a long period. As Mariah's family waited patiently, they asked around how their day was. In the meantime, Divine killed the railroad train operator and got control over the train. Since Mariah's family had a smart car, she took control of her car and slowly moved it upon the railroad tracks without the option of leaving. That's the dangers of smart cars and letting them drive yourself.

Divine sped the train so fast, that it was going lightning speed. As the train was approaching the car, the family got close and said a quick prayer. This made Divine feel sadness because she had rolled down their windows to see Mariah's suffering. Even though sadness came abruptly, this didn't stop Divine from executing her plan. As the train came closer, she saw a baby boy that was in a car seat. Before Divine could stop the train, it was too late. The destruction of the car was horrendous and since the car was electrical, it burst into flames. The flames were posing as demons as the smoke rise through the air. Before the police arrived, she noticed Mariah's mom, dad, Mariah, and her newborn child was all dead.

Mariah's boyfriend was on the same team as Aleem, so he wasn't present. Before anyone could comprehend what they just witnessed, Divine teleported to her habitation and quickly found her mom singing while doing some yoga. This was a hard pill to swallow and the fact that she has to tell her mom what happened, crushed her even more. Remember, Divine and Esoteric weren't in the best mood with one another since Esoteric didn't place a spell on Mariah. Divine told her mom the story, but before she could even say anything, the news anchor came up and the incident was getting reported and shared everywhere within minutes. That's the power of social media.

Esoteric noticed Divine in the room and said, "Hey baby, you saw what just happened?" Divine answered back saying "Yes" and she sat her mom down to talk about what had happened. Esoteric was shocked that she turned her back and did something to Mariah. Esoteric was in tune with mostly everyone and everything. She already knew she had a newborn child and that's why she didn't want to cast a spell on her for the baby's sake. Divine should've had an open discussion with her mom to let her know what was going on to gain insight into Mariah's life. She didn't and acted based on reaction and emotion. That's what the world wants you to do; react by emotions. If they can make you react based solely on emotions, then you'll be more passionate and would say anything at that very moment. Your emotions are being manipulated using project mockingbird to formulate words in copacetic to get your emotions to arise instead of thinking. You can say something that'll come back to haunt you. Divine didn't know and she'll have to pay.

Killing someone to protect yourself or your family is one thing but killing someone based on pure anger and emotions is pretty much a murder case. Since Divine is Esoteric's daughter, she wanted to help her as much as she can. She was going to receive karma from the spiritual realm because nothing goes without notice. Esoteric did a multiverse reversing spell. Although it worked correctly, Divine had to experience all the pain, loss, and hardship of all Mariah's friends and family. It's like committing suicide where you'll have to experience all that pain that you put people through for committing suicide.

Divine realized that Mariah was going through her issues and demons as well. She would put it all on Divine to try and escape. I mean, she was a teen mom.

Mariah tried to stay popular and had beauty standards that she wanted to meet. She was still cheerleading while she was pregnant but couldn't do some of the moves she used to do. This made the other girls laugh and pick on her while she was down. You shouldn't pick on someone or bully anyone without knowing what they've gone through. Most bullies experienced pain from their upbringing. All they ever experienced was pain. They get pleasure from other people's pain and hide their problems. Sometimes your pain gets misdirected.

They're not angry, just heartbroken because you both may have had a special bond with one another. Just give them time and space, and they'll come back around. People love to judge a book by its cover and never allow that person to fully express themselves to anyone. It's all pre-judgments and predetermined outcomes of what you think might happen based on overthinking. Some people know, some people believe, and some people project.

Divine saw this and felt her heart sink in sorrow. It was devastating to see what the three-month-old baby would've become. Divine had to deal with how people were affected by the tragedy. While the spell did work, she still had to face her karmic debt throughout her life. After three long years of therapy, self-realization, connecting back to self, and self-healing; she was finally done with her karma.

Divine is so peachy, peaceful, and full of light now because she doesn't want to enter that dark place once again. Now with polarity, you'll have to have a balance between the light and the dark. That's why she'll rather stick to being full of light instead of the darkness controlling her.

For Aleemic, it was easy to deeply fall enamored with spirituality based on his Bloodkin. Aleemic has a massive following that he helps through their spiritual journeys. He would then purchase a temple for motivational lectures and workshops. This was his calling, to teach and become a supportive person along other people's journeys. Aleemic would then purchase another building similar to the BLB Productions' building.

With a family like that, manifestation comes easy for them. It's the law of attraction; whatever you put your mind towards, you'll receive. For example, if they're craving vegan pizza, within a day or two, they'll receive some vegan pizza. If they said, "I'm an A-lister," and they kept saying it and believing in it, then it'll come true. That's how in tune they are.

Setting intentions and staying humble was a test for them. All this power comes with risks if not handled properly. Will this power come to bite Aleemic in the butt? Will his family's past affect how others view him? Would they not accept him since he was spiritual? We'll see about this later on throughout this book, "How to Overcome Apocalyptic Events".

Chapter One

LUCKY 7'S

Character 4: Joey

What can I say about Joey? Poor Joey, that's for one. Joey goes through it internally and externally. His self-worth is all over the place, he's trying to find himself, and already has a child. The craziest part is that he's only 16 and his baby mama is Aqua (a fellow main character in this saga), but we'll get to her when the time presents itself.

Anxiety, depression, suicidal thoughts, and this isn't even the tip of the iceberg. He went through so much, that he tried to fake his own death. Crazy right? Let's dive deeper into the life of Joey.

Joey has two older identical twin brothers who were named Mike and Cody. Since they were twins, his parents focused more on Mike and Cody than they did on Joey. Joey constantly felt like an unwanted child. He kept a lot of his feelings internally. Mike was a wrestler and a boxer. Cody was a soccer and hockey player. They love to go to the gym and mess with their little brother. Joey doesn't go to the gym because of his self-worth level, low self-confidence, and the problems he was facing. Not to mention that his brothers performed wrestling moves on him to add to the damage. His brothers thought it was funny, but not for Joey. He was hurting internally, and you can see it all on his face. He would attempt to tell his parents, but they kept saying "Suck it up" and "Be like your brothers." How can he be more like his brothers when it was problematic for Joey to deal with his issues?

Ashley (his mom) worked as an accountant while Michael (his dad) was a coach. Joey didn't have any bullies because they all knew he was the brother of the captain of the wrestling, soccer, and hockey teams at the school. Joey kept feeling this feeling of self-doubt and continuously compared himself to his brothers. This brought the issues of perfectionism, depression, anxiety, and other issues. Like how I said, we're constantly manifesting and whatever we put out in the Universe we shall receive back. Say, for instance, someone used to always talk about, judge, and make fun of people who have disabilities or a person being in a wheelchair for instance. Don't be surprised in another lifetime, that person ends up being in a wheelchair temporarily or for the rest of their life. I don't tolerate people disrespecting others and that seems like the norm nowadays. Being disrespectful isn't right and if you don't see the issues of what you say, think, or act, then you'll stay disrespectful towards people.

You were never created to live depressed, defeated, guilty, condemned, ashamed, or unworthy. Someone can't ruin you forever and you're not a tragedy waiting to happen.

Electromagnetic weapons are wireless manipulation of the human brain to change the induce moods from apathy to indirect aggression for example. Using electromagnetic fields, people can alter the electoral signals in the brains of humans and animals. Sometimes, you have to go through the worst to get to the best. Focus on the good in everything and remember to always breathe in stressful encounters. Be patient because you were created to be victorious because you're already the divine. You get to be you forever.

Joey usually gets A's and B's in school. He showed his parents his report card and basically, they said, "How nice" and continued doing what they were already doing. This crushed Joey's spirit and all the hard work he put in. While he was getting these good grades, Mike and Cody were telling Joey to do their homework to stay on the sports team at school. If you were failing, then you wouldn't be able to play on the varsity team. This made Joey way busier than expected because now he was doing work that was above his grade level.

He was experiencing depression over the fact that no one cared about him, loved him, or noticed him. Thus, making Joey enter a dark state of mind. This made Joey experience suicidal thoughts and he started to contemplate staying on earth. Like I said beforehand, if you commit suicide in the physical world, you'll have to feel all those emotions of the people who you impacted by your fatality.

I know right now with suicidal thoughts, it seems as if no one cares, loves, or is there for you. Trust me, you'll be surprised by how much your death would impact the people around you and those you barely talk to. You know how the saying goes; people don't truly love you until you're gone. That's why record labels, love when their artists end up dying because they'll get a bigger following, bigger sales, bigger numbers, and they can keep all that money to themselves, essentially.

Joey never thought of self-harm because he was scared of hurting himself. He wanted an instant death to not feel the pain throughout his death. Committing suicide physically is different from committing suicide spiritually. In the spiritual, dying from this system or letting go of this physical reality is an instance of spiritual suicide. Committing suicide physically for a physical reason is significate.

There are physical organic beings, then you have spiritual inorganic entities, and then you have those deities that dip in between both. Those are the people to look out for because they can cause the most spiteful damage to us. They like to hide in the shadows through the thin wall between the physical and spiritual realities.

Joey was ready, prepared, and amendable of the fact of committing suicide. He knew how to do it because he watched some videos on how to fake your death or commit suicide. Joey wrote a short death note to his family even though he felt like they wouldn't read it. He wrote that he wasn't feeling loved or cared for in this family.

You might have an attachment to people who are closest to you that makes you feel a certain way towards them. That's why you should practice detaching and disconnecting because once you're attached there's no coming back. Nothing wrong with showing love and care for people but having an attachment to something or someone is a craving effect. You need them, you desire them, and you cannot go through life without them. This can be toxic in the end and could hinder your spiritual growth. Everything on the outside is a reflection of the inside. It's your mirror reflection. If you're wanting anything on the outside, it's going in reverse. Once you flip the script, you'll begin to manifest an acclimated way. The difference between wanting something and having something is doing something. If you start now, you'll begin seeing results one day earlier than if you start tomorrow. If you're using the power of letting go and detachment, then you'll be able to let these things come into your life easier than ever.

Detachment is experiencing our feelings without allowing them to control us. We step back and look at things objectively. We let go and accept what we cannot change. We detach from others' choices, knowing that their spiritual work isn't ours to do. We choose how we'll act rather than just reacting.

Detachment is a deep breath of serene and forbearance in response to unexpected anger. We can listen without losing ourselves. With detachment, we see our mistakes honestly, make amends, and start afresh. Detachment allows us to be in the world, but not of the world. It frees us to lead our lives with grace. Detach from emotions and those physical traits that have been taught to us. We didn't come down here from the spiritual realm with all these emotions and other expressions. They taught us to focus on human emotions and physical characteristics instead of being detached from all those physical traits. No person, place, or thing has any power over you. Letting go means realizing that some people are a part of your history, but not a part of your destiny. Never apologize for being you.

Challenge:

Refuse to entertain negativity. Life's too big, and time's too short to get caught up in the empty drama. Healthy detachment has become the release of the subjective thoughts, emotions, or energy that's holding you back. This can be in the form of people, places, and things that have kept you trapped in dis-ease. It means that you can step back and observe what's happening to, in, and around you without being involved in it or creating additional drama. In doing so, you allow the feelings, thoughts, and energy to dissipate. You're then free to act with compassion, love, and acceptance.

Exercise:

Say this affirmation: "I allow myself to peacefully detach from anyone who has hurt or harmed me." Allow yourself to do what's best for you, even if it upsets other people. You get what you get, so don't be upset. Don't dwell on the seven deadly but show virtue to overcome them.

Although, this is true, look at it from Joey's point of view. He never felt that feeling of love from anyone. Joey didn't have many friends and the only time people talked to him was to find out more about his brothers.

Joey liked to draw and was super creative. He was interested in cartoons, anime, and animation. It's never too late to connect with your inner child.

Joey expressed his issues with depression and anxiety of trying to please everyone without gaining anything back in return. Joey didn't want to hang himself because that looked painful. He was thinking of getting run over by a car, but he didn't want anyone to find his body. So, he made the executive decision in drowning.

Joey didn't know how to swim, and he knew he wanted an instant death experience. So, instead of just choking on some water, he determined to get chains around his neck and an anchor to bring him right to the bottom of the ocean.

His parents were out at Cody's soccer game in the afternoon and then at Mike's wrestling match during the evening. Of course, Mike was there to support his brother and the same for Cody. His parents were always there to support their favorite sons and their accomplishments.

Wonder why some kids have a hard time connecting with their parents if they miss all the highlights of their life. Kids only have their 1st birthday, their first dance residual, the first-time walking, etc. All these moments are memories that children keep and whoever was there in that moment they'll have a deeper connection with them. Hence why most fathers don't have a deep connection with their children because some fathers were never there. The same goes for the women who decide to put their children up for adoption and then try to come back decades later. The child has a better connection with their adopted family, and they showed more care and love compared to their immediate family members. Also, the parents who opted in committing abortion never experience that baby or the accomplishments that'll achieve. What if that child was a key element for society to help people along the way? This won't be the case due to abortion. It's killing off the baby instead of embracing it. If people love having unprotected sex, get pregnant, and then say they're not ready for a baby; why have unprotected sex in the first place? So many people say they don't like condoms or other solutions, but then when they get pregnant, they're not ready for the baby to come. It's no measure of health to be well adjusted to a profoundly sick society. People would rather fight for abortion rights but won't fight for their human rights.

There are things one must unlearn to create the life one truly desires. Unlearn societal standards of beauty and diet culture. Unlearn seeking external validation over self-assurance. Unlearn to distract from hard feelings instead of processing them. Stay focused because not every distraction is a worthy detour. Unlearn to make yourself smaller to fit into social situations. Unlearn pretending like you're fine instead of asking for support. Unlearn to ignore your boundaries to please other people. Unlearn to believe your self-worth depends on your productivity. Unlearn to sacrifice your voice and beliefs to avoid conflict. Unlearn not to celebrate your accomplishments because "others have better ones."

Acknowledge your self-worth because your confidence is soaring. Never assume that loud is strong and quiet is weak. Observe the energies around you because the quieter you are, the less information they have against you. Your voice and heart matter too. Don't let the loudness of another person's opinion silence the fierceness of your spirit. The one thing that you have that nobody else has is you. Your voice, your mind, your story, your vision, etc. So, write, draw, build, play, dance, and live only as you can. Use your voice for kindness, your ears for compassion, your hands for charity, your mind for truth, and your heart for love.

Joey almost thought of faking his own death and leaving to go to another country or out of state. The problem with that would be that he didn't have a car, wasn't old enough, and couldn't receive his passport yet. So, Joey went to the safe where his parents' held money and other valuables. He then proceeded to take some money out of the safe so he could buy the chains, anchor, a bag, and call a taxi. He walked over to the store closest to him to buy the items. No one questioned it because they thought his parent was in the store with him or was outside. He then progressed to call a taxi to go to the highway and jump inside the ocean. He asked one customer to use their phone to call his mommy. The fellow customer felt sad for him, not seeing through Joey's acting skills because he knew how to act as well. Instead of calling Ashley, he called the taxi company by finding the number in the yellow book before he left. He waited outside for the taxi, and it was already getting dark. He didn't want to commit suicide outside when it was bright out because people would see him and try to rescue him.

The taxi finally pulled up to his location and Joey told the taxi driver that his parents got stuck on the highway and he needed to be with them. The taxi driver didn't ask questions because he was trying to get some money. Once the taxi driver let him off (before entering the highway), he sped off to get another ride. Joey walked to the highway and he loved seeing the clear deep ocean beneath the highway bridge. He put the chains around his neck and connected the anchor to the bottom of the chain. The anchor was heavy, but he could pick it up. Joey knew by taking physics in high school, that the force and pull of the anchor will make him throttle on the chains faster and while the water enters his mouth, he'll start drowning at the bottom of the ocean. Once he was impending to jump off the bridge, he got a notification from his current girlfriend Aqua saying "I need to tell you something." Before Joey could respond by saying, "What" she called Joey saying she was pregnant.

Joey was shocked and couldn't commit suicide after this. Joey was out in the rain hearing this news while calling for a cab. He eventually did make it home safely after calling the taxi company to bring him home. Now for Aqua and Joey's relationship.

While no one was paying attention to Joey, one person sneaked her way into Joey's heart. It was a girl named Aqua. Now Joey was 16 and Aqua was 18. They met because of all the homework he had to do for his brothers. He was in their class a few times to give them their homework before or after class. He noticed this cute girl and he was scared to approach her. Then his brothers would always throw parties while their parents were away, and he would see Aqua again. Aqua noticed Joey and went up to him while he was doing one of his drawings. They loved to draw together and talk about anime. When Joey was a child, he gained vivacious toward his favorite animated character.

Now with Joey not caring early on in his life, he became a professional raw dogger. Yes, he would have sex with women without a condom and not have any babies with them. It was the talk around town as Joey started to do it more because he was drunk and not himself. He let those dark entities enter his body and that's why they call alcohol spirits. Aqua wanted to experience that raw dogging experience from Joey as the other women talked about. This time it was different because they developed similar hobbies first before really stepping into that physical connection. Yes, the physical attraction was there for Joey, but he didn't know if Aqua felt the same way. For the other women, it was strictly physical and that's why he was professionally raw dogging them. This was Joey's escape from his problems to get drunk, find a cute female, and raw dog them. Aqua was the only one that truly showed that they cared for Joey and that led Joey to not be guarded and break those barriers of his heart to her. They both were opening up to one another and becoming more vulnerable throughout the process. Joey did imagine raw dogging her and cutting ties right after, but this felt different.

Fast-forward to the night they had sex. His whole family was out celebrating their championship victory against the opposing team. They didn't invite Joey to the dinner because he didn't play for that team and to his family, it didn't make sense for him to come. They told him that they can only bring two guests, but in actuality, the whole outside family went as well. This made Joey feel infuriated and he started drinking. He needed someone to distract him from the true pain he was feeling. He called Aqua and she came over with her car. Joey expressed his feelings for Aqua and it felt like the perfect time to have sex with one another. So,

Joey raw dogged Aqua that night and went about his business afterward. Aqua and Joey continued to talk from time to time, but not as frequently as before.

Remember having sex with someone who's still experiencing trauma that they haven't healed from yet, is a problem when it comes to having sex. Their problems become your problems, their issues become your issues, and all the people they used to have sex with, those demons latch onto you. Joey thought he was in a good spot with Aqua, but Aqua started ghosting him from time to time and wasn't showing any real effort or consistency in their relationship. Yes, Joey asked her to be his girlfriend the night they had sex and she said: "Si Papi" in her Spanish accent. When women speak in another language, that just makes them even sexier. It seemed like the energy was off because of her distance, so he proceeded to try and commit suicide. Once he got that text and phone call, everything changed.

Joey wasn't a professional raw dogger anymore and became an amateur raw dogger. Joey didn't care because he wanted to be a part of the baby's life. He would do anything Aqua needed him to do and was always there for her. This made Joey lose himself over another person. You always need to put and keep yourself first because this is your journey and path. Joey didn't know about spirituality, so he didn't know about this information. He didn't realize the subliminal messages she was throwing at him by not caring as much. Of course, she would be there for the baby, but not as much for Joey. After nine months of doing all that he can just to show her she's special; the baby came.

They named their child Brenna and what a beautiful bright star she was. Brenna came into this world full of life and was smiling right out of the womb. No crying, no hitting, and no pain; she was just smiling.

Brenna's middle name should be Calm because she was tranquil. They took pictures with the newborn baby and the family looked so good together. In Joey's eyes at least because this was only the beginning of their turmoil.

Joey took their family out to the park on the same day that Brenna was born. Joey was going to proposals to Aqua. Joey thought the right thing to do was to marry her because of the child's sake. That's the problem with most young people nowadays. They want to have sex so fast, get in relationships super-fast, and marry each other quickly after having babies. Babies won't always bring the family closer together. People would use the baby as a scapegoat in trying to stay together. Before you get married discuss bills, parenting styles, credit, debt, religion, how to deal with family, what beliefs will be instilled in your children, childhood traumas, sexual expectations, partner expectations, financial expectations, family health history, mental health history, bucket list, dream abode, careers, education, centrist, and whatever else come to mind. Love alone isn't enough. Protect your assets and get a prenup if you need to. It might be easier in separating instead of misleading the baby into seeing fake love. This will condition the baby of this ideology of fake love throughout their life. Most young people today, once they have a baby, they automatically think of marriage. People are young and don't know what they truly need from a relationship. They only go after their wants and desires. They quickly go through life while they're young. Sometimes it works and sometimes it doesn't.

When Joey asked Aqua for marriage, she was contemplating like she had something to tell him. Aqua told Joey that she was pregnant again. He was gusto not thinking if it was his kid or not. He automatically assumed that it was his kid again. Aqua was pregnant with another child from another man. We'll talk about this situation when we get to Aqua in her section.

This crushed Joey's spirit, and he began the downward spiral of his phobia once again. He started to fail his classes due to his struggles internally and being a young father. Everything was weighing on his shoulders. He had more responsibilities to handle and was barely getting any support from his family. The only person Joey truly loved became a baby mama to his newborn child. From always striving for a real family dynamic, he ended up co-parenting with Aqua. Would all these issues bring a negative vibe to Joey within the group? Would he ever express himself and all that he'd been through? How would he respond to seeing Aqua again? Never think that a small group of committed people can't change the world. It's the only thing that ever has. Can this group of beings, do it? Find out if they can throughout this book, "How to Overcome Apocalyptic Events".

Chapter One

LUCKY 7'S

Character 5: Indiniya

Indiniya is a kind beautiful spirit, but she usually puts a guard up to protect her heart over the past. What she had to go through in her childhood has hindered her connections and family member. She let those issues be at the forefront of her life. Through all of this, she still was a genuine soul, even though she carried some baggage that was holding her back. Let's dive deeper into the soul of Indiniya.

Indiniya had a sister named Becky, a brother named George, her dad was named Wayne, and her mom's name was Becca. Becky was the oldest and she wanted to be a doctor and a dentist. She had a lot going for her and that made her distant from her family. Indiniya had a deep disconsolate feeling in her heart towards that. It felt like she was moving on and experiencing life without them. Being the only daughters in the family, they used to be close growing up. It all changed once she started focusing more on her goals than on her family. Becky was starting a family, about to have a child, and recently got married. Indiniya didn't want to compare herself to her sister, but she did. She wanted that lifestyle for herself, and she would fantasize about the fairytales that she grew up seeing. Not by her own family, but through cartoons, television, and the idea of marriage. On top of that, Becky moved to a new state, so now they barely have time to chinwag, conversate, and interact with one another. Indiniya was scared to call because she could see how busy Becky was. This made their connection more distant and that affected Indiniya. Indiniya loves to connect deeply and freely, but since she didn't have a deep relationship with her family, it got tucked away and buried inside her. The only true connection she had within her family was her sister because she was always there. Once Becky started to move on, she didn't know how this affected Indiniya internally for the remainder of her life.

George was a trapper who sold cocaine, meth, marijuana, LSD, and some other drugs as well. He worked for the cartel and in doing so, he was in and out of prison most of his life. When George was out of jail, he would sell drugs, rob stores, and rap. He was a rapper who was rapping about what he was doing. This didn't end up well for George. People called George the "One Night Standard". You probably ask yourself, why do they call him that? Great question. They call him One Night Standard because he would rap about what he just did the day before. For instance, if he just sold some crack on the streets, made some money, went to the strip club, and had sex with a prostitute; he would rap about that. So, the police caught on after he was in and out of court. They used his lyrics for their gain and his downfall. George would smoke constantly and drink inside the house. His parents didn't say anything because he was old enough to make his own decisions, but they were ready to kick him out. Since he was in and out of prison, they welcomed him back into their house which was a bad idea. His lifestyle affected Indiniya because she thought in connecting with him, she'll have to do the same thing. So, she started to smoke with him, do drugs, and drink alcohol.

George showed her all the ins and outs of the business, but she didn't want to get involved in selling because that can be an eluding game to play. So, when George came back home, he'll bring the remaining goods to her sister to "connect".

People can feel peer pressure in doing something that they don't want to do. People would reject or think less of you if you're not doing what they're doing. Behind closed doors, peer pressure is just a form of competition for that person. They want to see how far you would let them control you. It's a toxic way of living and that's why so many people get peered pressured into doing something they know is wrong.

Indiniya kept experiencing toxic relationships because of her past. Her past wasn't the best and that has shaped her future.

Once Becky left, George came back from jail. Since Indiniya's parents were working, the only person she could connect with was George. Even though most of the time he'll steal money from his parent's savings account to have sex with sex workers. The only person who knew about this was Indiniya. George told her to not tell their parents. Scared tactics to the fullest extent because he was older than her and she didn't know any better.

No matter where you're from, everyone's buying or selling. If you can find out what a person wants, they'll buy anything you're selling. Most people base their choices on five emotions: greed, lust, compassion, humanity, and desperation. Customers are your target, the salespeople are your thrifters, and your coworkers are your shields. Step one is the bait; find out what they want. Step two is your hook; to attach what they want with what you're selling. Step three is the reels; gain their trust and seal the deal. Most people do stuff for power or pleasure.

One night, Indiniya overheard her parents talk about money and that they were struggling in keeping up with the house. Indiniya went up to her parents and told them the truth. Wayne busted into George's room and gave him a whooping like no tomorrow. He then proceeded to call the police to turn his son in. Indiniya was witnessing this horrifying event occur while her family was being dismantled by the inch. After the whooping, Indiniya would come out and creep outside the door. Wayne was already calling the police, so George barged into Indiniya's room and told her that she would regret this decision. George had this evil look in his eyes which were full of darkness. He called one of his friends while he was packing up to tell him what Indiniya did. She didn't hear what they were saying.

The eyes are the beholder of the soul and if your eyes are pitch black, then you might not be as organic as it seems. People who get burned by the sun, turn red fast, have issues with the sun, or need suntan lotion, you might need to find out where you came from. Having a connection with the sun is one of the most powerful things you can do in letting yourself know you're chosen. Not only do other races experience these symptoms, but even some melanated beings do as well. Everything's not what it seems because we live in the Maya through the illusion. You have to see who people truly are instead of automatically messing with them if the energy isn't pure from the start.

George tried to leave, but Wayne grabbed him to make him wait for the police. Becca was crying, but also supporting Wayne. Indiniya was in her closet crying over what's been taking place within her family. Wayne slammed him to the ground and tried to restrain him. George was from the streets, so he knew how to fight because he fought almost every week. One of George's hands was free, and he punched Wayne right in the face. George went on top of Wayne and started punching him. He was punching him so hard that Becca didn't know if Wayne would still be alive. He legitimately smashed his skill in about 15 times. Right before the 16th punch, Becca attempted to pull George away from Wayne. As she was doing that, George didn't know it was his mother and he pulled out his pocketknife and slashed his mom. Now you probably wondering if he slashed his mom on the leg or thigh. Since George was tall, as he turned around with the knife, it reached his mom's throat.

Crying can be a very healing and spiritual experience. It's a wonderful way to release stagnant and unpleasant energy, especially if you're empathic. We've been conditioned to view crying as a weakness but in other cultures, crying is collectively seen as a very enlightening experience. In Japan, they have classes (called "rui-katsu" which translates to "tear seeking") dedicated to regular sessions of crying to provide people a safe space to process and grieve their more difficult emotions. Don't grieve when people fail to recognize your ability; grieve for your lack of ability instead. Even tears of joy can be very energetically, purifying, and uplifting for the spirit. Remember this, the next time you need to cry… you're not weak. Sometimes we're tested, not to show our weaknesses, but to discover our strengths. It truly takes a strong person to be vulnerable in today's world.

When George saw his mom gasping for air it brought this rush of emotion over him, but he still was furious because the cops were on their way. Indiniya was currently 14 years old when all of this was happening. George was on the way out of the door when a random car pulled up. It was George's drug dealer.

George didn't pay his dealer for three months straight and he was expecting the money today. Of course, George didn't have it at the moment, and he was scrambling since the police were almost there. The dealer and his gang kicked down the door and demanded the money. George could take the money from his parents, but with everything that was happening, he wasn't thinking straight. The gang came in and saw all the carnage of what had just taken place. The dealer was about to call the police on George over what he did and then leave the premise. The police were already on their way, but the gang didn't know. George attacked the dealer, and they went into a tussle. The gang was there to help the drug dealer. They decided to torture George because he didn't have the money. They knew they weren't going to receive the money and the police should be on their way over the damage that's already been done. The dealer took out his gun and shot George right in the face.

Cold blood rushed upon George's face. Indiniya was scared of the sound of the gunshot that she let out a scream. The dealer told the gang to find whoever else was in the house, so there won't be any witnesses. The gang followed the sound of the screaming noise and found Indiniya in the closet. They took her hostage and put her in the trunk. The police sirens were coming closer and closer. The gang had a self-driving car believe it or not. As they pulled off, it ran over an elderly woman who was trying to walk her dog during the night. It was a hit-and-run assault. Watch out for those self-driving cars because they can easily take over and do something we didn't want them to do. The police saw them run over the lady and leave the crime scene. The assistant police officer had enough and decided to take out his gun and shoot the driver. The gang came out of the car and started a heavy fire shootout with the police under the streetlights. Multiple police cars came, and it was too much for the gang to handle. They all died during the shootout.

They inspected the car and were shocked in seeing Indiniya in the trunk. Indiniya had a busted lip because she screamed out for help as they were taking her hostage. So, one of the gang members punched her right in the mouth to shut her up. As they covered her mouth, Indiniya was experiencing lots of torment. Not only with her family in the past, but also with what just transpired. She told the police that her family was inside the house. They saw George with a gunshot wound in his temple dead; they saw Wayne not moving at all, and they saw Becca with her slashed throat and her eyes closed.

George's friend Woody finally came after George made the phone call to tell him what happened. He knew the police were already there, so Woody dressed up for the occasion.

Woody told the police that he was Indiniya's uncle and that he can take her. Woody said that it'll be best for her to get clearer evidence of what happened tomorrow since it was already midnight. The policemen agreed and told him that they'll have to be at the police station in the morning. They took down Woody's information including his address. Indiniya barely knew Woody, but she saw him periodically when he hanged out with George. Indiniya used to smoke, drink, and do drugs with not only George but Woody as well.

Woody took her to his trap house and instantaneously it smelt like smoke. Woody would try to make her comfortable by offering her a drink or two. Indiniya just wanted to go to bed and try to process everything that just happened. It's important to go to bed earlier and get enough rest. When Indiniya fell asleep, the worst had yet to appear for her that night.

The times when Indiniya and Woody would smoke together when George would go to the bathroom or get more alcohol, Woody would enticingly look at Indiniya. He would then subtlety flirt with her a little bit, but not too much where she would feel uncomfortable. Mind you, she already had alcohol and drugs in her system, so she didn't care as much or realized it. Now that she was sober today, she got to feel her emotions.

George could tell that George had something with her sister by the way he looked at her when he looked through the bathroom mirror. Since Woody was his ride or die, he didn't pay any mind to it, but once George got crossed by Indiniya, he told Woody to do what he wanted to her.

As Indiniya was sleeping, Woody would then tie her up against the bed and put duct tape over her mouth. Woody would rape Indiniya senselessly as the true rapist and pedophile he was.

By the time Indiniya woke up and realized what was going on, he was already inside her and it was too late to try and fight it. After hours upon hours of seemingly endless rape, he finally went to bed beside Indiniya. This traumatized her in a way that should never happen to anyone ever. What she had to go through shouldn't be cast down upon anyone on this planet.

Woody slept in because he didn't get enough sleep last night. Indiniya didn't sleep and was up all night paralyzed, shattered, and emotionally and physically scarred. Remember they had to be at the police department in the morning and if not, then there'll be a problem. An hour went by, and there was a knock on the door. The police slammed into the door with a crew of swat members looking for Woody and Indiniya. A smoke bomb and a smoke grenade entered the room and he started to cough. Woody finally awakened to see what was going on. By that time, they already put a gas mask over Indiniya's face, and she told them what happened. It was pretty suspect as he was over-aged, in nothing but boxers, and in the same bed as an underage teenager. They brought Woody into prison for life and started to question Indiniya about everything that transpired over the last 24 hours.

If a cop tells you, you better talk, that means they have nothing on you, and you better keep your mouth shut. Police officials love to do scare tactics and try to manipulate the situation. Saying your friend ratted you out or someone already confess when they didn't. Stay true to yourself and don't back down from the fight. If any of them or any security guard starts to pressure you, just speak another language.

Indiniya told them everything she could remember or comprehend. Indiniya stated that she did some drugs with Woody in the past, but she regretted it. She was too young at the time to throw her in jail, but they did keep it on file. She also had to do community service, go to rehab, and go through a jail initiative program. She accepted the charges and went to the rehab center. Four years went by, and she became clean by the age of 18. She stepped away from drugs and only used alcohol when parting or on special occasions. *Crowd asked, "What happened to the parents? Where's the sister?"* I thought you'll never ask, but let's look at the relationship between Indiniya and her parents first.

Becca was a hard-working middle-class woman who was truly a boss in her own right. She tends to make sure other people were good before herself. She was there for Indiniya, making sure she had food, clothes, etc. Once Indiniya was old enough to get a job, Becca did less for her and Indiniya had to start doing it all by herself. It became a roommate type of vibe instead of a mother-daughter connection. The only time she would connect with her mom was if they had a deep conversation about something.

For Wayne, he was more like a roommate of Indiniya. They would say wassup to each other, do stuff for one another, but not connect deeply. They both didn't see the need to connect deeply with each other, but they always had love for one another. In life, there are people you easily gravitate and connect with. Then there are people who it'll happen over time. Then there are people you don't need to connect deeply with, or who you don't mess with.

After the shootout, the ambulance arrived on the scene. Indiniya didn't see her family before Woody took her away. Once the ambulance went inside the murder scene, the gang members were already dead outside due to multiple gun wounds. They took Becca and Wayne to the emergency room. For George, it was too late for him and died because of the bullet in his temple. During the car ride, they noticed that Becca was dead. The slashed wound on her neck was an instant kill and they didn't find out until they got inside the ambulance. The only person who had hope of surviving was Wayne.

They rushed Wayne into the surgery room and let a robot surgeon operate on him. Doctors wanted to try out and see how robots would operate on patients. Since Wayne couldn't sign the waiver and the consent form, the doctor said, "F it" and let the robot operate on Wayne. After the robot performed surgery on Wayne for a few hours, the doctors all went on their lunch break, letting the robot handle it. The robot had malware and rebooted the wrong system, so it lost the code and programs in doing the operation correctly. The warning signs popped up on all the cameras, but all the doctors and nurses took the same lunch break. By the time they finally arrived back in the operating room, Wayne already had passed away.

This just shows you how society puts so much trust in robots and technology that they want them to control our everyday lives. Jobs are getting taken over by robots, cars are getting replaced by self-driving cars, and robots are now knowing how to feel emotions and have babies. You can power a car with just water, but people wouldn't try it because it's outside the norm. Electric power cars are better than fueled power cars as well.

There are stereotypes based on discrimination. No matter your race, age, gender, veteran status, disability, etc. People try to find employment with an employer, but the company might base your hiring status on one of these options. For example, if someone just came out of college looking to jumpstart their career, they get turned down based on not having enough experience. How can youth have work experience when they spend all their time getting a degree that they needed? They're already in debt from all the money they had to pay; so now looking for a position, they barely get their foot in the door. Why do an internship when you already developed those skills personally or in school? The same goes for the elderly. Someone thinks they're too primitive to work for that company. The whole system is made for you to fail and to slave your life away. They give you small benefits to make you think it's all okay and that you're doing something in this world.

Indiniya never said bye to her family and the next time she saw them was at their funeral. They didn't know the spiritual meaning behind cremation, so they just buried them. Cremation would help you to remember all the knowledge from your current life if you needed to reincarnate into another being. We're not going for reincarnating anymore because this is my last lifetime, am I right crowd *Yessir*.

Your heart has to be lighter than a feather. It'll be in an inquisition of purgatory amongst the Gods for Armageddon, doomsday, and judgment day. You take this time to look back at your life and see everything you've done. You feel every emotion you may have caused someone in the past and if you can't accept it or move on, then you'll be stuck there until you learn. Unless you automatically want to reincarnate and go through the process all over again.

How many grudges did you take to your grave? When you weren't liked or followed, how did you behave? Look back on the things you thought you owned; do you even remember them well? Would you ever live through and accept your regret and pain? Heaven is for those who let go of regret and when you're not ready to let it all go, you'll have to wait until you come into acceptance. Heaven is in this moment in your mind, body, and soul. You don't reach for bliss, you are bliss. All you have to do is unwind your mind and train your soul to align. You have to be Heaven to see Heaven.

With no family, Indiniya had to go into foster care. This was the start of her feeling abandoned and abused by friends, family, and boyfriends while feeling worthless. Indiniya had to process everything while she was seeing the other children get picked by families over her. She was asking the Universe, why me? Why was this all happening to me? Why do I have to go through this? As you may know, we shouldn't question why anything is happening to us, but instead, ask what this is teaching us.

Being curious even in the worst situations will be beneficial for any person. Being openly curious about "I don't know" and sitting in the "I don't know" is a good position to be in because it allows you to continue to be open, to learn, and to hear perspectives on all sides of the spectrum. It's when you become so dogmatic and entrenched in one position and you start self-identifying with it. This will make you defensive with anything that comes against that position. Everything's temporary and it's all based on your perspective. Bad is a made-up concept, so being spontaneous is key to everything. Follow your intuition based on your perspective and cognizance. Why do you react to this type of criticism? Go in the back of your mind and analyze everything.

Who you think you are or want to become, you have to say that a thousand times per day. Not only do you have to truly believe in that manifestation, but you also have to truly feel that manifestation for it to work. Your subconscious mind would make you see the reality you're currently in, but your conscious mind sees past it. Don't let a memory mess up your life. Accept it and move on because life's too fast for you to keep thinking about the past. So, you went through a little breakup, a minor setback, but let's be honest. You don't need this right now. You're strong and independent, you look great, and now you have all this extra time to focus on yourself. Keep changing, elevating, and gaining abundance in your life. Everything happens for a reason and the Universe wouldn't place any challenge in front of you that you won't be able to handle. When it felt like all hope was lost for Indiniya, guess who showed up? Becky.

Becky found out her little sister was in foster care and no families were adopting her. Becky knew about her family and was actually in the waiting room during the operation on Wayne. Of course, she couldn't be in the actual lab where the robot did the surgery on Wayne. She had to wait in the waiting room and Woody sent a text to Becky that he had

Indiniya. She was actually at the police station waiting for Indiniya to arrive and she never showed. By the time, Indiniya came to the station, Becky had to go pick up her child from school. The police station told Becky everything that Indiniya told them. She knew that Indiniya was going through a lot, so she just went MIA as she went to rehab.

Once Becky knew where she was, Becky and her family came to visit her. They had a long three-hour heart-to-heart with each other about everything that they've gone through and how Indiniya truly felt. After the head-to-head, Becky already predetermined that she and her family were going to adopt her. Indiniya was so passionate about spending more time with her new mom (who's her sister). Even though she spoke about what she had gone through with her sister, that doesn't truly mean that she properly did the shadow work to fully get past those situations. Would Indiniya keep all of her past issues to herself and let them get in the way of the group? Would she make predetermined judgments about people without fully knowing them? How would she view relationships now? Would her past affect her future? I'll answer all your dying questions throughout the book, "How to Overcome Apocalyptic Events".

Chapter One

LUCKY 7'S

Character 6: Bastet

Bastet is a unique character in this story. She wants everything right now and wouldn't take no for an answer. This stemmed from doing black magic and not healing from her past. It was arduous for her because of everything she went through while keeping it all inside. She would act as if nothing was wrong, and she did all this healing before. You can see it on her face that something was bothering her.

She tends to become desperate for a man and desires marriage. She would mess with guys for them to have a baby with her to make them stay around. In her eyes, if they had a baby with her, then they'll have to marry her. She would tell them she doesn't like using condoms. Those men easily agreed with the circumstance to have some fast sex but ended up getting her pregnant. She thinks of guys as a trial run. If that guy doesn't stay, then she'll find another one. That's how some women act when having sex with men. This type of mindset and acting like she knows everything will affect her and her future relationships.

She tends to only see things from her point of view instead of others and how it'll impact them. This started in childhood acting through her ego. This theorizes for Bastet since she now has multiple children with multiple baby daddies. Brian, Joe, Kevin, and Chantelle to be exact. Bastet lost a different child throughout the process. Even though this was making Bastet hopeless, Bastet wasn't giving up on love.

Bastet was an only child just like Apollo. Her mom was named Victoria and her dad's name was Vinny. Vinny was never really there for Bastet, and Victoria had a problem Bastet was young and she only knew her parents and a few friends from school. Bastet couldn't comprehend at the time what was going on, but as a child, she was in tune. Children remember how someone made them feel and who was there for them throughout their life. If someone wasn't presently there throughout their life, then they'll remember that and be reminiscent of the fact. That's what Bastet was realizing, but since Bastet was an alpha woman, she didn't want to ask for help or appear weak.

The Universe doesn't give you what you ask for with your thoughts. It gives you what you demand with your actions. She wouldn't share her true feelings with anyone or leave any situation without discussing it. She was strong and able to hold her own. Behind the smile and soul, there was still stuff that needed to be fixed. Anyone who recognized and shared the information with Bastet in a respectful manner made her enter fight or flight mode. She would assume everything was great, but then deny, deflect, and try to defend herself as much as she can. She would use small talk and sexual interactions to intrigue and entice men. She would think about negative situations using her ego instead of listening to her intuition. This was a hindrance for Bastet and the people who she interacts with.

Her father wasn't there most of her life. This caused issues for Bastet in the worst way. Since she didn't heal from that situation, it's a recurring effect on her relationships. The Universe was showing and telling her what the root cause was, but she wasn't fixing the predicament. Root causes let the names of all disorders be the limbs jointed together with the trees. Work on the root and that subdue, and all the limbs will bow to you. The limbs are cholic, pleurisy, worms, gravel, gout, and stone. Remove the cause and they'll be gone. That's how the Universe works. If they notice an issue you need to fix, you'll experience the same situations throughout life until you fix, heal, and overcome the dilemma. That's why all of her baby daddies left because it was a recurring effect.

Healing from the past can be difficult, but it's necessary on your path. Without healing, how can you burgeon and elevate? That's where shadow work comes into play. Most people try to avoid their shadows, their dark side, and their dark night of the soul. The four phases of a dark night of the soul are an identity crisis, shattered belief systems, withdrawal, and transformation. To do that isn't by the mind, but by the heart and the ability to feel. Does this person's energy feel right? Does this make me feel good? Something about this person's energy is heavy. I don't like how this makes me feel. Or something about this doesn't sit right with me. If you have to think or question it, then that's your red flag right there. People don't learn their lessons; they just repeat the same mistakes. It's like their inner computer system got a glitch and it keeps them repeating the same programs. They tend to live at bars drinking, smoking, doing drugs, pills, sex, masturbation, short-term pleasure, and other forms of temporary relief to take their pain away.

Wonder why pedowood or what people like to call Hollywood, always tries to promote sex and lust? Pediwood is full of mortala beings roaming around this whole planet. Hollywood is a child pedophile organization.

Some creators and directors of these kid shows have fetishes that they want the kids to perform. If they don't then most of them won't receive the role they were auditioning for.

Wonder why some webcam women use red LED lights? Red is a form of lust that some demons use in trying to steal your energy, light, and power. What's your highest form of energy you may ask? Your sexual energy (which is your semen) helps power your kundalini energy. Your sexual energy is sacred and should be used sacredly instead of being wasted. People love having sex but having sex with the wrong person, you're only gaining short-term pleasure which can last for a few minutes to an hour. Wonder why most men don't last long in bed? They only look at sex as short-term pleasure through the physical reality. Some people who take care of their energies and use it wisely can go for hours. Making love and having sex are two different things.

People can have sex with anyone they want and not necessarily have a connection with that person. Making love with that person shows that you do have a connection with them, and you know how to control your sexual energy. Most people who do have a connection with a person but haven't mastered their sacred energy can still fall under short-term pleasure. Especially if that person doesn't have a connection to their three brains. The brain/mind, the heart/soul/spirit, and your genital area. If two people who are spiritually in tune with their mind, body, and soul have a deep connection with each other; then they can make love for eternity.

Love someone, even more, when they seem least deserving. At that very moment, they're most in need of your love. Having sex can help speed up your manifestation as well because you're entering each other's portals to create something beautiful. This could mean a newborn child, manifesting powers, or diving deeper together. Most people don't see sex in this way and only look at it through the physical. They look at sex as short-term or to create a baby instead of viewing it as a sacred energy exchange.

Yes, people have different paths, purposes, and missions from one another. The spiritual journey is like grade levels and people are operating on whatever grade level they're currently in. The more you go deeper into the rabbit hole, the more knowledge you'll obtain. The more you go deep into the ocean, the freer you'll become. That's why I said it's important to save your energy and not waste your semen on anyone or anything that's operating on a low frequency. Not to mention with these injections/implants; people now have aids, STDs, lower immune systems, blood clots, and infertility. STDs can transfer that injection to another person by transferring bodily fluids. If someone got the injection and has sex with someone who didn't, then that person who didn't get the injection will now have the particles of the injection. Nanotechnology particles eat the body alive and the mutation forms. If that person then has sex with another person who didn't have that injection or test, then that person will have it as well. Watch who you sleep with and metal detox when necessary. The same goes for people who got the implants as well. A mandate isn't a law.

There's no healthy aspect to any drug that you put into your system whether by ingestion or injection. It's all different levels of poison. Your body's first reaction is to find a way to rid of that toxin. The more you feed your body with these poisons, the harder it becomes to remove the toxin through normal means. Once you reach a certain level of toxicity, your body has to find more desperate measures to remove them. If you hinder your body, this will lead to much more severe measures like chronic diseases, tumors, cancers, or worse.

When someone wants to commit suicide in a movie, they often head right to the medicine cabinet for medical poisons. No one is trying to kill themselves by heading to the fridge and eating four heads of organic cauliflower. If a whole bottle of medical poison can kill you, how can taking the same amount of poison, over a longer period, make you healthy? It's time to start connecting the dots. Most people would rather blame germs and genes for their illnesses than accept that it's mostly their diet, beliefs, mindset, and overall lifestyle to blame. Most people don't have the stomach to deal with what's really going on. So, they just disregard it and fall back into the illusion.

You shouldn't take health advice from people who are unhealthy, from companies that profit off of the perpetual disease, and from corporations who accept money from fast-food chains. Fast-food chains are genetically modified and mind-altering food. You can't catch a disease, the same way you can't catch health. Understanding this fact alone can completely change your life.

If you go to a medical doctor just for a routine check-up, he or she would likely find something to put you on medications for, and create a problem. If you go to a medical doctor with a problem, they'll certainly put you on medications, which won't fix the problem, but ultimately create new ones. Sickness isn't a physical symptom. Sickness is an ideology that makes you fear touching a doorknob or think that hugging your best friend can make you sick. The germ theory is a sickness that has infected your mind and distorts the way you experience reality. People don't learn how the body really works. Rockefeller medicine taught you bs to shill their petroleum-based pharmaceuticals. Prescribing drugs isn't health care. Look for something positive every day, even if some days you have to look a little harder.

Growing your food is like printing your own money. Fasting (when done correctly and for the right reasons) does something to you that cannot be explained with human language. You become very aware of just how habitual the act of eating has become. Are we taking the nutrients of food and water if we just end up going to the bathroom? When you fast, you don't feel the urge of going to the restroom, so what's the value? Many of us don't eat for hunger, we eat for pleasure. The absence of perpetual pleasure-seeking (in all forms) exposes you to the emotions you mask with your quixotic habits, and you're finally exposed to who you truly are. This is where the healing starts physically, emotionally, mentally, and spiritually.

The individual has always struggled with being overwhelmed by the tribe. If you try it, you'll be lonely often, and sometimes frightened, but no price's too high for the privilege of owning yourself. If you feel lonely and have no friends; it's okay. You came into this world alone and you're careful about sharing your energy with people who serve you no purpose in life. Needing nothing brings you everything.

Every 90 days we have new blood. Every 11 months, every organ in our body is new. Every two years, every bone in our bodies is new. We are regenerating ourselves every minute of every day. We get rid of a billion dead cells an hour, and each one of those cells is replaced by a new cell. That cell will be replaced by what you eat.

There's a theory that every 100 years a pandemic happens. At first glance, nothing seems strange, but the accuracy with which these events take place is outlandish to notice. 1720 Plague, 1820 Cholera Outbreak, 1920 Spanish Flu, and 2020 Coronavirus. There are about 7,000,000,000,000,000,000,000,000,000 atoms in your body that are billions of years old. At the deepest level, you're the Universe in human form.

The real New Year starts when the cycle of life begins again with new blossoms and exponential growth. The new beginning is spring, called "Vernal Equinox" which happens on March 20th. So, the real New Year's Eve is March 19th with New Year's Day being March 20th.

The awakening has gone mainstream and there's nothing to stop nor halt it. Not even the plandemic, fake alien invasion, NWO, Project Bluebeam, weather modifications, and climate cooling. The elders have strategically placed 144,000-star workers all over the world as beacons of the awakening. The beacons have connected, henceforth we're all connected. Awakened star seeds are currently hearing a whirring sound and horns in their ears. Some are experiencing their ANKHCESTORS' memories, pains, emotional imbalances, or feeling like everything's falling apart. Some are experiencing and witnessing so much synchronicity through patterns and numbers. Some are experiencing vivid dreams, lucid dreams, in a trance, and astral projection. You'll feel this rush of excitement after your euneirophrenia dream. Don't worry it's the Universe communicating this to you thus you're aligning with its frequencies.

Watch out for the blue and artificial light that messes up your vision and brainwaves. It's like a microwave trying to attack your brain, but this time you go to sleep with the lights on. That's why most people need complete darkness to fall asleep. It's time to beat the drums, invoke our ANKHCESTORS, honor the elders, and do the warrior boogaloo around the fire as we chant spells to cast NRTERU.

If you constantly lose your energy over what you view on your computer, television, or your phone screen, then it'll make you fall at your lowest point. You were ascending high but then crashed and burned. That's why they wouldn't necessarily promote actual porn (in most cases) but will entice you with nudity, television sex, or the words they say to make you think about lust. Then once you think about lustful action, you go and do what you do on your phone screen. This lowers yourself and completely squanders your creative energy. You'll feel no motivation, no inspiration, and no elevation because you'll feel your lower self creep into the mix. This is a form of short-term pleasure because at the moment it feels good, but right after, you'll most likely feel horrible. Just like anyone who experienced having bad sex. It'll feel pretty good at the moment, but then afterward you wonder why you did what you did in the first place.

They don't want you to pulsate your mind and think outside the box. When there's no enemy within, the enemy outside can't hurt you. They want you to stay in prison within your mental box imprisoning your mind so you can be controlled. Realize it or not, most people aren't controlling their lives. They're allowing outside forces to control the actions, behaviors, and thoughts that run through their bodies. All tyrannies rule through fraud and force, but once the fraud is exposed, they must rely exclusively on force. All you can do is warn people to wake up. If they don't listen, don't waste your time or energy arguing with these people. All you can do is exulansis because people have so much envy, they'll not understand. Move on so you can warn others.

Ask yourself all the time you masturbated before it occurs, was it your true thoughts going into your head, or was it some demons pushing out mind control tactics for you to lose your seed instantly? Instant gratification, right? Well, if it's instant, then it'll be a short-term stimulus. You're focused on the short-term premeditation, and you'll never have a clear head.

All in all, people would always try to have a quick escape by not feeling their true emotions or going through the dark night of the soul. People tend to lie to themselves and that's why most people can't look in the mirror (especially inside their eyes which is the beholder of the soul). They're scared and their ego will kick in and say, "What am I doing, or this feels weird." Hence, why most people cannot meditate for more than a couple of minutes.

Challenge:

Take your time and say your mantras, tantras, and your affirmations. It only takes a skillful person in meditation to not listen to anything, sit in silence, and be in a calm state. Most people need something external for them to feel that sensation or reach that point. Everyone's path is different, so do whatever works best for you.

Exercise:

Staring into your soul in the mirror is called mirror gazing. Mirror gazing is most powerful when closing the door, turning off the lights, and having a staring contest with yourself while saying words of affirmation.

There's sun, nature, star, moon, or ship gazing as well, but for more information on that check brandonbass99 on YouTube (https://linktr.ee/DoubleBYouTube) for more details. You know I had to do it crowd *crowd laughs*.

Bastet was having problems with this because she was never the picture type. She likes to take pictures but tends to judge herself on her appearance. She would take multiple pictures and only keep one. Most women would take 25-100 pictures (for example) and only keep about two or three and only post one or two. Most women make small remarks or say degrading comments about themselves through the process. In hindsight, this will plummet your confidence and then they'll make judgmental comments or gossip about other people. See how it all unfolds and comes back into play. This is why I said shadow work and getting to the root of the problem is essential in your personal and spiritual growth.

Reminder:

All situations are neutral until you place judgment and label them. You define the situation; the situation doesn't define you. It's not the situation that's the problem; it's your thoughts about the situation that is the problem. A problem isn't a problem until you mentally decide that it's a problem. Your thinking isn't the problem, but instead, you're thinking about your problems is what creates the problem and also redefines your thinking relating to the situation. Someone else's thinking doesn't matter without you thinking about their thinking. Your thoughts add value and it's not the other way around. Your thoughts possess all power; it takes the power within you to create the perception of power outside of you. Your thoughts about reality aren't always true. Study, observe and question your thinking about your thinking, which is your judgment of your thinking. Also, known as meta-thinking and meta-cognition. Your thoughts and emotional projection can bend reality, "re-define" situations and reshape the reality of future events.

Be impeccable with your words by speaking with integrity and saying what you mean. Avoid using your words to speak against yourself or to jaw at others. Use the power of your word in the direction of truth and love. People would bad-mouth you for hours and they don't realize what they're truly doing to themselves in the process. Don't take anything personally because what they do isn't because of you. What others say and do is a projection of their reality and dreams. When you're immune to the opinions and actions of others, you wouldn't be the victim of needless suffering.

Pain is physical and suffering is mental. Beyond the mind, there's no unscathed. Pain is essential for the survival of the body, but none compels you to suffer. Suffering is due entirely to clinging or resisting. It's a sign of our unwillingness to move on and to flow with life. Don't make assumptions, ask questions, and express what you want. Communicate with others as clearly as you can to avoid misunderstandings, sadness, and dramatic expression.

Always do your best because your best is going to change from moment to moment. For example, it'll be different when you're healthy as opposed to sick. Under any circumstance, simply do your best, and you'll avoid self-judgment, self-abuse, and regret. You deserve the best, so only accept the best.

People can call you whatever, but you know who you are. People don't have to show you love because you already know that you're loved. They're mad when they can't distract you anymore. Discipline is the choice between what you want now and what you want most. You're going to have these friends and past relationships coming knocking at your door. You're going to have these thoughts of going back to your dated ways. You're letting it come right back to you. Everything you did before is dead now. You're moving to your new self, and don't go back to your old self. Stop allowing people who do so little for you, to take up so much space in your mind. We cannot build our destiny by carrying rented thoughts in our minds. If they do care, they should be able to focus on your small fastidious because the little things count the most. The person who's meant for you is going to listen, hear you out, and understand instead of blocking you. It's all a game and a simulation. Don't take it seriously and play it as if it's a game. Nothing should surprise you anymore. You shouldn't feel affected by anything that's going on in this world. You're just experiencing it. You feel the sadness of this rare lacuna for this person, but it's a trick.

Anybody who's eating that bs, smoking that bs, drinking that bs, or doing that bs, let them go. Learn how to say no and stop saying yes to people when it's a no for yourself. Don't submit to authority, step into your power, and reclaim what's yours! Stop allowing people to take advantage of you. You don't have to do what everyone else is doing on the planet. You are your own free being outright. Take every chance you get in life because some things only happen once. Find something you enjoy. If you do something you don't enjoy, then you won't put your all into it. You won't be consistent because you don't enjoy it. The human brain knows what makes it happy and it'll push you to do those things. It won't push you into doing things you don't want to do in life. Do or do not, there is no try.

Bastet always wondered why her dad and mom didn't get along and why Vinny barely was there for her. It wasn't like Vinny was in and out of jail like George, but he was always in the same state. Victoria was always present in her life, and she cared for and nurtured her. Victoria was trying to be her best friend than a mom. Victoria was doing it in such a way that seemed suspicious, or she was trying too hard to develop a connection with Bastet. Now I know what you're thinking, she had to because Vinny wasn't around. She had to become the mother and the father in Bastet's life. Why wasn't Vinny present in Bastet's life when he lived in the same state as her?

A few years after Bastet was born (I would say around two or three years old), Vinny had a reason to leave Victoria. Victoria was the biggest part of Vinny's absence because he was there for the first two to three years of Bastet's life.

Victoria would go out at night and return home either late at night or early in the morning. Victoria would say, "Oh I was out with a couple of friends living the nightlife." This wasn't the case because Vinny would then check her phone when it was unlocked and he saw some messages. Now, I wouldn't suggest going through another person's phone because that's an invasion of privacy, and they would lose trust in you. You don't know the full story, details, or information, so don't overthink to where you act out of rage and anger instead of calmness, and listen to what they have to say. He went to the group chat of her friends and noticed they didn't talk about going to the club last night. He kept scrolling and he saw something astonishing.

Victoria had another person's contact name as "Secret Admirer/Lover". Vinny was so outraged with anger that he started to smash holes in the wall, break precious items, and destroy other stuff in the house. Victoria woke up in shock over Vinny's tantrum. Victoria was concerned about the baby since Bastet was already crying. After Vinny settled down a bit, Victoria checked in on Bastet.

Vinny told her about the secret admirer she had on her phone. Victoria knew her secret was going to come out that night. All those times she went out to the club, she was seeing her secret lover. She didn't sugarcoat anything since the deed had already been done. She got straight to the point and told him that she had a secret admirer which was her lover. Vinny and Victoria had been married for over 12 years. Vinny was shocked and told her that he wanted a divorce. He still loved her though because of how long they've been together and the family they built. He was a bit considerate with the information that was given to him and what she had expressed.

Victoria had this pale look on her face while listening to Vinny because she had to tell him something else. Audience you might need to cover your ears because viewers' discretion is advised.

She stated that she had a secret child with this secret lover of hers. Her secret child was born a year after Bastet. Vinny couldn't believe what he just heard. He was devastated and Victoria had a rush of guilt that entered her body. Vinny was crying his eyes out. He was asking Victoria what'll happen for Bastet. Surprisingly, Vinny was still trying to make light out of the situation. Not for Victoria because Victoria had more news to share with Vinny. Vinny was getting angry once more and started to ask who's the father. She proceeded to let Vinny know that her secret lover was his best friend Pauly. *Crowd said "WTF!"*

Yes, it was his best friend Pauly, and she knew eventually he'll start to ask questions about it. Victoria was smart and she knew what she was doing. She told Pauly to get another phone and have a secret number to communicate with her. This will make Vinny think she's texting a random person, but all this time it was his best friend. Watch out for people who have boy best friends and girl best friends because it can cause some underlining issues. Victoria also put his new number as a secret admirer because she knew eventually, she couldn't hide the truth from Vinny anymore. That's why she purposely left her phone unlocked, so Vinny would see it firsthand instead of Victoria having to tell him. Victoria was a sneaky and conniving master at what she did. Love is love and that love would make you do some crazy things.

Once Vinny found out it was his best friend, he stormed out of the room and was about to exit the front door. Bastet would come out of her room and cry out the word "Dada." Vinny looked back and stared into her eyes and left without even saying bye.

Vinny wanted to punish Victoria by having her take care of their responsibilities of Bastet way more frequently. He thought it was a form of her remembering the family dynamic they once shared. They got divorced and Victoria had most of the custody over Bastet. Vinny went MIA but was still able to be around her whenever he wanted to with Victoria's approval. Victoria was still dating Pauly and was ready to build an everlasting life with him.

Victoria had a secret daughter that she kept secret from Bastet all her life. That's why she tried to spend the most time with Bastet, so she wouldn't pose a question or feel jealous of her not spending enough time with her. In Bastet's eyes, she was her only child. Bastet had a sister-in-law which was around her same age. Would Bastet ever find out? How would Bastet's childhood affect her life? Would she ever change, or will she always be in her suborned ways? Find out soon throughout the book, "How to Overcome Apocalyptic Events" continues.

Chapter One

LUCKY 7'S

Character 7: Aqua

Wow, this book is getting juicy. I wonder how it'll turn out in the end. This chapter was needed to have you connect deeply with the characters and have your relationship with them. Speaking of characters, this is the last main character. You either love her or you hate her; yes, I'm talking about Aqua. Let's hop right into the eolith of Aqua.

Aqua was the youngest in her family having two older sisters. One was named Alex and the other was named Tori. Alex and Tori were the definitions of mean girls. They were skinny, better than you, and you couldn't tell them otherwise. They had self-confidence issues that ran so deeply that they had to make as much money as possible and run around telling everyone how much money they made. Then they would break people who were weaker than them to make them feel better about themselves.

No one had a chance to talk to them because of how they acted. They had their posse of "yes women" obliging to what they tell them to do, say, or think. Both sisters were both semi-popular and got into a lot of drama. Alex and Tori didn't join any cheer or sports team because they were better than them. No one could say or do anything when they gossip because their parents were the biggest investors in the school they went to. Even though Alex and Tori barely did any work and just chewed bubble gum and did their makeup; their parents were the investors. This means if their parents stop giving the school money, then there'll be no school.

They would take frequent bathroom breaks to look at themselves in the mirror. Wherever they went, their posse went as well. At least for their posse, they get invited to sleepovers and parties. They only talk to them in the 3rd person; for example, "Come on girls" or "Let's leave." When they're at their sleepovers, they are acknowledged, but Alex and Tori did most of the talking. Aqua felt neglected because she was never able to amid into their sleepovers. When the parties ended, Aqua was the one to help clean up because if the maid were to clean up, then the maid would tell their parents. So, Aqua had to clean it up by herself, so they wouldn't get grounded.

Vicky was their mom, and she was a realtor and a real estate agent. Jordan was their dad, and he was the CEO of his own tech company and had his own car dealership. Jordan was busy, so he didn't care if they threw a party or not. Vicky was out and about fixing up homes (called fixer-uppers), putting homes on the market, and selling houses. She was always searching for new homes, working with her team, taking calls from clients, and making their dreams come into reality. Not necessarily the dream life their children had hoped for or imagined, but for her clients, she did.

Yes, they live and have the finer things in life, but that doesn't necessarily always bring you happiness, just comfortability. Most people who have a lot of money are really lonely. That's why they sometimes need a posse of people that are always around them. Some people will look after the ones who helped them along the way, but most people get lost in the money and end up turning their backs on the people who helped them get to that point. Wonder why, when someone who's considered to be "rich" always has to throw parties and hang out with people constantly? It's because they're trying to hide the fact that they're alone, maybe lonely, can't be by themselves, and they're hurting inside while not dealing with it. People buy big mansions, and they're the only ones who live there. With the massive buildings they built and all the money they have (without paying taxes most of the time due to write-offs), we could provide food, water, clothing, and shelter to everyone on this planet. With all the land and resources, we have, this can be done, but remember, people are sellouts. They don't care about us and would barely give, but mostly take.

Rich means realizing I create happiness, so people who say they're rich are just wealthy.

Some people don't reflect on what they have and show humbleness and gratitude. You should live in a constant state of gratitude because it's the best attitude. That's why when people start to gain a little clout, a following, and some money, they tend to act differently. Boasting and bragging are different from being humble and confident.

Most people aren't honest with themselves and would try to avoid the pain as much as possible. For example, if one just got out of a relationship and then days later, they start developing a connection with another person and automatically make it known publicly on social media. This will make them look childish and immature. They haven't fully healed from the situation and would rather drag the other person's name in the mud. People know the intention behind a post or what they do or say on social media. They're intentionally hurting that person while they're in their healing stage. Someone should wait about a month before starting to post about another person to be respectful.

Seeing a woman try will help make a man feel more appreciated for his doings. When he feels like you're not even trying to contribute, that's when he feels used. Any guy who's confident and self-respecting and that woman isn't trying to contribute, then he feels like he's being taken advantage of. It has nothing to do with money. It has to do with the lack of gesture. Women want a man who can be vulnerable and open with them, so they can trust him. How you view other people and place perspectives on them, your thoughts project and transmit to other people. People will subconsciously connect to your thoughts, so be aware that you can alter people by the way you view them. You should have no judgment on no one.

People post money on social media, but they don't have it. You don't have to flash something unless you're trying to act as if you have it. People post these things because they want to feel and validate to people that they got it. They don't have it like that because you don't have to post it all the time. If people say something like "I'm cool" in their bio, they're not cool at all.

Anything that wouldn't make you money, why do it? Find ways in which you can be compensated for your skills, talents, and what you love to do. If it's not a necessity, why buy it? What do you love to do and are good at whether you're getting paid or not? Nothing comes easy, you have to work for it. You have to put in the energy, and you'll get something back for it. If you decide to be real, be prepared to lose people.

The reason why certain people aren't taking off even though they have the talent to do so is because of the realness and humbleness. They wouldn't switch up. Once a person blows up or gains notoriety, they can easily be misled right back inside the matrix. They pick and choose who'll blow up. Most of them sold out or signed their souls away. They sometimes get it wrong with some people who blow up who are coming out with the truth. That's why most of them died throughout the process, placing fear tactics on them, or bringing them to celebrity jail. In most instances, the archons get it right. They target them when they're at their most vulnerable state or point in life. That's why they love bringing kids into the system. The kids see all these celebrities doing what they want to do, but they don't know any better. Their parents don't care as long as they're doing something productive. It's a setup in giving away their whole life for the industry. It's a toxic cycle and Hollywood is a dangerous ideology that most people follow because of the lifestyle. They don't know the price it may cost them in living this lifestyle for the rest of their lives.

Don't care how well people think they used to know you unless they're in your life right now. They don't know anything about you, so they'll place predetermined decisions and other instances based on what they believe. Instead of changing people, change yourself. Don't accept the things you cannot change. Change the things you cannot accept. Accept people as they are but place them where they belong.

The capacity to be alone is the capacity to love. It may look paradoxical, but it's not; it's an existential truth. A person who's okay with being alone is powerful. Without possessing the other, without becoming dependent on the other, without reducing the other to a thing, and without becoming addicted to the other. They allow the other absolute freedom because they know that if the other leaves, they'll be as happy as they are now. Their happiness cannot be taken by the other because it's not given by the other. You're responsible for your happiness. Happiness starts within yourself first and foremost. Forget about just doing it and instead just be it. It's all within you, but you have to know it for yourself. If you expect others to make you happy, you'll always be anticlimactic. The goal is to grow so strong on the inside that nothing on the outside can affect your inner wellness without your conscious permission. Stop waiting for Friday, for summer, for someone to fall in love with you, or for life. Happiness is achieved when you stop waiting for it and make the most of the moment, you're in now.

Affirmation:

If they're toxic, they got to go. This is my life, this is my happiness, and I cut off the necessary people to achieve this statement.

Practice:

Put your energy where you choose to put it and don't allow the media, the government, or anyone else put it where you don't need to put it. Put up your spiritual shield to branch out, tap in, and enter that dominant vibration. All bots are agent smiths. Learn how to communicate with these beings without wasting your energy. Don't feel like you have to dumb yourself down to talk to these people. Keep it to yourself because words are spells. Don't interpret anything too much. This is time waster number one. The fewer people you deal with the fewer bs you deal with. The fact that you're staying positive after all the bs you've gone through proves how much you've grown. Don't waste any minute of your 24 hours. Make the time.

You didn't come here to make the choice, you already made it. You're here to try and understand why you made it.

Don't eat and drink at the same time. Practice mindfulness when we eat. Absorb the nutrients by chewing slowly. Respect your body when it's asking for a break. Respect your mind when it's seeking rest. Honor yourself when you need a moment for yourself. Your happiness is the most important element in ascending. Everything that's meant for you is coming your way. Be thankful for your struggle, because without it, you wouldn't have stumbled across your strength.

Since their parents weren't always home, the only people around the house were their maid and their chef. Alex and Tori didn't see value in talking to them. The person Aqua developed a deep connection with was the cleaning lady. The cleaning lady was there most of the time and if she would've told their parents about their parties, they would've gotten her fired. So, instead of talking to Alex and Tori, she would connect with Aqua.

Aqua and the maid talked about life, relationships, played games together, etc. The cleaning lady's name was Maria. For Maria, she looked at Aqua as another daughter of hers; and Aqua looked at her as a motherly figure. Aqua wanted this same connection with the chef as a father figure, but he leaves right after cooking their meals.

Maria had to wash the dishes, but Aqua would help her as well to talk more. Aqua valued quality over quantity, unlike her sisters. Her sisters viewed quantity over quality for the people they associated with. For materialism, they wanted quality and quantity. Aqua didn't care about materialistic items because she was minimalistic.

Aqua was still jealous of her sisters because they get all the attention, and she would be overlooked. This brought issues of self-worth and self-confidence, and she judged her appearance. With motherly instinct, Maria knew Aqua was going through something. Aqua became more of a quiet storm, experienced shyness, and had a problem with body positivity.

For Aqua's self-worth, it stemmed from comparing herself to her sisters. Her sisters had people always around them, were popular, and were the center of attention. Aqua didn't experience that, and now she felt like her self-worth was demolished. Aqua's self-confidence began when she started to gain a lot of weight. At first, she tried to be like her sisters, wearing all the finest medallions and losing a lot of weight. She thought by being like them, she'll receive the attention she wanted. This wasn't the case because they still looked past her. Aqua would try to act, talk, and be like her sisters, but people viewed it as being fake. Word got around and they started to call Aqua a fake and a fraud. Alex and Tori didn't care because the more people who try to act like them, they'll receive an ego boost. Although they didn't care for them, they still talked negativity about her sister and where it all stemmed from. Now her private business is becoming public. She was getting some attention, but not in the way she would imagine. Aqua would spend time in the bathroom crying and she didn't want to go to school anymore.

She would take online classes she gained a lot of weight. Aqua was devastated and felt hopeless. This made her view her body in a negative manner. She didn't feel the desire to go to the gym because when you're in a dark place in your life, you're not motivated enough to work on yourself. Aqua was cute, but when she constantly compared herself to her sisters, that's when it all derailed.

Aqua would go on dating sites and act like she was one of her sisters. This was a form of the temporary pleasure of getting that attention she so desperately needed and desired. When it was time for them to meet up, she would say she was busy, or something came up.

She would instruct the men she was hooking up with, with instructions. These instructions stated: leave the door open and cover their eyes. She would then proceed to go over and handcuff them to the bed, put a cloth in their mouth, and duct tape their eyes, so they wouldn't be able to see or feel Aqua. She knew she was a catfish, but she didn't want them to leave her. She felt empowered when some men approved of it since some of them were desperate for free sex. Some men thought it was too creepy. She didn't have to take any of their money or items because her family was already wealthy. She would then let them loose and run out the door without them noticing.

Not everyone who approaches you is who they say they are. Learn how to use discernment because it's hard to stay committed when your heart isn't in it. Focus on yourself and don't get lost in other people. No person, place, or thing has any power over you because you're free.

Everybody's fighting over a realm that was created for beings to come and live out their karma. If you take a step back and look at this from a different perspective without your emotions and feelings attached. Why would you even want to be bothered about it? Everyone on planet earth has karma that they're outliving throughout their lives. Everyone here is a flawed individual; no one here is more perfect than the other. No one here is better than anyone else. You're not separate from anyone else. When we talk about unity consciousness, and you understand the duality; no one's disconnected from anything. We're connected to every single thing on this planet. When you know that and plug into that frequency, that's when you begin to manifest.

Maria had a sit-down conversation with Aqua and she felt the passion that Maria brought. Maria cared for Aqua, and she saw her falling apart. Sneaking out, getting home late, and failing school. After a long deep observation with Aqua, she helped her enter a better place of self. She was starting to become more confident within her skin and started to promote body positivity. At this time, she went back to school and noticed this guy who kept coming into her classroom that wasn't alleged to be there. This guy was named Joey.

Aqua would recognize Joey when she went over to their house for house parties or around the school. Joey didn't care about her body because he knew he had a genuine connection with her. This made Aqua become more lovable, confident, and happy within herself. Joey was considered the nice guy and Aqua wasn't getting her needs met in the bedroom. Remember how she started to become distant from Joey after he raw dogged her. She then went back on her dating apps, and she forgot that she was still talking to this guy who was coming into town this weekend to see her. She forgot that she used Alex's profile picture for this particular dating app and that she would have to catfish him. This was months after being pregnant with Brenna.

Aqua continued to go with it because she wasn't receiving what she desired in the bedroom with Joey. This guy who she was talking to would be considered a bad boy, but ultimately, he was just more impudence compared to the average man called a nice guy. Don't be fooled by the terms "nice guy" and "bad guy" because most of the time it's all just a confident level.

Aqua didn't want to lose this opportunity with this guy because he was her long-lasting connection on this dating app. When an opportunity presents itself to you, you take that opportunity if it makes sense.

She performed for him and wore a bag over her face as a sign of guilt. She knew it was awkward since he wasn't hard. The guy's name was Johnny. Aqua said "F it" and sat Johnny up and told him the truth. She felt ashamed and embarrassed to tell him, but she needed to. Johnny supports body positivity and shows Aqua that he cares for her. This was the boost of confidence she needed. While Aqua was aroused, she told him to stick it in. Her needs were met, and she felt like Johnny listened to her.

Fast forward a month before Brenna was born; she took a pregnancy test, and it was positive. She thought it was for Brenna. After Brenna came out of the womb and before she left the hospital, she took another pregnancy test. It read positive again and she asked the doctors to check, and they stated that she was pregnant again. Aqua already knew from the beginning who the daddy was. She called Johnny to tell him the news and everything that happened between her and Joey. Johnny was okay with it once she said she was going to move on from Joey. She wanted to start a real family with Johnny. Johnny was excited and told her that they'll celebrate because he was moving down to her state tonight.

As you know, Joey brought Aqua to the park and asked her to marry him. She declined because she was pregnant once again which led to dissolution. She knew it wasn't from Joey because after that first night, they only had sex once in a blue moon and she faked her orgasms.

She stayed in contact with Joey because they had to co-parent. Joey still loved Aqua since she was the only person to show value in his life. He didn't care if she was trying to start a family with another man. He was going to fight for her. She told him she was forlorn with him and her needs and wants weren't being met. Joey started to change and become better in doing so. It was just too little too late for Joey.

Johnny on the other hand was out and about doing God knows what. Aqua noticed this and felt an urge of red flags coming along. She wanted to stay with Johnny because of how he made her feel in certain situations. Plus, they just gave birth to their newborn son named Elias. She still felt deeply for Joey and the connection they once had. Johnny still cared for Aqua even though he was doing whatever behind closed doors. Come to find out, he was hooking up with other women and never told her. Joey tried to show her proof and receipts after his FBI investigation. Johnny was a believable person, and she could never see Johnny who cared so much about her doing these things.

This whole relationship is like a Bermuda Triangle. How can Aqua trust Joey when he barely knows anything about Johnny? How can Joey still want Aqua when she legit got pregnant from another man and told him the same day she gave birth to his child and when he was proposing?

Why is Johnny not one of the main characters of this book? Why is Aqua acting so innocent in this situation?

Now, I know y'all got some unanswered questions you're asking yourself and I told you Aqua was lowkey a juicy character, to say the least. Most readers and listeners would either love, hate, or don't know how to feel about Aqua. Trust me, this is just the beginning of this love triangle between Aqua, Joey, and Johnny. Find out what happens throughout this book, "How to Overcome Apocalyptic Events".

Ah finally, the end of the introduction of the characters. This was indeed necessary for the book as a whole. When it comes to this book, don't expect anything to be superfluous when it comes to this excerpt. We have reached the end of our spectacle and pentacle night here in the live audience. I'll still be hosting and illustrating the book for everyone at home, but I thank my live audience for the stupendous night in getting to know these characters. You'll never know when I'm creeping in the shadows and when I'll appear. Grand night everyone and let's get right into chapter two which is entitled "The Beginning".

Chapter Two

THE BEGINNING

It was a hot summer afternoon. The birds were singing, nature was glistening, the sun was radiant, and the earth was exuding that good ass prana. It seemed like a normal day throughout the world. Here in the present moment, let's catch up with these characters and see where they are now.

Indigo was finishing up some of the programs that he was involved in. He works so hard to achieve his goals, but sometimes he tries to distract himself instead of healing from his pain.

At the end of high school, he wanted to get straight A's throughout the entire year. Throughout elementary school, he wasn't able to reach that goal due to his disability. Throughout middle school, he wasn't able to reach that goal due to his bullies. This brought shyness in the first two years of high school. Junior year came and that's when he started to be involved in those programs. Senior year came and he finally accomplished his goal of getting straight A's, but it came at a price.

Indigo knew how to multitask and was observant of energies even when he didn't know. He knew when he needed to talk and when he didn't need to speak. He knew exactly what to say and that was one of his hidden gifts. Most people saw him as being shy (which he was), but he wanted to protect his energy. At the moment, he didn't know, but now he was realizing it.

Since he was taking all this time to focus on himself, he gained more confidence, but people viewed him as being selfish. You can't please everyone, so you might as well please yourself. It came off the wrong way to some people, and he took their comments to heart. He was affected by what others said about him, thought about him, and those who judged him. People would make slick remarks about him throughout his life. He wasn't opening up to people due to the fear of people judging him. Right out of the womb with his tragic birth experience, to now allowing people's words and actions to get the best of him. He started to get into a spiral of trying to impress, focus, and please others instead of himself. He was going back into his old ways. Even with this statement alone, he was still accomplishing his goals since he can multitask. He was just losing himself through the process.

The more he helped people, the more he was losing himself. Once he tried learning more about himself, he thought it was wrong. He'll be losing time being there for other people than himself. The people Indigo dwelt with wanted his time and attention at all times. Even though it wasn't being reciprocated back to Indigo. This made Indigo a bit coldhearted, and he was entering his savage-like ways. He tried his best to try to please everyone and make everyone happy, but internally he wasn't happy. Externally he seemed happy. Look at what he accomplished, look at everything he's doing, look at his pure beautiful white smile right? Nope, that was a mask for him, and he performed it well.

He constantly told himself that everything was okay because look at everything he accomplished. Just like celebrities, even though they win all these awards, that doesn't mean they're really happy. That's what Indigo was going through which was a battle within himself. He constantly kept battling himself time and time again. He overthought every situation and possible outcome based on what he was thinking. He let outside forces govern his life and have them make decisions for him. There was a difference between what he wanted to do and what his thoughts were telling him to do. He was following his mind and ego instead of his heart and spirit. He was gaining so much confidence and was heading in the right direction, but ever since that situation, hardship took over. It was like a drug; he was addicted to his thoughts and gave more trust in external thoughts instead of his true self.

He was also experiencing heartbreak throughout his relationships. Indigo barely had relationships because most of what he experienced was situation-ships. Situation-ships are people you have a connection with, and you think it's going somewhere, but it's not. It doesn't progress and they're presently there for a few weeks or a couple of months. Seeing all these people just randomly go and spectral him broke his heart even more. He thought they had something special with each of his connections and were building towards something, but he was easily mistaken. He used to put his all into someone too fast and place all his eggs in one basket. That led to him being heartbroken even more. So, all of this upon his past, his thoughts, and other external forces taking over his life made Indigo go into a panic attack.

Indigo had a panic attack while he was at the mall. At that time, he walked for a long time with no food or water in his system. During this encounter, he was still stressed about everything that was happening in his life. He wanted to run away and avoid it.

He was in this store inside this huge shopping mall but then blacked out. He was standing up during that time and it felt like he was in a trance. His body became numb, and he felt like he was dying. Might've been an out-of-body experience subconsciously, but he was still operating his body consciously. He called out to Sherly, and it felt like no one could hear him. Sherly realized that Indigo wasn't behind her anymore and she saw him near the cash register. Sherly took him by the hand and tried to find a chair. For Indigo it felt like everything was happening all at once. When Sherly was bringing him to the bench, Indigo saw the clear emulsion of light.

As he was walking, it felt like he was walking towards the light. He was accepting of it as he took his last breath before he dies.

He finally sat on the bench, and he took some deep breaths and tried to gain his sight back. Once he gained his eyesight back, they went and ate some food. He was fine by then, but something changed.

Since he had this spiritual instance that happened in his life, he became more religious and more interested in different topics. Can you blame him? He never really had a real connection with spirituality because his parents placed him in religion. So, that was the first thing that came up because he didn't tap into spirituality before. He seemed more interested in aliens, knowing more about the planet, and the sky. He wanted to see if these interesting topics were true or not. That was the official start of his spiritual awakening, but he didn't know this.

Indigo was now getting ready for college. He was excited to go to college because he knew he was going to meet new people and make "long-lasting friends" as everyone says.

We know the truth about college: putting people in debt, preparing you to slave your whole life away, to only find entry-level positions. Companies ask you to have education, but work experience as well. How can we gain work experience when we've been in school all this time? That's how they trap you and sell this American dream of being successful, but you have to be asleep to believe it. Everything's upside down and in reverse in this whole society. Know the truth, stand by the truth, and use deception when dealing with people who tell you something's true or not. Once you let your thoughts wheel you in and you entertain them, they'll have control over you. You know the difference between your inner voice and your thoughts. It's an inner knowing, your intuition already knows, and your gut feeling never lies. Don't second guess or overthink your intuitive spirit.

Indigo went to three proms in total that year. Through his troubles, he was still confident enough to do his own thing. Indigo could've gone to four proms that year, but something happened with the fourth one.

Indigo was in a relationship at the time when he was about to go to college. Indigo was tired of seeing the same people and doing the same things every single day. His new upcoming experience in meeting newer people was college. He was already checked out of the relationship because she was too attached, rushed things, wanted promise rings, and her family knew Indigo's family. It's bizarre and pretty awkward when you see someone of interest, but you're with your family members. They'll talk about that experience to other friends and family all day and then check in on seeing how it went.

So, Indigo dumped her two weeks before her birthday and a week before her prom. He was officially in savage mode. He loved wrestling and developing the character he wanted to be, and he was slowly turning into his alter ego. In wrestling, he would've been the heel instead of the babyface because heels can do or say essentially anything they want. He found power in that, so he started to become this character.

At one of his proms, he went by himself with a group of friends. The other two were with two other women. He had a fun time, but he was entering a savagery state of mind. He started to not care as much. He lost that nostalgic touch and emotion towards things. He didn't know how to feel anymore, but only showed his emotions when it was something joyful. If that thing, person, or place wasn't bringing him joy, then he wouldn't care. Internally he did care about things, but why care for something or someone when they're not bringing you joy? He kept in contact with things and people who brought him joy or interest, but for everyone else, it slowly started to fade out. Even though he tried to work things through with those people, it just didn't work. That made him go through heartbreak again and he's now going through the same cycles as earlier. He would be guarded and not open up to people once again. Whatever you put into the Universe you shall receive. So, everyone else wasn't opening up to Indigo either. This made Indigo become a hopeless romantic.

He thought he'd never find love, and no one was meant to be with him. Even though he constantly dreamt of his dream girl, he thought it'll never come true. His dream girl will come into his reality sooner or later, but of course, at that moment it was tough for him.

He was a lost soul. Some people called him a lost boy. He was trying to go through life not bringing up his past or all the pain he endured. He would still put this persona up of nothing being wrong and letting his new "character" control him. He was becoming more than one character. Indigo was going through a personality disorder and that made him latch on to psychopathic and egotistical tactics. He knew which character to portray in a given situation. There were multiple beings within himself that he was becoming. He liked the cockiness, the arrogance, the attention, and all the awards he was getting. He was high off life and was about to embark on his college journey.

Then he saw a flyer about an exclusive escape room event taking place in Los Angeles for a televised reality show. They wanted to try and use newer technology like VR and the metaverse in the game. The auditioners didn't know this because they kept it a secret. They gave people limited information on the flyer, but it was from a reputable company. Indigo called in and had the interview right there. A few hours went by, and they called him back. They wanted him to come down for the casting call event.

Before college started, he took a trip to Los Angeles by himself. This was his first time traveling on his own with no one else. He loved the concept of escape rooms but never got the chance to participate in one. He showed enthusiasm but was nervous at the same time.

Apollo was living his best life at the moment. He was currently in his junior year of college and was barely passing. He almost dropped out a couple of times, but he didn't want his parents to be angry since they paid for his schooling. So, he made sure to pass his classes at the bare minimum. He went to an HBCU that had thousands of students, a humongous campus, and had parties every weekend. He went to every party and had a new woman every week. He had friends that were his hype men.

Apollo was becoming a top-tier A-lister now. People started to recognize Apollo globally. He didn't live with any regrets and wasn't getting attached to the women he had sex with. Apollo's pull-out game was strong, but he knew he wasn't going to get a girl pregnant. He knew some women only wanted him for the clout. He was becoming an icon, trendsetter, and guru. Apollo was clever and careful when using ingenuity to entice women. Some women can be erratic when dealing with Apollo's inventiveness. I'm surprised he doesn't have children at the moment due to all the women he ran a train with. Most people use sex as a gateway for pleasure to not focus on the real pain inside them.

One night, he had a threesome with two drunk college girls. After that, he did the necessary actions to not have a baby at that time. After he flushed it down the toilet and threw the condom outside the bathroom. When he came out of the bathroom, he saw the women trying to have sex with each other using the condom he just used. They tried to see if any of his seed was still left inside. He quickly grabbed it and dispose of it.

Women tried other ways in having Apollo become their baby daddy by being on their period or using birth control. Birth control harms the female body internally and externally. Apollo was smart and was getting quicker on his feet.

In another instance, he went to the bathroom after he did the deed with a woman. He put hot sauce inside the condom, mixed it up, put it in a bag, and then placed it in the trash. He left the dorm for five minutes knowing she might do something when he came back.

Since college kids were being grimy, Apollo put his valuables in a secured safe and left most of his items at his parent's house. When he walked back into the dorm room, he saw the woman who he just had sex with being in immediate pain. Her yogi was scorching, and it felt like there was a bomb explosion in her body. She took the condom out of the bag and put it in her vagina. Not knowing there was hot sauce in it. As she poured it in, she let out a scream like no tomorrow. She went to the hospital and transferred schools because she was too embarrassed. Apollo laughed it off and continue doing the same thing. His newer women were conscious enough to not do what that other girl did.

Apollo was already gaining people's attention and energy. He was diving into some acting roles and was actually on the big screen. There was a strip club down the street from the university, so he'll spend most of his time at college parties and the strip club. He was also smoking, drinking, and doing drugs as well. He still didn't do his inner work or healed from the past. He was living the good life, so he didn't think of changing his ways at all. He was going through life with all the finer things coming to him. He was drowning himself with the fame, fortune, inclination, and all the attention he was gaining.

Don't get it twisted, Apollo is very smart, but he only cares about the things that bring him more fame and fortune. He was flashed with all this glory, and everything being handed down to him, that it was difficult to connect with anyone who didn't come from the same background as him. He would treat people like crap and a lot of women caught feelings for him, but he just used them. Some of his short-term connections turned out to be long-term. At times, he tried to change for the better, but the more he focused on other people, it felt like he was wasting his time. That's why he stopped caring because he wanted the best of both worlds.

It was spring break, so he went down to Miami. He went jet skiing, went to block parties, and ordered an Airbnb to throw a house party. He had to create a new Airbnb account after that house party. They banned that current email from Airbnb because of all the ruckus it caused.

During his time in Miami, he saw an advertisement for this new reality TV show. This was right up his alley. He called in, did his interview, and immediately got offered to come in for casting. He was on his way to LA which he was familiar with. He went to modeling events and acted in LA, so he was used to this. He was excited to elevate more through his television persona. It comes naturally for Apollo because he was already used to the glamorous lifestyle. He wanted everyone to know who he was and what he got going on. Some call it arrogant and full of himself, but he calls it persistent and confident.

Some people get jealous because of how much confidence someone exudes that people don't understand why they're so confident and the person judging them doesn't. People love to compare themselves to other people due to the fact they take social media too seriously. Some people wouldn't post certain things due to how people will view that post or themselves. Jealousy comes when they see other people doing something they want to do. Apollo calls people his clones because he's the blueprint. Whatever he does, people copy or want to do the same. He's one of the first to do it in his own unique way. Most people won't acknowledge Apollo for setting the standard for people. He inspired people to be creative, to spark inspiration, motivation, and imagination for people to step into that creative space. He doesn't get all the praise he deserves.

Apollo exudes creativity with everything he does. He is articulate and has masculine traits that make people nervous around him. When Apollo talks to you, he can tap into his divine masculine and divine feminine traits whenever he needs to. He knows the balance between both, but he uses his masculinity more. When Apollo walks through the door everyone stops and forgets what they were doing and stares at him.

Most people say they're a leader, but they're following in the footsteps of Apollo and what he's doing. Why are people jealous of Apollo? He's what everyone wants to be and hopes to become. He's living out most of everyone's dreams and desires. Everyone thinks he was handed everything on a silver platter, but that's from the outside looking in. They don't know what he had to go through to get to this point.

Most people forget where they came from after they got famous. Instead of focusing on their journey, they're focused on the fame, glamorous lifestyle, and all the attention it possesses. They forget where they come from and where they were headed. Remembering where you came from, doesn't mean you cannot change your life for the better. The key to happiness is staying true to who you are no matter where you are. I'm not saying it'll be easy, but it's possible. Now at this very moment, it's all on you. All these possibilities and choices are right in front of you. No one's here to make that decision for you. So, you're the one that has to make that choice.

Currently, Aleemic is living his best life as well. As we mentioned before, he had this temple where he was giving his motivational speeches. Aleemic was living through his purposes and missions in the world with no regrets. Aleemic branched off and he was outliving his dreams and aspirations.

He used his platform as a tool to get his messages out there. He was a successful businessman who owned multiple businesses. Whatever he dreamt for his business, he was going to achieve it. This was in the form of clothing, social media platforms, podcasts, music, art, books, technology-driven, restaurants, food trucks, and of course his mega building. This building was the multitude of everything he had ever created. He was so successful that he placed multiple buildings around the entire world. He was now well-known, but when he started, he only received a few peak moments. Once he stepped into his power and ascend past it all, that was when the Universe blessed him by the billions and become a billionaire.

Aleemic always knew he was going to become a huge success, but he didn't always recognize it yet. He didn't recognize it because he kept getting turned down from positions, people not noticing his worth, and the limited success he gained. They put curses on him to hinder his success and limit how successful he'll become. Aleemic realized the trickery and made the executive order to have those curses and spells be sent back to the sender. With that being said, now if anyone puts a spell or curse on him, it won't work.

Aleemic knew he had his spiritual team behind him and no matter what, he was going to make an impact on people's lives. No matter how many people it was, as long as he helped people, that's all that mattered to him. The Universe noticed that and rained down blessings upon his life for eternity. All that work he put in ever since the beginning is now turning into abundance. He was living and experiencing the highest of realms and dimensions since he was operating at the highest vibration, frequency, and energy.

Aleemic never switched up on anyone or didn't let the fame get to him. He stayed true to his word and stayed true to Christ Consciousness. Now you may ask why did he become such a success when you said some people wouldn't blow up due to their realness? Great question. He grew so massive because he was living and experiencing the healed version of the 5th-dimensional new earth golden age. He had put in the work on earth and stayed true to his roots to be able to make it out. A few times he gets to travel back to earth and either uplift people or do work for his businesses. He chooses to live in the new earth, but he still has access to the ancient earth for business purposes only. Not to mention, he does some of the same business ventures in the new earth as well. He can tap into both frequencies, and it won't drain his spirit because he's so divine.

Aleemic purchased land and created his own running city on his private island. He wanted to live on the beach and be close to the sun and water but still live near the mountains. Even though they're warning visitors to stay away from some public beaches. That's the trick to getting all the beaches controlled when they paint a bad picture of these public beaches. Then the government will step in, take over, and deploy their fees and restrictions.

Aleemic runs a successful and sustainable city and those who get invited bring something to the table. People would have to pay to live there or work to stay there. He has gardeners, construction workers, holistic doctors, intuitive readers, chefs, etc. Aleemic wanted to do what he always dreamt of, which was to go on a world tour. He already went on a world tour for business and as a motivation coach, but he wanted to go on a music world tour. Let's circle back to see how all of this was spoken into existence.

Aleemic just finished college and was proud to receive his diploma because of all the naysayers and doubters in his life. He let other people's judgments and opinions take control over his life. These dark entities will place people in your life to either help elevate and make you learn something, or they'll tear you down and suck your energy dry. Just like the saying goes, "God can speak through other people, or the devil can speak through other people." The devil can bless you just like how God can bless you. The Most High communicates to us through us. Remember whenever you're in a position to help someone, be glad and always do it because that's the Universe answering someone else's prayers through you. Just watch out for the scammers. Not everyone's truthful, righteous, or they can pray for your downfall. Some people out there just want to see your worst and don't have the best interest for you. Then, there are a few who wants you to succeed and have your best interest. Keep those types of people around and cut off the dead weight. It's the dead weight that'll bring you down and lower your vibration. They're weighing on your shoulders to pull you down and that'll hinder your success. It's these people who want to lower you to make you stoop to their level.

Once people gain power, they love it so much that they don't want to lose it. Just like superpowers; if someone gains superpowers, some people will abuse their power and cause pain and suffering. That's how they portray the good vs. the evil or the superhero vs. the supervillain. It all turns out to be the same in all the stories. Hence, some people haven't unlocked their full powers yet, because they may cause hatred instead of spreading love and protection.

After college, Aleemic stepped into his purpose of helping others. He became a teacher, and he taught all walks of life. The joy he receives from helping others was always a marvelous feeling. He was helping people so much, that he lost himself through the process. While he took more time helping people along their journeys, he started to find less time to take care of himself. He was helping people day in and day out that he barely found time to sit and meditate. Aleemic barely had time to go to the gym because he was doing consultations back-to-back-to-back. Aleemic witnessed his wrongdoings a few months after college. He decided to go off the face of the earth. He stayed on airplane mode and DND to go on a retreat of self-healing, self-realization, and self-care for a whole six months.

During these six months, he went on a spiritual retreat and hired some spiritual therapists, coaches, and mentors to go through this process. He could've done it by himself, but he knew it'll be more beneficial with a team of people supporting him along the way. He knew he would get distracted if he tried it alone because he might be tempted to go back on his phone, message people, or help others more than help himself. That was Aleemic's problem. Going back on social media to check in with people instead of checking in on himself. He was more involved with other people's issues trying to guide them on the right path but wasn't guiding himself. He was becoming too attached to people. For instance, a detective stays on a case outside work hours. He's deeply invested in other people that it'll take over his life. That was happening for Aleemic, the same precision occurrence.

Aleemic went completely off-grid, with no contact, and the only people he saw were his therapists and healers. They showed him the way to balance between helping yourself and helping others. Putting yourself first and not allowing people to become more important than yourself. Sure, that may sound selfish, but it's the truth, no matter how you take it.

They taught him the power of healing yourself while healing others. You can't show genuine love and support for others if you haven't done that internally for yourself. Most people tear people down and strip them apart because they don't have a true genuine love connection with themselves. Sure, it's easy to say that you love yourself, but it needs to be more than that. Just like manifestation, not just knowing or saying something, but also believing in it, being it, embracing it, and feeling it as well. Multiple factors play into self-love. Fill up your self-love bubble and watch how your life grows and changes.

One may be negative but then turns positive after gaining more love for themselves. The reason why so many people are so negative is that they don't have positivity flowing throughout their bodies, their veins, or their blood vessels. A negative person will be negative. A positive person will be positive. A purely "evil" person would only be "malice" based on what happened to them or all that built-up anger and microaggression that's being held deep down inside them. It's like a pot of boiling water with a lid trying to hold it in. Once that lid comes off, there's the true person that comes out. Everyone has both sides, the light and pure vs. the dark and shadow side. It's all about controlling both sides while operating your mind, body, and soul. Not saying you have to always be positive or negative. It's the Universal law in having both sides since we're chaotic beings of the Universe. Just look at The Hulk. He gains his supernatural powers after being mad and causing chaos. We're the same way.

It's about not letting people get under your skin to where you'll burst out of pure anger and outrage. For example, if someone cuts in front of you on the road and you're so outraged with anger that it pisses you off for the rest of your day. This allows people to easily change your mood in a matter of seconds by one action. They'll move on in life not thinking about it, but you'll be mad for the rest of the day. Letting your emotions and feelings get the best of you without using logic. It'll cause you to have mood swings while risking yourself having a cyclothymic disorder. Anything people say, do, or think about you, will make you angry. Take control over yourself and don't allow others to govern your mental stability. Life's too short to stay angry or hold resentment toward people. Today choose happiness and become free.

It's not always about being positive all the time either. There's a duality with everything. Say if someone spits in your face, are you going to smile in their face and say have a good day? If you could do that, then you have no self-respect for yourself. You might feel mad and upset during that altercation, but don't do anything that'll harm you in the long run. If people pick on you, stand up against them. If people bully you, stand your ground and fight back. If there's a person you want to talk to, gain the confidence to go up to them and speak your truth. You're so much stronger than you give yourself credit for. If an evil spirit were to continuously attack you, will you keep allowing them to do so? No! You're going to stand in your power and take back your ownership of yourself.

Aleemic found out how to control his triggers that were eating him up inside. He healed and dealt with all the issues he faced from past lives, childhood trauma, and anything else in this lifetime. He knew he only had a few triggers that were in the way of him becoming his healed version. He allowed people to get under his skin and over time it affected him. He told me that one day he was on the phone talking to someone for four hours straight. During this time, the other person kept badmouthing him. Endless wordplay to get under his skin to receive a reaction from him. Over time these little instances caught up to Aleemic and instead of being positive about himself, he was focusing on all the negative comments people said about him. No one truly knows Aleemic, but how would you feel if people constantly disrespect you, bad-mouth you, spread rumors, put dirt over your name, gossip about you, and call you out your name? Keep poking the bear and eventually, the bear will have its breaking point. They're portraying an image in their mind of who they think Aleemic is, but that's not the real image of him.

Don't fall for their hate. They are beneath you. At the deepest level, they're trying to drag you down to their lower wavelength. Don't fall for it. Nothing or no one is worth lowering your vibration for. Recognize that those people ultimately can't see you clearly from where they are. None of their stories have 'you' in them. They're simply viewing you through the lens of their pain, fear, and hurt. All the insecurities and what they think they see in you, are ultimately a reflection of themselves. Some people cannot get past their ego, trauma, and pride. So, they project their negativity and insecurities out on you. They will bash you if you don't fall in line or act like them.

People will talk about you, people will judge you based on how they view you, and people will assume who they think you truly are, but that's false accusations. Aleemic had people spreading false rumors about him and that hurt him. After all the work he's done, after all the people he'd helped, and all the success he gained, there were still people trying to tear his image. They overthought everything he said, every word that came out of his mouth, and everything he did was judged based on how they viewed that message. It was toxic for Aleemic, and he needed to break away and escape from that reality. Even though he was doing so well, certain people still had the chance to affect his life for the worst. He allowed those people to enter his life and let them stay around which essentially broke him. If they're disrespecting you and degrading you, then why keep them around? They loved his energy, so they always came back around. Aleemic would let them come back based on their words and say they loved him. Once they came back, it was a downwards spiral once again. For him and these people, it would be makeup and break up over and over again.

Aleemic finally had enough and took this time to better himself. He was working out once again and getting his body in shape. Now he was jacked and full of muscle. He learned how to deal with those triggers and heal them, so those triggers wouldn't be triggers anymore. It's all about healing those wounds, trauma, the past, and those triggers, so you won't be affected by them anymore. After six months of working on himself, he began to manifest at a faster rate. He was on a whole new wave link and jumped on a faster and higher timeline. He was achieving that higher power and he ascended to the new earth. Once this happened, he decided to stay an extra three months to live and rejoice in this new blissful state. He wanted to learn how to use his superpowers, how to manifest correctly and make that transition into the new earth. It was a total of nine months (which nine represent the completion and end of a chapter). This was necessary for Aleemic and his journey as a whole. Once he finished the nine months, he announced his world tour.

Aleemic always loved music and just like Apollo, he was the God of music (which also means the God of frequency and vibration). This was Aleemic's biggest achievement that he wanted to complete. Since he was well-known everywhere, he went on tour globally and it was a massive success. He had multiple number one hits on all the charts; world tours sold out in all countries, received awards, and was getting the recognition he rightfully deserves. All of this happened because he took the time out for himself instead of putting his focus on other people. Blessings and abundance were flowing in his life like running water. After the world tour, he started to develop his plans for his building.

He knew exactly what services and what he wanted to provide for the community. He wanted to do so much that no one could stop him. One new venture became another venture, which led to another business, that led to another creative avenue. He was doing everything so fast because he knew how to manifest instantly.

After the world tour, he gained so much wealth and abundance that he was creating random items he thought of and was making them come alive. It was like he was on Shark Tank pitching his ideas to the sharks, but he was the sharks as well.

He placed everything he had ever done in these buildings including the inventions, the services, and all his branded items. He placed his first building in the United States, and it was instantly a success. Some may call it an overnight success, but it wasn't. Some may call him a one-hit-wonder with his music, but his gold and platinum records tell differently. After one building, came another one, then another one, another one, and it just kept going. Now his building was everywhere, and people love it. He then purchased a private island to start his city and that was a success as well.

Nothing Aleemic has done was a failure. Yes, he learned along the way and some things didn't go as planned, but once he fixed it, that problem never came up ever again. No repeated cycles, no repeated loops, and never was bored or stagnant. He let go of that old part of himself and elevated himself to the next level.

After all these wins, he came back and started teaching again. He held an event in Dubai to help anyone who showed up. With the little promo he did, he sold out the Sheikh Zayed Cricket Stadium. After his nine months of healing, he wasn't teaching or doing any consultations while he was on tour or creating his buildings. Even though he gave his services away at his buildings, he hired people as employees to provide everything he offers. Now, he was prepared to teach and help people once more. This was great for Aleemic in all possible ways. He got back to working for the people but didn't allow it to control him.

After the function, one kid with his parents gave him a flyer that he brought from America when coming to this meet and greet session with Aleemic. His parents said they wanted to give him something. The child wanted him to do whatever the flyer was offering in a way to expand and get the word out. As Aleemic looked at the flyer, he saw it was for an escape room television show. Aleemic thought he could bring his cognizance to the show and awaken more people throughout the process. He called in and they wanted him to come for a casting call in Los Angeles.

For Joey, Aqua literally and figuratively broke his heart right after having a child and asking her to marry him. Joey went back to that downward spiral he was so familiar with before. Joey started failing his classes, stopped doing his brother's homework, and barely ate or drank anything. Now it's good to go on a dry fast from time to time, but for Joey, this wasn't for that reason. Joey isn't eating or drinking because he was too sad to do those activities. The only thing that brought him joy was Brenna. Without Brenna, he would've easily never looked back and committed suicide. Since he still was raising Brenna, he made her his responsibility.

He didn't want to go to school because of the embarrassment and the fact that he might see Aqua. He hasn't spoken to Aqua ever since that night. The only palaver they did was about Brenna. They never had that sit-down conversation that they truly needed.

His life was falling apart due to him being a young father trying to go through everything he experienced. He hasn't healed from any of his pain, his past, or his relationship with Aqua. He never had the proper closure, and I'm not sure if he'll even want it at this point. Like we said before, he still has feelings for Aqua and he did research on Johnny.

Johnny was a unique person, to say the least. He was gothic, emo, and had lots of piercings. Johnny was a biker and had a motorcycle. Aqua loved riding on the back of his motorcycle and saw how confident and good-looking he was. This is what Aqua wanted, that feeling, that submissive way of being. She was done playing the masculine role with Joey and she wanted to go back into her feminine role.

Aqua and Joey were co-parenting, but Joey had to take care of Brenna more since Aqua was pregnant. Now that Aqua was moving on, it was hard for Joey to create that family dynamic that he once dreamed about. He thought it could never happen and all his dreams were fake reality. Surprisingly, he knew what generational curses were and he wanted to break those cycles.

All he drank was alcohol when he was by himself. When he was around Brenna, he would drink water or juice just like his daughter. He wanted to show proof to Aqua that he wasn't going down his toxic spiral once again and that he was okay. When he was around Aqua, he didn't ask for any drink or food because he was in denial about her.

When Joey was with Brenna, he showed her all the creative stuff he enjoyed. He still loved creating art, cartoons, and anime. Joey was making his cartoon as a distraction from thinking about Aqua. Even though the main story and plot were basically about his relationship with Aqua, it was therapeutic for Joey even though he never sat and healed from the situation. Just like how people make music, art, or anything creative to get over something that happened to themselves.

He wanted the characters to be animated because he used to like anime characters sexually. He would also use artwork to tell a story and to paint a picture of everything he experienced. Believe me now, or believe me later, that man Joey was talented. He sold his artwork online because he didn't want to show his face or have people ask who he truly was. He sold so much; that he gained the confidence to have an art show.

The art show for Joey represented his truth and his experiences. On the day of the event, he had so much enthusiasm. He finally went back to school to promote his art show. The day has come, and Joey was ready to tell his story, but no one showed up.

20 minutes passed, and no one showed up yet. 35 minutes went by and there was someone that came in and Joey was ecstatic. It was the janitor cleaning out the trash. After 45 minutes, Joey was about to give up and walk out the door. Right after that, people from the anime, gaming, and esports clubs came and supported him. Joey was involved with these clubs when he was in a good state of mind. Once everything transpired, he wasn't going to the club meetings anymore. Also, people who bought his artwork online started to show up as well. Joey was happy that they showed up and was grateful for them. One of the esports players gave him a flyer about a TV show he'll be good in called 'Escape Room'. Once he said it was a TV show, Joey crumbled it up and put it in his bag with zero thought in mind. The only thing on his mind was the people he wanted to see which were Brenna and Aqua.

Aqua had Brenna this weekend and Joey told Aqua about the event. The day passed and they never showed. It tore Joey's heart once again. This was a big deal for Joey, and this was how he provided for his family. The fact that they didn't come, showed Aqua's true colors.

Joey decided to go to the bar instead of calling Aqua and asking where they were. Joey was drinking and getting high. Aqua called Joey multiple times in seeing where he was, but he wasn't answering. Once he picked up (in his alcoholic breath), he expressed how they didn't come to his art show. Before Aqua could say a word, he hangs up. He was so upset, that he looked in his bag and called the casting director of the show for his audition. He was already drunk and not himself, so of course, he would do good for his audition. He nailed the audition and they wanted him to come down for a casting call. After he said yes and goodbye, he booked his flight to Los Angeles. Right after it said confirmed, his battery died.

As he was driving home, it was precipitation outside, and he was swerving due to the alcohol in his system. Joey went off the rails and crashed right into a tree. As his life was in the palm of his hands, he thought it was all about to end. At this point, he didn't care anymore, and he wanted his life to be over with. As he was about to make that executive decision, a truck came by and saw the crash. The guy came out and called 911 instantly. He decided to perform first aid and CPR on Joey since he was a veteran. Once the police came, they brought Joey right inside the ER.

After a few days in the ER, Joey was cleared to go back home, and he lived through the crash. Joey wondered how he made it out alive, and the doctor told him that it must've been a miracle. Due to the car crash, he asked his brothers to pick him up. His brothers came and brought him home. Mike and Cody were asking him what happened? Joey said nothing and he didn't want to talk to his brothers or family since they didn't show up. Once they got home, Joey said thanks and slammed the car door. Even though he lived in his parent's house, Mike and Cody waited until Joey calmed down a bit before heading inside. Ashley and Michael were busy, so they made Mike and Cody pick him up. Once Joey entered the house, he saw something shocking.

Once Joey walked through the door, he saw balloons, pictures of his artwork, food, and drinks all around. He walked up and saw a cake that said 'Congratulations, Joey'. Joey was wondering what they were congratulating him on. He then saw multiple cards on the table and one of them said the name Aqua. Joey didn't even touch the envelope and he ran to charge his phone. Joey was playing images throughout his mind of wondering what could've happened. Once he charged up his phone for a little bit, he went to his chat messages with Aqua and he saw multiple unread messages.

Aqua took so many videos and pictures of the surprise party for Joey. It was all Aqua's idea and the thought behind it was to surprise him with a surprise party instead of recognizing him at his art show. Everyone was there from Aqua, Brenna, his immediate family, and his outside family. With Joey not coming home that night, he missed his whole party.

Joey called Aqua to apologize for what happened last night and expressed he didn't know about the party. Aqua was telling him that it was a surprise. Joey felt bad towards Aqua, his family, and his brothers specifically. Once Mike and Cody came inside, Joey hugged them both like he never hugged them before. This made Joey more hopeful for a love connection with his family and Aqua. This was his chance to go after what he desired. His feelings for Aqua became stronger and the love he had for her was remarkable. He knew Johnny wasn't good for Aqua, but he just needed to prove it to her. Will he do it in time or will he be too late?

Joey remembered he had to go to LA for his audition since he already booked his flight. Maybe he needed this time to get away and reflect. His family agreed to take care of Brenna when he was gone as well. He assumed he wasn't going to get the role because he was really shy, quiet, and awkward. He'll be surprised at what happens next.

For Indiniya, she was a part of her new family. She always wanted to spend time with Becky, since she was the only person, whom she had a deep connection with. Once Becky left and started to create her own family, Indiniya felt alone. Then, she tried to connect with George, but we all know how that turned out for her. She felt like she was left in the dark, but now being a part of this new family, she can have a fresh start. Even though she had that three-hour talk with Becky about everything she was going through, she hadn't healed from those past experiences. She just talked about them. Becky wanted Indiniya to go to a therapist, but every time she dropped her off at the clinic, she would leave. She would then come back to the clinic to get picked up. She just told Becky that the session went well. Becky was skeptical because she hasn't seen any progress from Indiniya. Maybe she wasn't ready to talk about those past experiences, or maybe they'll haunt her for the rest of her life.

All Becky could do is encourage her since she was overage and could make her own decisions. She couldn't force her to go because that's her life, and she was going to do whatever she wanted.

Indiniya portrays an image that everything's good, and she is healed from her past. You could see in her eyes that she was still hurting and grieving from her past. She tried to bury it to try and forget about those experiences that ate her up inside.

Since then, opening up to people and becoming vulnerable was difficult for her. She tried to be open with people, but she holds certain expectations and standards that'll hinder her from connecting with people in a genuine way. Her past got in the way of what people said to her, the words they used, and the actions that followed.

Straight out the gate, anything she was involved in was serious. She needed everything to be serious because of her upbringing and not always having people there for comfort. This played out as she started to grow up. Would Indiniya keep running from the past because she always brings it up?

Indiniya gets frequent downloads of who she truly is, but she pays little to no attention to it. She can reach that point, but the shadow work is getting in the way of it all. Would she allow herself to fully overcome the past or will she be stuck there forever?

Indiniya was listening to music while drawing in her room. Becky came home after treating one of her patients who showed her a flyer for this new show called 'Escape Room'. Becky took a picture of the flyer and thought it'll help Indiniya to get outside and try new things. It's all about new beginnings, new adventures, and new experiences with cherishable people.

The patient who she treated was Joey, can you believe it. When Joey was admitted into the hospital, the first doctor on the scene was Becky. He still had the flyer in his bag, and he already called for his interview. After Becky was speaking about her daughter, Joey gave the flyer to Becky in case Indiniya was interested. Joey thought it'll be a good idea to have her try something different in her life, and Becky agreed.

As she came home, she knew that Indiniya might not be interested in the show. So, Becky took the audition for herself and acted like Indiniya. She performed well enough that she got the call back to come in for an audition. Becky now had to announce they were going on a trip.

Indiniya loved seeing nature in different areas of the world. She didn't care where it was, she was just excited to see nature in its prime. Becky gathered everyone together to head to Los Angeles. Indiniya was afraid of planes, so she thought they were going on a road trip. Becky already booked the flight and when they were in the car driving to the airport, Indiniya thought it was the start of their road trip. Little did she know, she was about to go on a plane. After a few hours of the plane ride, Indiniya faced her fear of planes in just a few hours.

Once they landed, Becky still didn't tell her about the audition she'll have to do. She didn't know how to tell her, so she'll tell her when that time comes. Becky just wanted her family to enjoy their time and live in the moment.

Bastet kept having people enter her life to try to steal her energy. She would easily let them in and have sex with them, but something changed. She started to feel this sorrow feeling from her parents. Not to mention, that Victoria was hiding having a child with Pauly from Bastet. Vinny left everything behind due to what Victoria did. Vinny thought about killing Pauly, but he was his best friend for decades now. There are always two sides to every story and then there's the Universal truth.

Now that Bastet is grown and could comprehend information, she wondered why Vinny left her all this time. The only real parent she had was Victoria because she was always there. She wondered why Pauly didn't take her in as his own. That was because they were hiding the secret of having a child. It was hard to tell Bastet because all this time had passed, and her sister-in-law was a year younger than her.

Bastet saw how secretive they were becoming, and she started to question what was really going on. She felt them holding a secret from her, but she couldn't figure out what it was. She didn't feel comfortable talking to Vinny, even though he started to put in an effort. He just missed all the important parts of her life, so Bastet was thinking what's the point? What was he going to say? Why wasn't he there and never showed effort beforehand?

Vinny wanted the best for Bastet, and he truly cared for her. He just didn't want to break her heart. Bastet always wanted a sibling. If someone comes out saying she had a sister, that'll break her heart. Vinny knew about the secret because of the fight he had with Victoria. Remember Vinny was trying to fix things, but once she told him about the baby from his best friend, he had enough. That was the icing on the cake for him to leave. Remember this happened when Bastet was young. Now being an adult, still, no one told her about her secret sister.

Bastet had a lot going on due to all of her baby daddies and children. She had to deal with children all the time. Her baby daddies acted like children, her kids are children, and her parents were acting childish and weird around her. Luckily, Bastet was in touch with her inner child, so she knew how to deal with them all. Some people called her needy and self-centered, but she just saw it as having a genuine connection with her inner child. With her already having children, people perceived her as being mischievous (showing fondness) for playfully causing trouble.

Bastet was working so hard, that she barely took care of herself. She was always tired and worn out from working and taking care of her family and friends. She was working nonstop, day in and day out. She tried gaining some energy back from working out. After the gym, she received some downloads. The best times to receive downloads are when you're working on yourself, working out, meditating, sungazing, etc. Bastet was kind of spiritual at the time, so, she felt her spirit relay a message of going to an intuitive reader or a tarot card reader for some answers.

Bastet was nervous, but she knows she needs the truth. Was she truly ready for the raw uncut truth though? She heard about tarot card readers, but she knew some of them can't be trusted since they could be putting spells, curses, and/or body snatch you through the process. It's all about if they set intentions, use the proper sage or incense, and then when the spirit speaks, it speaks. This made Bastet neurological, and she started to drink gallons of water back-to-back nonstop. She knew she needed to go, but the cold-hearted truth can be disturbing to many.

She knew this shop up the street that provided a free intuitive reading if you purchased more than five items at the store. Bastet's stomach was aching because of all the water she just put in her digestive system, but she was fine at the moment. When she got into the store, she purchased five random items for herself and her kids. They asked if she wanted a free reading for purchasing all those items. She said "Yes" and that was the start of the truth-seeking.

Since Spirit moves in miraculous ways, the intuitive reader didn't put a time limit on being with Bastet. The intuitive reader was the owner of the store, and her name was Sara. Sara brought Bastet in and sat her down to make her feel comfortable. Bastet told Sara her name and Sara started to decompress Bastet's personal life. She got all the answers right so far about the baby daddies and the children. That was surface-level information, but you know you have to ease in the truth. Sara told Bastet that she had a sister-in-law. Bastet was defensive right out the gate saying that could never happen, but it was the truth.

Sara told her all the information and showed her proof, but she didn't want to accept it. Sara grabbed Bastet's head (respectfully) and sent her a vision of her seeing her sister before something happens. Sara saw a vision that was tragic for Bastet, but she didn't want to tell her that type of truth because she didn't know how she would've taken it. She didn't want to bury herself in sadness. You'll under, inner, and overstand what I'm saying as the story progresses.

Sara sent her a vision of her sister being right next to her, but before she got to see her face, Bastet took Sara's hands off her head. Bastet was so paranoid that she had a panic attack. The last thing Sara told Bastet before this happened was her sister-in-law's name was Sincere. Once Sara said her name, Bastet blacked out and fainted in the store. Remember she was already having stomach pains, and that went to the extreme while having her panic attack. She drank so much water that she pissed her pants right before she fainted. She didn't remember anything after that.

Sara called the ambulance, and they took her to the nearest hospital. This was the first time Bastet ever needed to go to the hospital. When news broke out to Victoria, she thought it must've been something serious. She knew it might've been the right time to come out with the truth about Sincere. Victoria brought Sincere with her to the hospital, and they went to Bastet's room. It was so nerve-racking for Victoria that she almost had her own panic attack. Why would Bastet want to know the truth while she was laying on a hospital bed?

When they went inside her room, they noticed that Bastet was still sleeping. Victoria's nerves calmed down while seeing her asleep. 12 hours passed and she was still sleeping. Victoria and Sincere had to go, so Victoria decided to whisper in her ear that she had a sister named Sincere and they'll meet one day. Victoria named her Sincere because she thought Bastet and Sincere could bring serenity to each other.

After that, Sincere brought her a gift which was a flyer to have a chance to go to Los Angeles because she needed a vacation and time to herself. Victoria and Pauly were going to take care of her kids and their baby daddies. She left the flyer on her table, and they acted like it was a gift from Victoria. Sincere called in for her audition to spend time with her sister, but she didn't receive the call back to come in for the casting call. She thought Bastet would have a better chance to get on the show and go on this trip to LA. Right when they drove off, Bastet awakened. She saw a flyer that said it was from Victoria. She wanted her to call in and see if she can make it on the show.

Bastet just realized Victoria came and tried to visit her. Bastet felt whiplash from everything that had taken place. Her doctor came in to check on her. Bastet almost had a near-death experience, but she knows she needed time to herself to process and either accept what had happened or not accept it. The doctor doesn't know if Bastet even remembered what had happened.

The doctor told her that she needed to get her stomach pumped because of all that access water she had in her stomach. Sara told the paramedics that she had overwatered herself and they could tell. Sara was tapped in about what was going on in Bastet's life. Sara knew the water helped caused her to faint, but the real panic attack started because of

Sincere. Sara called the paramedics since she fainted, but Sara didn't tell them about the reading session.

The doctor told Bastet that her mom and another person came to visit her. They left a flyer behind stating she should apply. Once Bastet realized the doctor said her mom and another person, her heart started to beat faster. She looked outside and didn't see her mom's car. The doctor suggested that she should apply because she was getting stressed out. Bastet called and received her call back and was now on her way to LA. Will this mystery sister tear her apart? Will this pain eat her up inside? Will this be destined to happen, or will they never meet? Find out soon throughout the book, "How to Overcome Apocalyptic Events" continues.

Ah yes, the final main character Aqua. Aqua still has love for Joey. She knows these tendencies about Johnny that aren't adding up. She was still in her fantasy honeymoon phase, so this seemed all surreal. Through all of this, she still loved Johnny. The million-dollar question is who does she love more?

Through all the good and all the bad, Joey didn't technically do anything wrong. She decided to find what she was craving at that moment. She finally realizes that Johnny might be a player, but of course, she doesn't fully know. The decision between her desires versus what she needs was eating her alive. That's one of the toughest decisions to make in people's lives. Whether or not they'll fulfill their needs, wants, and/or desires. Truthfully, you deserve it all.

Aqua was raising Brenna and Elias all at the same time. Aqua applied to be on the show Teen Mom, but she got declined. Some people have babies solely to try and be on that show. They don't realize that they only choose a couple of people to be on the show. Thousands presumptively applied and only a handful get selected. On top of that, she had to deal with people at school judging her because she had two kids before graduating high school. She received unpleasant looks and stares from people as she walked by. Some people threw trash at her. That was when she was with Joey, but once she moved on with Johnny, all the haters backed off. They were scared of Johnny and his presence at the school. Being with Joey, Aqua became more creative and expressed what she enjoyed. Being with Johnny, she tried new things, but it wouldn't be something she necessarily wanted to do. It's good to explore and change, but is it a positive change or a negative change?

Joey was constantly showing her all the FBI work he'd done on Johnny's past, the crimes he committed, past relationships, and much more. At first, Aqua didn't listen to Joey because she felt like he was trying to break them up. Once, she started listening and asking people around town, it seemed like Joey had something up his sleeve. Aqua didn't want to rush to conclusions, so she just went with the flow. Aqua didn't want to come off as a stalker type, but Joey didn't care if he was. Aqua slowly started to watch Johnny's every move just like Joey. Aqua didn't take it as seriously compared to Joey. Aqua now was evocating over Joey and started to contemplate on which person was the best to settle down with. She was getting mixed signals and mixed messages from Johnny because ever since Elias was born, he started to change his ways. He was showing her that caring side of him like when they first met. She was becoming delusional and denialistic. It was like someone was playing mind games on her, manipulating her, or doing spell work.

All in all, she was having a hard time choosing and didn't want to make that decision any time soon. She enjoyed the company of both Johnny and Joey.

Aqua wanted a third child because all of her family trees had three siblings/children. Hence, Aqua's parents had three kids: her, Alex, and Tori. Would the daddy of the third child be from Joey or Johnny; or will there be a third guy in the mix? Maybe someone from her dating sites might reach back out to her.

After the investigation, Johnny cheated on Aqua with another woman without telling her. Joey had the proof and showed her the evidence. Ever since then, Johnny apologized to Aqua for what he'd done. Aqua accepted the apology from Johnny because she remembered how understanding Joey was towards her. That was when Johnny started to change for the better. People will solely base you on all your negatives and wrongdoings and barely focus on the positive side of a person. After Joey heard that Aqua accepted his apology with the possibility of things working out; that was when Joey had enough.

He was thinking, that after all the information he presented to her, she still was trying to figure things out with him. Joey then started to become distant and went through a downward spiral as we touched on before.

After the surprise party they threw for Joey, Aqua went back home and decompress while she Netflix and chilled with ice cream and cake (what a guilty pleasure). She received a call from Joey apologizing for everything that happened. Aqua stated that it was a surprise for his art show. Joey expressed his true feelings towards Aqua and she considered it because she wasn't fully committed to Johnny. She spends more time with Johnny instead of Joey, which clouded her judgment and mind. Our minds can get so clogged up with all this massive amount of non-stop information, that we have no energy or clarity left to focus on doing something that'll have a powerful impact on humanity.

Aqua felt since Johnny was there most of the time, the obvious decision was Johnny, but she remembers what he'd done. She wanted to hang out with Joey more to see who'll be the best fit for her. Essentially, she had two men fighting for her love.

Don't ask me why Joey is still trying, but when you truly love someone and exchange that type of energy all the time with that person, it's a bond that'll be hard to break.

Aqua told Joey that they need to spend more time together and Joey agreed. Joey remembered he was going to LA for however long the casting call. Aqua was bummed, but she had more time to spend with Johnny during Joey's trip. They ended the phone call in a good way right before Johnny walked through the door.

Johnny came through the door sunburned and was coughing like crazy. Aqua asked Johnny what was going on. Johnny told her that he was doing a prank video driving his motorbike through the sand at the beach. The sun was so blazing that it burned him, became red, had blemishes, and his skin felt like it was on fire. Not to mention that his bike tipped over and the sand broke his tooth.

After sneezing a couple of times, Aqua quickly took Elias to bed and called the nanny to take care of Elias for the rest of the day. Aqua didn't want Johnny to become contagious to Elias since he had certain allergies.

She quickly checked Johnny into the hospital to check his fluids, his vitals, and his blood pressure. After the nurse did the correct measures on

Johnny, he was awaiting the doctor to come in. The doctor was Becky. What a small country right?

After Becky cured him (after two days), he was all cleared to go back home. Then he told Becky about his tooth and asked if she knew of any good dentists around town. Becky was a dentist as well, so after two days she fixed his teeth.

As Aqua was waiting, Becky gave this flyer to her to see if she was interested in signing up for this TV show. Becky saw the beauty of Aqua and thought she'll be great on television. So, Aqua took a picture of Becky's smartphone because she took the picture of Joey's flyer. Becky didn't know that Joey and Aqua knew each other and Aqua didn't know she treated him as well. As Aqua was waiting, she called in for her phone interview and got invited to the casting audition. She just realized the casting director said it'll be in Los Angeles, and she remembered that Joey was going to LA as well. This was her chance to rekindle things or spend more time with Joey. After she accepted, Johnny was all cleared to leave the dentist.

Aqua told Johnny about her trip to LA and Johnny said he'll drive her. Johnny wanted to go because it was just something to do. She didn't want him to come because this will interrupt her from connecting with Joey. Johnny didn't pay attention to the disgusting face she had and automatically called the nanny to babysit Elias for a while.

Aqua didn't say anything because she usually lets him make the decisions. She never really dared to step up and say what was on her mind all the time. Not only Aqua will be surprising Joey in LA, but also Johnny as well.

This love triangle never dies. What will happen next? Would Joey be humiliated by seeing them both? How would Johnny react to seeing them both plan a trip to LA? What will Aqua do?

As this juicy tale continues, sit back, relax, and enter the whole new world of chapter three, entitled: 'Time to Play the Game'. Let the games begin!

Chapter Three

TIME TO PLAY THE GAME

Everyone was excited about this substantial event that was taking place in Los Angeles. This new change in scenery will bring more opportunities either good or bad. The new location, new people, and new blessings could be on their way. For a few, it might be the best decision in their lives, but for some, it might be the worst decision of their life. Find out who because you'll never know what's coming next. For right now, let's go through each character starting with Indigo.

Indigo was a brave soul going to a whole new state by himself right out of high school. Since he just graduated, he was preparing to go to college. For the summer, he wanted to go on a trip, and to his surprise, here was his trip. Indigo used some of his graduation money to make this trip come into reality. He didn't want to use his savings because he was a good saver.

Indigo was excited to audition for the escape room television show because he was started to get into modeling and acting. This could be the big break he needed to make his dreams come into reality. He knew he wanted to be a model and actor because he always had that type of skill and talent. He knew it only took confidence because anyone could be a model if they took care of themselves and had that self-confidence.

On the plane ride, he kept overplaying and practicing what he'll say in front of the casting directors. They didn't give him a script, so he knew it'll be based on his energy and personality. For practice, he turns to ask the person next to him some questions to spark up a conversation. Once he turned over, he saw that person sleeping.

On the plane ride, he would practice talking to himself and the flight attendant. The flight attendant was so amazed by his personality that she told him to meet her in the back where they held the snacks next to their bathroom. There were three bathrooms in total and two snack stands where the flight attendants were at. So, you have one bathroom for first-class, one for commercial use, and one specifically used for flight attendants. She was talking about the bathroom where flight attendants would hang out around. Once Indigo got up, he was confused about where it was because he didn't know what to expect. He finally found it and was surprised at what happened next.

The flight attendant threw him in the bathroom, started to undress, and undressed Indigo. Indigo was shocked over the fact that this was happening because this type of stuff only happens on screen in movies or TV shows. This told Indigo that anything was possible, and he could achieve his goal of becoming a movie or television star.

After they got physical for a bit, the flight attendant was about to have sex with him. Indigo was currently on his semen retention journey, and he was a virgin. Even though Indigo had the nerve to be physical with women, he never went to the extreme of actually having sex with them. From the outside looking in, people would assume he wasn't a virgin based on all the experiences he had with women. All of those instances never went into having sex, but it was quite close.

As she tried having sex with Indigo, he examined and sensed her energy. What energy could it be? Indigo wasn't in full-on spiritual mode at the time, but remember, he had the power of reading people's energies. Every time he was about to have sex with people, there was this pull of his Higher Self that came into the picture, and decided to not have sex with them. It could've been because they weren't valuable enough to gain his energy, could've been their energy level, weren't established enough, or their status wasn't up to par with his. This was devastating to the women and lowered their self-esteem. Some of them ghosted Indigo after this fact alone.

Indigo knew some people weren't valuable enough to gain his energy because it's like entering a portal. Would you rather enter a pure, divine, and clean portal or a not secure, uneven energies, and a dirty portal? With Indigo being a virgin, he's fully cleaned, and no one has entered his portal. Most people who have sex allow other entities to enter through their portals, so it's dirty. When I say dirty, I don't mean not washed or cleaned via soap and water. I mean, dirty by the energies and demons attached to it. They'll surround them since they have entered through their portal. It's so important to watch who you have sex with because it can become toxic, but your mind would only assume it's for pleasure. That's the duality between pleasure and what associates them as well.

The reason their energy level isn't up to par with his was that when you're vibrating on a higher playing field and the other person isn't; then they'll drain your energy. When you think about it, if you're on a 432hz frequency for instance (which is a healing frequency) and the other person is operating on a 440hz frequency (which can cause more harm than good), they'll essentially be stealing your healing energy. If their energy is low, say if they ate a cheeseburger beforehand. All that energy from that cheeseburger and the demons, fears, and flaws from that cow (even if it's really from a cow or not) will be entered through their mouth portal. Which then will be entered throughout their system. Then when you exchange bodily fluids with that person, that same energy will be transferred into your system as well.

From the established or not point of view, since having sex is exchanging energy, then all your worth and establishments rub off on them as well. If one isn't established, has nothing going for them, or hasn't experienced certain things in life at an age where these experiences are crucial to have under their belt. Why lose your energy to someone with who you'll have to teach basic everyday knowledge? Some people don't have that experience, so why waste your time babysitting when you could find someone on your level or who could raise you to the next level?

Indigo was in his head thinking about all of this since his Higher Self took over in this situation. He was more conscious than subconscious in this scenario. Indigo was hard in the midst of this situation but then became soft after he realized this information. The flight attendant felt a type of way toward Indigo and felt like he bashed her image and character. Indigo left the bathroom and went back to his seat.

The aftermath for Indigo was to not let anyone steal his precious energy no matter how they look, what they say, or what they do. Who's the real person on the inside? Most people put a mask on to convey an image of what they want to be portrayed to people. Get to know a person to the fullest extent before diving deeper with them because they could be darker instead of being pure light as they say they are.

Indigo didn't care as much because he was more focused on his audition than getting women. Indigo was now focusing on himself than putting others before him. This was the start of his awakening journey of true power and self-love that he once dreamt of having.

For the rest of the plane ride, he went over his self-tapes, looked out the window as they flew by, and started to connect with the sleeping passenger next to him. He finally woke back up and Indigo started to have a schmooze with him. Come to find out that he was going to see the wall of fame. It shocked Indigo because he was going there as well. Indigo knew that one day he'll be on the wall of fame.

They continued to chat for the rest of the plane ride. Once they landed, since this was Indigo's first time flying by himself, he had no clue where anything was. Good thing Indigo made this connection on the plane with his passenger because he then asked where they could find their bags. Indigo followed him and found where the bags were supposed to be. The bags didn't come till 20 minutes after the plane landed.

During this time, Indigo turned his phone back online (off airplane mode). He received two missed calls and multiple text messages from his family members checking in on him. He then responded and began to watch parts of the escape room. He wanted to get in the zone even though his audition was the next day. Indigo likes to skip through movies if they're not talking about anything or just skips to the good parts (sometimes). He wanted to rewatch and relive the memories and the rooms of the escape room.

Once he received his bags, he then waited for his Uber to arrive. Since he hasn't been to an escape room before, it made him more ecstatic to join. He got dropped off at the hotel and gathered his stuff into the hotel room. Indigo was a good organizer because he wanted to become a minimalist but hasn't achieved that goal yet. Indigo was ready to have some fun.

Indigo's first location was the wall of fame as he stated before. The funny part was that he saw the guy he flew a plane with there in real-time. The guy's name was Frank. Frank and Indigo connected once again and shared some fun memories once more. This was so destined to happen, that they exchanged numbers and they are now travel buddies. Frank had a condo in LA and let Indigo stay in his condo for today and tomorrow. This was due to California being an expensive place to live.

Indigo told him about his audition and all the other destinations he had to go to. Frank was willing to take him. Indigo and Frank were practically best friends. They made sure to look out for one another and spent time with each other. Frank was leaving LA after tomorrow, so he lends Indigo a stashed key just in case he needed to stay longer.

Indigo and Frank explored LA by going to the mountains, hitting some nature spots, fine-dined, going to the club, and going to the strip club. After they traveled to a few clubs that night, Indigo was tired and beat from the whole day. Plus, he wanted some sleep because of his busy schedule tomorrow. Frank wanted to go to the strip club, but Indigo didn't want to go.

One thing about Indigo was that, if he doesn't want to do something, he won't do it. If Indigo wants to do something, he'll find a way to do it. Since he didn't want to go to the strip club, Indigo took an Uber to Frank's crib and crashed on the bed. Frank came home at midnight PST time with two strippers. Indigo automatically woke up when they entered because of his marvelous hearing skills.

Indigo thought to himself, poor Frank because these strippers only want him for his money. So, he grabbed his pair of headphones, listened to some vibrational frequencies, and went back to bed.

Indigo woke up around 2:00 AM because he had a modeling fashion show (which he was a part of), that started at 4:00 AM. He got dressed, prepared himself, and was about to leave for the event. The only person who wasn't ready was Frank.

Indigo tried to wake him up by dumping water on his face and even slapped him. The strippers stole all of his energy that he wasn't getting out of bed. Frank then pointed at his wallet and said, "Take as much money as you need." Indigo grabbed most of the money to call an Uber. Even though Frank couldn't take him, he was still excited about the modeling event he was going to be in.

How did Indigo find out and become a part of this modeling runway show? Indigo watched an ad during his time streaming the movies from yesterday about this modeling event to cast a premium model. It was open to the public and he was excited to go and show off his talent.

Indigo arrived and was ready to conquer his first modeling event. Indigo signed in, gave him a number, and then took some pictures and videos of him. This was his chance to practice his skills on camera to get ready for his real audition later on.

It was a sunny bright day and Indigo was waiting in line for his turn to go on stage. Once he got up on stage, that man Indigo killed it. He showed off his personality with flair and style. Indigo did so well that once he got off stage, people were still clapping and cheering for him. Indigo had five different women come up to him and gave him their phone numbers.

The event was getting ready to end and they were about to announce the winner. The winner was Indigo and he got to sign with a major modeling/acting agency, won a cash prize, and was going to be on the cover of their newly issued magazine. Indigo was about to embark on a new journey of modeling and acting, which he always wanted to do. Just imagine, after two days of being in LA, you win a model runway showcase, won a cash prize, sign with an agency, and be on the cover of a future magazine. He had so much momentum that it boosted Indigo's confidence tenfold for his audition to be on TV. This was a huge moment for Indigo as a small-town boy acting like he was country all the time. Now he was outliving his dreams of becoming a model and actor. After he signed some paperwork, took some pictures for the magazine, and exchanged information with the modeling agency, it was time to go to his audition.

He got dropped off at his audition and the building was massive. It had 14 different studios and people drove golf carts to get around. The audition took place in studio seven and Indigo saw so many people auditioning to be on the show. This made Indigo a bit impatient, but he remembered he was an official model and actor now, so he gained some courage in his time of need.

He saw some drunk people, nervous people, and people who flashed designer clothing. The demographic was at its highest. There were teenagers, young adults, males, females, and adults presently there.

The casting directors came out and explained if they saw something in you, you'll then proceed to meet with the executive producer. If they made it past the executive producer, then they'll meet the creator/CEO of the show.

They gave them an introduction to the show, what it'll be about, and what they'll have to do. Indigo and the other participants were still interested in the show. They were only casting seven people, but that doesn't mean they won't put you through to the next round if they already chose seven. The executive producer was the one to choose between the rest that'll make it through. In the final round, the creator of the show will boil it down to seven candidates.

The casting directors watched the energy in the room, felt the vibration they were giving off, and if they were interesting characters. You cannot have a show with non-interesting characters. The casting directors were looking for fun, unique, and different characters for the show. They didn't want people with the same personalities to be on the show because it'll become boring and too much of the same.

It was Indigo's turn and the casting directors saw something special in him. They viewed him as the brains of the escape room since he loved the actual escape room game. The show needed a smart person to keep the show on track with its goal to win.

They loved the story he told when he was on the airplane coming to LA and everything that transpired till now. Indigo went raw, uncut, and told them about everything. The casting directors cracked up laughing and saw Indigo being a comedian as well. They would never believe any of that happened, but it was indeed the truth. One of the casting directors said he was a comedic expert. He was a comedic genuine since he was originally a funny person who loves to crack jokes. The casting directors chose him to move on to the next round.

Once he got into the next round, he was then faced with the executive producer of the show. The executive producer had all the candidates that made it to the next round. The casting directors did thousands of phone interviews with people who were initially interested in the show. They then trickled it down in the hundreds for a casting call event. Then it trickled down in the fifties once it reached the executive producer. They weren't playing around and were set on picking seven unique characters for the show.

The producer was mainly looking at how different they were and what stood out for them. They want to develop a character, but also have that rooted unique feature that makes them stand out. Since the show mainly wasn't scripted, they'll have to go through different parts of the show where they'll have to act on the fly.

The producer was testing their acting skills and seeing if they were a good fit for the show. Also, if they've had modeling or acting experience (which was a plus). Since Indigo was a model and actor now, he was already stoked that he met those requirements as well. The producer, for example, randomly threw something at them and saw how they responded. Indigo instantly caught it and threw it back without the producer saying anything. The executive producer thought Indigo was bold by catching and throwing it back in an instant. The executive producer progressed Indigo to the last and final round with the creator of the show.

Now it's time for the last round with the CEO. We'll keep the names of these characters unknown for right now.

As we stated, the executive producer interviewed around fifty aspiring cast members for this show. The executive producer placed 15 characters in the next and final round.

For the final round, the CEO would interview all the participants and then have a chitchat with the casting directors and executive producer to see which of these 15 candidates can be cast down to seven. Making the first impression on the CEO was a huge deal because the CEO had the last say on who'll get casted.

The CEO would say it's a different form of an escape room because they'll do it in virtual reality. The CEO would ask the remaining 15 competitors if anyone wasn't interested anymore. Two people weren't interested in the concept, and they left. The CEO noticed two more people who were faltered about the idea and the CEO threw them out. Now it's down to the last 11 participants.

Since this was a game of escape room, the remaining auditioners would play a real-life escape room to show off their knowledge, skills, and teamwork. This wasn't an original escape room; it was a haunted house full of terror.

One person was scared of haunted houses, so that person was out. Now it was down to ten.

Once they got in the house, the CEO locked the door and the timer appeared. They had 20 minutes to find a way out and collect all the clues. An unassigned door suddenly opened, and it was a clown sitting on a rocking chair letting out one of his red balloons. Most people were freaking out, but some suddenly enjoyed the experience.

The red balloon popped and out came a rattlesnake. One person who was afraid of snakes yanked the door to come out. Noticing the door was locked, they sat in the corner and said, "I quit." The creator came and unlocked the door to get the contestant out. Now it was down to nine.

After going through most of the clues, the CEO witnessed someone who was barely participating in the game. The CEO then took that person out of the game and now it was down to eight.

The show only needs exactly seven in total for production purposes. After they completed the game, everyone else succeeded. The CEO couldn't decide, so he told them to sit tight, and they'll call them in one by one. After discussing it further with the casting directors and executive producer, they told the participants if they had made it or not. It was Indigo's turn and he got cast for the show. He was then placed to go to studio 13 for further instructions.

Indigo felt a rush of relief and blissfulness for being cast on the show. Since studio 13 was in a different building, they brought him via golf cart to the next building. He then waited with the other six cast members of the show to await further instructions.

Indigo was thinking about how this trip had transformed his life for the better. He couldn't wait to participate in this exciting new show (which everyone was excited about). This will skyrocket Indigo's modeling and acting career since he'll be performing in front of millions of people weekly. This show was gaining so much buzz that it was available on all streaming platforms while still being available on cable television.

For Apollo, he had a unique experience going to LA. Apollo took his private jet (well his family's private jet) to LA. Before boarding the plane, he took some flicks for the gram and then allowed people to board the plane. He invited his crew of yes men and some women on the plane. Apollo recorded a music video while the plane was in hyperdrive.

Most people think Apollo's dumb and just flexes money, but there's more than meets the eye. Apollo was smart, but all of his decisions aren't necessarily the best decisions. Will Apollo ever learn from his mistakes? We shall see.

During the music video, they were popping champagne, and he was wearing a gold, black, and red robe with red bottom shoes, since their jet was gold and black. Since Apollo was gaining more recognition, he became famous in the public eye. Apollo was getting recognized for his music, acting career, and being a fashion designer.

Right after they finished the music video and it met his standards, he went to a fashion designer modeling event that he was performing in. Since this was LAFW (which means Los Angeles Fashion Week), he was one of the influential fashion designers to perform. The event will be held during the evening, so once they land, they'll have to set up. He had his team there to help along the way and the models started to pile in. These high-end fashion models used to work with Gucci, Victoria's Secret, and much more.

Apollo scheduled a three-day trip. On the first day, it was the fashion show, the second day was his other business ventures, and the last day was for the show's audition.

The models recognized Apollo and were asking for pictures and autographs. Apollo turned it down and said that he was working. Yes, don't forget Apollo's still a savage. Apollo then chose the models he wanted to use, and the event was about to start.

After hair, makeup, and them getting dressed, the event was ready to begin. Apollo loves to multitask while performing multiple tasks simultaneously. Apollo let his team handle the models because he knew the crowd was going to enjoy his clothing anyways. Apollo had the final say, but he was mostly focused on editing the music video he just did to be uploaded by tomorrow.

The show, either way, was a success for Apollo and he was named the designer of the year. Apollo went on stage and gave a marvelous speech that he found on Google, and he received a standing ovation. That just goes to show if you have confidence in the words, you say or the things you do, then you can easily influence people to believe the same things or the words that are coming out of your mouth.

Apollo went home and his team finished editing his music video for him to post it at midnight. Everything was all set and ready to be published. Once the music video went live, Apollo went to bed. That was after day one.

Day two arrived and it was indefinitely a timeless moment, and you'll see why.

Apollo had a busy schedule for today due to all the events he has to attend. Apollo checked his music video, and it was already number one on trending. That was the only thing he needed to see for that day to become a successful day.

The first event he had to go to was the music award show where he was being honored as the most legendary music artist in history. It was surprising because Apollo only started making music a few years ago and was already getting an award of that magnitude. Apollo was performing at the event as well. This was a morning event leading into the afternoon. Apollo gathered his team together and got dressed. He wore one of his new designs from his clothing line to perform. Apollo hopped out of his limousine and stepped right onto the gold carpet.

Apollo loved the lights and cameras, but sometimes it became too much for him. Apollo loves to do it all, but ultimately, he's a chill person. Once the cameras are rolling, he became a different person. Apollo likes to portray different images of himself in different situations. When Apollo is working on his multiple businesses, he gets serious. When he's by himself, he's chill. When he's around people, he's social. In different instances, you wouldn't know which Apollo you'll get unless you see what he's doing. That'll determine the Apollo you'll get in that situation or scenario. Some people don't want you to win, so they'll lie saying something you put out was trash when it was fire.

With all the fame and success, sometimes Apollo questions why he goes to these events. If he could be at multiple places at the same time, he would. The fame, fortune, and celebrity status made him numb. This made him not feel emotion towards things or people. He'll only show emotion and feelings when he succeeds. When he succeeded so much, he was losing that touch of feeling once more.

While on the gold carpet, he was starting to give his model face to the camera, and the photographers loved it. One interviewer tried to kiss Apollo on the lips, but he told her to kiss him on the cheek. The cameras loved Apollo, but does Apollo still love the cameras as he once did? Or was he just used to them now?

The music event started, and they passed out awards and had some people perform. It was time for Apollo to perform for the crowd and he was never nervous when he performs. No man, woman, thing, animal, place, or item could bring a phobic upon Apollo. Apollo performed all of his gold and platinum hits for the fans. When Apollo performed, most would compare him to the greats. He never compared himself to another person and just viewed himself as being himself. Apollo's performance was by far the best performance of the night. He introduced fire, the mist of water, dancing, and nature in his performance. Right after his performance, his longtime friend (who he mostly collaborated with) gave him the award. Apollo gave a similar speech as before, but this time it was different since he found it on Bing. Right after he received the award, he left because he was going to the next award show.

The next event was held in the afternoon which was a television award show. Apollo was getting an award as the best new actor of the year. Now you're probably asking yourself how does he know he'll win already? All these award shows are scripted, and they already know who'll win regardless of the fan's vote. The fans could all easily vote for one person, but then another person wins. The fans will go and listen to their music, watch that TV show, or watch the movie that just won the award. Even though they give people the chance to vote, their vote doesn't matter. They portray your vote as like it matters to make you think you helped generate who's in power or who'll win an award. They already know who they want to win or be elected no matter what the ballet says. Election fraud is real, and it happened by them throwing away most of the ballots. Fairytales don't always begin with 'Once upon a time.' Many of them begin with, 'If I'm elected, I promise…"

So, Apollo proceeded to get out of his limo, but this time it was a long black rug. Artistes would come out up to Apollo wanting to collab, but he will direct them to his assistant. Apollo just wanted to receive his award and get up out of there. Most men have a woman assistant because they're like a motherly figure, they're more organized, and they make sure everything's in order. His assistant was very precise, and his team helped him a lot. His team was like family because Apollo's parents weren't always present for the majority of his life.

Apollo would then receive his award and gave an acting speech that he found on Yahoo. He left the event early because, in his eyes, there wasn't a point in staying when you received all your awards and performed your songs. Unless you wanted to chat with another actor, actress, director, producer, or artist about collaboration. Apollo was busy throughout the whole day, so this was just the beginning.

The next event he had to rush to be a part of was the red-carpet premiere for his upcoming movie called Apollo. Yes, it was essentially a biopic of Apollo, played by Apollo. Apollo wanted to create a documentary for himself and his journey through life. He was going to walk through all of his experiences till this point in his career. He plans on making Apollo 2 when he gets older. Part one was about his life from ages 0-25 and then the next one would be from the medieval ages of 26-50. Apollo wasn't even 25 yet, but he added it in for good measure.

The event took place during the evening and ran through its course into the night. All of Apollo's friends, supporters, and family were present at the event. He was happy that he saw his family because he thought they wouldn't care as much. His family came to show their support and proof to Apollo that they loved him. They all got together, took some pictures, and headed right inside the theater. After the movie was done, his assistant reminded him about the birthday bash he was throwing for his long-term friend named Kevin. This was the same friend who gave him the award earlier. That was where he was going next.

Apollo went to the Airbnb house that he reserved under another email address since the last one got banned. Kevin had helped Apollo with his music career tremendously. Last year, they made a collab album together and it went number one on the Billboard Hot 100 charts for 52 consecutive weeks in a row. All Apollo had to do was send him an address and he was going to be there.

Once Kevin went to the Airbnb spot, they surprised him. He already knew after driving down the street and seeing how many cars, people, and loud music that was playing, that it was all for him. People were drinking, fighting, smoking, having sex, and doing drugs. Random people came over and tried to enter, but security stopped them from entering. Once again, good thing Apollo has an assistant and a team that helps him with all of this. Plus, it was good that they chose a remote location, so people wouldn't call the cops about the disturbance of the party.

Apollo and Kevin partied all night and everyone began to leave around 1:00 AM. By 11:00 PM Apollo and Kevin were already inside with a bunch of women having a good time. Apollo's assistant and his team went to a hotel to get some rest instead of parting like wild animals.

Apollo's team went back to the house in the morning because Apollo had to be at his audition by 5:00 sharp. Apollo's assistant got him to wake up even though he had crashed for the night. He couldn't remember what happened, but his assistant didn't care as long as he was ready for his audition. Apollo was still practically drunk due to what happened last night.

His team went and called the cleaning services, so Airbnb wouldn't ban his new account. His assistant got him prepared and since he was becoming more conscious, he remembered his audition was today. He got himself together was he was still off the Henny and whiskey.

His assistant finally brought him over to the building and all these fans were screaming because they saw Apollo. His security had to back people away, so he could enter the building. They thought he was a producer of the show or the host of it, but it was the executive producer who did that.

Apollo was still hungover from last night, so he had this fun interactive spirit with everyone. When you're drunk you let other entities enter your body, so you wouldn't act like yourself. For Apollo, you couldn't tell the difference because that was his acting persona. The casting directors called him in first to get all the attention off of Apollo.

Once Apollo went inside to meet with the casting directors, they told him that he bypassed the first two levels of the casting call. The casting directors knew of him and the big following he could bring to the show. They advanced him to the final round after calling the executive producer in confirming his spot. This is what fame can bring you.

He waited until the final round started. During this time, Apollo drank water to overthrow his drunkenness. Once they entered the haunted house, Apollo went on go mode since acting was his cup of tea. He knows how to capture an audience's attention and entertain them.

After they had gone through the haunted house, the CEO automatically cast Apollo for the show. Apollo was the best actor in the building. The CEO brought him and the remaining cast members to await further instructions.

After all the success Aleemic gained worldwide, he was ready to spread that same message to a broader network of people. That's the goal, right? Spread the truth to see if it sticks with the person, so they can change their obsolete ways for the better. If it doesn't stick with a person, then at least you tried, so move on to the next person. You don't want to waste your time, energy, or vibration on trying to convince someone who doesn't want to receive it. We shouldn't force anyone in believing or knowing anything because that's just like religion. Spirituality is a lifestyle. People get motivated by seeing your lifestyle and how pure, positive, loving, and calm-hearted you are in every situation. What you do daily can help change people if they see your progress. That'll motivate them in knowing more or giving spirituality a try. Don't judge a person on where they're at because they're just starting and getting their feet wet first.

That's what Aleemic did for his brands. He didn't need to individually text people or generate ads saying you need them to join his webinar. He wants pure and organic traffic coming his way from people who genuinely wanted to support his endeavors. He gained more success this way instead of forcing people to attend his webinar.

Aleemic doesn't care about social media tactics but uses social media strategies in getting the word out there. He doesn't want to force someone to listen to his music or join one of his services. Instead, he focuses on having genuine people checking out his services who are interested. That was how Aleemic became a massive success.

His love for teaching came back after his huge event in Dubai. Aleemic was a jack of all trades because he offered and provided various services through his buildings and on his private island. Aleemic was doing great for himself, and he knew he was going to reach this point eventually. He received constant downloads through meditation, sungazing, and his dreams to confirm this statement. No matter how many people he helped, how big his business was at the time, or what business ventures he went into next. As long as he was doing it through his authentic self, that was all that mattered. The Universe will reward you ten-fold if you do your mission or purpose while being your authentic self. It doesn't matter about trying to wake up millions of people, not about the attention, not about the followers, and it's not about the fame or fortune you'll receive from it. Of course, that'll come through abundance from the Universe, but that shouldn't be the main focus at hand. The main focus should be on helping people through the skills and talents you obtain that tell a powerful story.

The Universe did indeed bless him in marvelous ways. He became the youngest billionaire in the world, and he retired at a young age. Aleemic still worked because the work that he does was fun for him. You should have fun doing the work that you do instead of dreading it. If you're not having fun doing the work that you do, then why are you doing it in the first place? Don't say it's about money because money doesn't bring happiness. Don't say it's about bills because most people will be in debt for the rest of their lives. That's why people are always waiting for the weekend to get a break from their current jobs. Then you have some people who continue to work every day because they enjoy the work that they do.

That's why you have to know your purposes, missions, and the things that bring value or joy in your life. Life isn't all about paying bills, working multiple jobs you hate just for money, and living stagnated. Then when you go on a vacation barely once per year, for a couple of days just to relax. Then you'll head right back into your "normal" routine. That's why vacations are subjective because you just escape from your current reality and then go back to that reality once you're done. Find ways in which you could take multiple trips per year or try and live a vacation lifestyle for the rest of your life. Vacations could be boring after a week or two, so be an entrepreneur, so you could do fun work on the side that you love. If you're leaning towards multiple trips per year instead of living that vacation lifestyle, then do it that way.

Do what you need to do: no trips, excessive spending, and budget correctly for a couple of years to pay off all your bills, debt, and payments, so you can achieve multiple trips per year while still working. You'll then just be working just to do something instead of working because you have to. Aleemic knew this, so that's why he became a billionaire and got to retire early. Once you retire after 65 years old, you'll be too old, and your body would be worn out to go on multiple trips per year. Depends on the person because some 65-year-olds are in great shape. Take care of yourself physically, mentally, spiritually, emotionally, and financially.

After his break from helping others, he focused on his brand's image and did things that'll uplift his career path. As we stated before, he focused on himself instead of focusing on others. This made Aleemic lose people through the process, but after his retreat, everyone wanted to be in his life once again. He didn't pay attention to these distractions because he was ready to build himself back up and help others through the process. Spirit knew he needed time for himself to find himself. Once he figured that out, he was full of overflown energy and abundance, that he could share with others without feeling drained or losing any of his energy.

Everything should be flowing just like the Universe, animals, the ocean, the waves, and nature just to name a few. That's how to not overthink a situation, not focus on the past or the future, and not be present in the present moment. Life goes fast, so enjoy each moment in your life. You don't want to look back at your life and say you never really enjoyed every moment because you were doing too much. When you try and do so much, you wouldn't be as present, wouldn't be able to remember much about that experience, or wouldn't enjoy that moment to the fullest extent. You can do multiple things or achieve multiple achievements at the same time because we all have 24 hours in a day. Spend your time wisely and make sure you enjoy every moment in life. Life is like a video game and a simulation, so treat it as such, a video game.

When the kid gave him the flyer, Aleemic was ready to spread more of the truth to a broader audience.

Celebrities have to be ringed in and controlled or they don't get the platform or voice that they have. They want them to distract the public and coax the population to do something without questioning. That's why sports entertainers receive millions of dollars per year while police officers, firefighters, or EMTs only get paid in the thousands. Why aren't we questioning these things and asking for more money? People put their livelihoods on the line for the work that they do but have celebrities who get paid millions of dollars to essentially distract people from themselves.

The government is in trillions of dollars in debt due to the inflation rate bubble that's about to burst. They still find a way to send more money to other countries in crisis but give the American people per se less money. That's why prices on everything are skyrocketing. Not to mention these controlled corporations that the elite runs, receive more money and benefits than smaller companies, especially black-owned businesses.

These non-profit organizations don't have to pay taxes if they remain in the right spending and saving ranges. If they went below the margins, then they'll have to pay taxes. So, these non-profit organizations like the NBA or NFL can collect money from people and all they need to do is not reach a lower saving amount in the bank for example. That's how they can pass out millions of dollars because it's not always just based on talent, but it's merely focused on the persuasion you have on people. Not to mention they rig the games for bidding and gambling purposes.

Aleemic got prepared to fly back to America. Aleemic could've taken his private jet, but he decided to go first class to Dubai just because he wanted a different experience. This time flying back to America, he was going to fly commercial just for the heck of it. Aleemic wasn't always too flashy and try to prove that he had money and/or abundance. That's the difference between millionaires and billionaires because while millionaires go out and buy designer clothes, billionaires go and buy a button t-shirt. They would rather spend money on buildings and investing in other companies instead of wasting their money on materialistic items that wouldn't make them more money. That's the difference between smart shoppers and people who just waste their money. For example, why does someone need seven cars? Now someone might say, a car per day, but let's be realistic though. Buying seven cars that are worth thousands of dollars will easily add up in the million-dollar range.

Just because someone has enough money to buy anything they want; doesn't mean they need to spend it recklessly. It's the 1985 effect. These rappers are falling off because they placed their focus and attention on clout chasing, flashing what they had, and acting recklessly. They focus more on gaining followers on social media than producing quality music that'll last a lifetime. Trap music and talking about sex, guns, killing, and doing drugs isn't legendary. That might be cool at the moment because it's hot right now, but it wouldn't be in the next five years. Change and adapt to newer technologies and what's relevant at that current moment. Or just make quality lifelong music. That's why some people fall off and can't retain their audience because they gained those followers by doing dumb stuff that made them pop at the time. Their young audience got older, and they're not feeling that type of music anymore. Pass the truth to the next generation and teach them early on what you've learned. Fame and money don't bring talent and skill, it just brings a following and attention.

So, Aleemic got ready to board his flight, but it got delayed. Why are so many flights getting canceled and postponed nowadays? You could spend lesser time driving instead of traveling by plane sometimes due to these delays. It gets delayed and canceled because of 5G. We saw once they put out 5G, how it affected people, the motor vehicles, and nature. 5G causes the plane to malfunction and it does something to the atmosphere while the plane goes towards the dome. So, to keep people "safe", they'll procrastinate on why it got delayed or they'll cancel it until the 5G goes down in radiation. Safe means control in their eyes. 5G won't only read your thoughts, but it'll also insert thoughts and feelings. They make sure it reaches every home across the country. There's a threat to our world that none of us could ever imagine. It's real, it's being activated worldwide, and because of how far advanced they are with their plans, they no longer hide it.

Aleemic should've taken his private jet because he wouldn't have to wait. Good thing Aleemic booked his flight to LA a couple of days before his audition. The delay of the plane cost him a day in LA. The delay was around 14 hours, so that was already practically a day. Traveling from Dubai to LA takes 15 hours, so when Aleemic finally lands, it'll be the night before his audition.

That's why Mother Nature and Mother Gaia are fighting back against these dark entities. Since the dome has been cracked, we are now seeing ships, angelic figures, and the radiation pouring out from the suns.

Yes, we have multiple suns and there'll be another one called the destroyer. 2022 the return of the Gods (the Anunnaki), 2023 blue comet will rise in the air, and in 2024, the biggest solar alignment ever. The conjunction of the big four: Jupiter, Saturn, Uranus, and Mercury. This will eliminate the rest of these toxic beings who are still down here. This will cause these dark entities to go to their underground caves where they've been taking children, celebrities who spread the truth, and where they record their news broadcastings. They love to do their crimes near Halloween, so they won't show their true identity while performing MKUltra. There'll be a lot more celebrity deaths and people will start to vanish or die. They'll try and come back in 2028, but it'll be far too late.

Remember the ascension takes place in the mind first. It already happened in the spiritual for their demise, but it's now manifesting in the physical. They're delaying their Judgement Day because they created time to delay manifestations. That's why they're scrambling because their time is up. It's like an hourglass and they're operating on their last grains of sand. Let them have the season finale of their TV series, but don't ask for a reboot or stick around after the show. None of these preplanned objectives will be accomplished because the truth is coming out. There's no more running, no more hiding, and their judgment and karma will be something to behold. This wouldn't matter anyway for the chosen ones because this will be their reality, not ours. Even the phrase, "The Chosen One" has been brought to the mainstream and is now played out. There's a difference between wokeness and consciousness.

Due to the delay, he wanted to expose some corporations as the frauds they are. His first stop was at the biggest corporate grocery stores in LA. Having people buy food and water when it comes naturally from nature is ridiculous. Having people eat all these processed, GMO, and unhealthy foods that are tarnishing their immune systems. Pretty insane that 90% of foods in grocery stores didn't even exist 100 years ago, and neither did 90% of the diseases.

They called the cops on Aleemic and he was banned for a year from that corporate grocery store. Aleemic then secretly made it into a UFC fight.

Aleemic was smart at sneaking into places without getting noticed or questioned. He used to act like a construction worker to get into movie theaters. He used to use AirTag to get into festivals, but this time Aleemic climbed into the cage, went on stage, and grabbed a microphone. He exposed the government for what and who they truly are. Security grabbed him and brought him to the back. Aleemic was arrested and got placed in jail for speaking about the government. It wasn't so much tailgating the event because they could've just banned him just like how the grocery store did. This time, they threw him in jail because he was awakening people's minds that it caused a riot. Most people looked at him as crazy, but the information was sticking with some people. They started to leave the event and riot outside. He was in the back of the police car laughing at how much chaos he started.

Aleemic was supposed to be in jail for eight hours, but if he spends eight hours in jail, then he'll miss his audition. While the police officer was walking back and forth, Aleemic was planning to escape. They could easily find the hotel that he was staying at, but he was planning on going to his beach house. The police officer was sleeping in his chair while the keys were right on the table. The prison cell was close to the table but wasn't close enough.

Aleemic used his telekinetic powers to levitate the keys into his hands. He was in a shalom state while activating his powers. He escaped the prison cell and was about to exit through the backdoor with the officer's badge. The other officer was on sight roaming around the premise, so to not get caught, he swapped clothes with the officer who was sleeping. Aleemic knocked him out, so he wouldn't be conscious during the act. After Aleemic changed clothes, he grabbed some markers and made a joker face on the officer's face. Then, Aleemic unbuttoned his shirt, and he put the words, "Good riddance, I'm Vengeance…" Aleemic left the building and ran into the woods.

Aleemic wanted to spend time in nature, so this was perfect timing. After a while, Aleemic finally found a road after walking through the woods. Aleemic called for a Lyft and surprisingly they were still operating at this time.

While Aleemic was waiting for his ride, he looked over and saw a figure standing in the middle of the road. He flashed his phone's flashlight on the figure, and it was a creepy older man who looked sick. He told Aleemic that "He'll float too." After that statement, it got quiet.

Aleemic noticed an abandoned house where he probably lives. A few seconds passed and another figure appeared and grabbed Aleemic's ankle. Aleemic ran into the woods as he'd never run before. These beings were chasing after him, but even though he was shocked at what was happening, he was still conscious. All of that adrenaline came up and he tricked these beings, so they won't be able to find him. Aleemic's ride finally came, and he went to his beach house.

Before going to bed, Aleemic called Esoteric for some help in erasing the camera data, the minds of the police officers, and what he's done. He didn't want to be on the wanted list because that could affect his image and opportunity to be on the show. Esoteric answered immediately and aided Aleemic in his situation. After a powerful ritual, the deed has been done and he thanked his mom and got some rest.

While he was sleeping, he forgot to turn off the location after getting a ride back to his beach house. There was a figure that tracked his location and was secretly watching him through the window menacingly.

Aleemic woke up and got prepared for his audition. He noticed he still had his location on, but he didn't care since he now took a Lyft to the audition. They brought him to studio seven and he was now in front of the casting directors. Aleemic told them the story of what he'd experienced last night. No one believed him since it wasn't on the mainstream media. The casting directors thought he was acting or portraying a story as a storyteller. Even though all these events were true, the casting directors thought of him as a conspiracy theorist and the thinker of the show. They were so impressed with his audition that he bypassed the next round and went right to studio 13 with the CEO.

During the roleplay, they saw Aleemic thinking outside the box and going against the norm. After the game, the CEO told Aleemic that he was being cast to be a part of the show. He placed Aleemic in the next room to go over further details of the show.

Bastet was now leaving the doctor's office after she got called to do an audition. Victoria was the one to pick her up to go to the airport. During the car ride, the fact that Bastet might have a long-lost sister was slowly eating her alive. Bastet couldn't wait any longer and told her mom that she knew about her sister. Victoria knew this moment was coming and confirmed that she does have a sister. Before Victoria could say anything else about Sincere, Bastet stopped her from talking.

Bastet wasn't ready to face the facts. The fact that a random intuitive reader had to tell her first instead of her own family was dreading.

Bastet stayed quiet for the rest of the trip. They said their goodbyes and Bastet was on her flight.

When Bastet was on the plane, she got air sickness. She wasn't used to flying and her stomach was still hurting from earlier. The pain started before boarding the plane, but it got worse when the plane took off. Was it the thought of being in the air that caused the pain? Was it from the water again? I'll let you determine what you think the outcome was based on.

Bastet was taking a two-day trip to LA. Saturday was the first day of her vacation, and Sunday was the audition. Since she had an extra day before her audition, she went on a dating app and started to match with random people from the city. Before she landed, she matched with a guy, got to know him, and set up a date right after she landed. The power of the internet, right? Right before the plane landed, she had to turn airplane mode on, but they both agreed to have a date.

When Bastet landed, she turned her phone off airplane mode and grabbed her stuff. By the time she got herself together, the mystery guy was five minutes away. Bastet was excited to see him because they genuinely connected, and she had a free ride with a free date. Bastet went outside as she waits for the mystery guy.

She saw the guy from the profile picture, and they locked eyes. The mystery guy wasn't a catfish. Once Bastet got in the car, he introduced himself as Cameron. Cameron was a genuine guy who was passionate about love. He wanted to share that love with his new fling Bastet. Cameron and Bastet connected better in person than over the dating site because it was love at first sight. Bastet was relieved that he wasn't a catfish, it was daytime, and it was around a public area. Just in case something goes wrong, she'll have witnesses.

Cameron showed her the love and care she searched for. Bastet wanted to have someone that listens to her with zero judgment about her past or her flaws. Bastet knew she wasn't perfect, but she acted as such. During these times people called her a hypocrite or being hypocritical by the way she acted. If Bastet didn't get her way, then she'll throw a fit and a tantrum. This made people view her as a kid and they didn't take her seriously. Bastet would use sarcasm to crack jokes on people, but most people didn't get the jokes and thought it was pretty offensive. Some people can't take a joke and that's how Bastet operated.

Bastet freely opened up and told Cameron that she loved him. She felt this feeling internally that she couldn't resist or describe. Cameron was weirded out at first but remembered the reason why he was there. What were his motives?

Cameron brought Bastet to a five Michelin star restaurant. Bastet loved seafood, and this place had the best seafood in the state. Once they arrived at the restaurant, they got early access to a table because Cameron knew the owner. Bastet drinks as well, but she knew how to control it. Food was flying, drinks were flowing, and they were having a fun time. Bastet went to the bathroom, and she was conscious enough to bring all of her stuff with her.

While Bastet was in the bathroom, Cameron got her another drink and placed drugs in that cup. Cameron knew she might question what happened when she was gone, but their connection was so strong that she trusted him. If Bastet let a random person pick her up from the airport, then she must trust him a bit.

Bastet felt this intuitive spirit rise feeling like something just happened. As she came back from the bathroom, she was happy that the waitress brought her another drink because she was questioning if she wanted to drink the rest of her current cup. Not knowing that Cameron put the drugs in her new drink instead of her current drink.

She continued to drink and have a good time with him. Bastet felt her stomach getting wobbly and uneasy. She was losing her vision and became dazed. The one who was most concerned was Cameron. As people started to look over and ask if she was alright, Cameron told them it must've been something she ate. He painted a picture of Bastet trying some of his food which caused the reaction. Cameron paid for the meal and brought her back to the car. He told the restaurant that he'll bring her to the emergency room, but that wasn't the case.

By this time, it was getting dark, and he brought her to his house. Once inside, Bastet was gaining back some of her consciousness. She was asking him what had happened because they were having so much fun. He explained that she ate some of his food and became sickly. She became unconscious and he took her to the doctor's office. He told the doctor what happened, and he prescribed some pills for you. Cameron grabbed the pills and gave her some water (that was already drugged) to take with the pills. Bastet believed his story because Cameron was highly believable, and he used this power for manipulation. Once she took the pills and water, she passed out once again. Cameron decided to rape her while she was senseless.

After Cameron was done, he took her to this secret location where auctions are held. He brought her to the basement of the building, and everyone was excited to see Cameron with a female. Cameron ducked taped her mouth, stripped down her clothes, and tied her to the pole (on stage) alongside the other women. The group of guys was on the floor ready to bet on them. The host of this toxic horrendous scene would begin the program.

The fellow women were conscious, but as Bastet was awakening, she was shocked. The event began and they were auctioning off these women based on who had the highest bid. It was finally Bastet's turn to be auctioned off to these men. Cameron didn't pick her because he stated that her sex was useless. Cameron had already chosen another woman and as he walked out, he winked at Bastet.

No one was choosing Bastet and the host noticed, so he went lower in price. This gay couple who already had two other women, choose Bastet as well. They wanted Bastet in the mix to perform an orgy upstairs. There was a security guard positioned at every station if any of the women tried to fight or run away.

As they headed upstairs, the women knew how to perform sign language. While they were tired up, they used their fingers to communicate with each other. The plan was to have the security guard join in and catch them off-guard.

Once they got inside the room, the couple untied their arms, took off their duct tape, and demanded a show. One of the women started showing off her body in front of the couple. Bastet and the other woman started to entice the security guard. The security guard fell for the bait and Bastet grabbed a weapon from his belt while the other woman distracted him. They started to hit the men with all the weapons they grabbed. Music was playing in the background, so no one heard the banging sounds of the weapon. The men were trying to fight back, but the three women hold their own. The men became unconscious, and they took their clothes, keys, and money. They jumped out the window and drove the security officer's car to the nearest gas station.

They told the owner of the gas station what happened. The owner called the police, and they were on their way. The men back at the house awakened and couldn't find the women. The women left the gas station right in time because they knew the men would be out to get them. They grabbed some materials and headed to a hotel that was far away from that building.

Bastet let the two women fight over who'll keep the car because all Bastet needed was the extra money. She didn't want to drive around in a stolen car anymore. Bastet decided to get some rest to prepare for her audition in the morning.

That's why you can't trust everyone you meet because you don't know their true intentions. Watch your drinks, go to the bathroom before you leave somewhere, and make sure you have pepper spray or some sort of defense weapon or tactic handy. Before rushing into something, think before you do.

Bastet had to go to bed reliving everything that just played out. Not to mention, she was still grieving about her family and her so-called new sister. Each woman had nightmares and the other women comforted each other. This was another traumatic experience for Bastet, but how could she get over all these situations?

Bastet got up early to ask the women if they could bring her to her audition.

This group of women made a bond over this traumatic experience. When you have a traumatic experience with another person, you instantly create a bond between each other that can't be broken.

They brought Bastet to her audition and waited for her to get out. It was Bastet's turn to meet with the casting directors and she shared her story. The casting directors appreciated her creativity and the imagination she had. Bastet was telling the truth, but the casting directors didn't believe her because she didn't have any bruises. The only bruise she had was on her leg from jumping out of the window. The casting directors put her through the next round without hesitation.

Bastet then namaste with the executive producer, and she told the producer the story as well. The executive producer saw how passionate she was about her story and all the details she brought forth. He thought the story came out of a movie. The executive producer put her through to the final round because she had the vision of coming up with unique ideas for the show.

Bastet was getting angry and when the CEO placed her in the escape room, she broke down. She started to cry, scream, and break objects. The CEO needed a character who'll go beast mode and be dramatic in the show to boost ratings. The CEO saw that in Bastet and she was cast as the newest cast member. Bastet made the executive decision to go through with it to share her story and spread light on the issues she faced.

Indiniya experienced a tough life and now she was on her way to Los Angeles. Becky and her family had two days to experience LA.

On the first day, they went to multiple parks around town. They created life-lasting memories through the pictures they took.

As they stumbled upon the last park, Indiniya told her family she was going to follow this mockingbird she heard. Becky told her to stay close. Indiniya looked straight up following the sound of the mockingbird as she wandered off into the woods. These woods weren't a part of the trail. The day was turning into night and by the time she realized it, she couldn't find her family.

Someone randomly grabbed her from behind and started to cover her mouth. This guy stalks the woods and tries to find people who were alone. He saw Indiniya in the shadows and flung his way upon her. Becky heard Indiniya's scream, and she ran after her. Becky did cross country while she was in high school, so she knew how to run in tough terrane.

The guy brought her to the basement of his house. Becky's husband called the police as he and the kids were catching up. Becky didn't want to wait for the police. Since Becky was a runner, she made it in time to find his shack. Becky did mix martial arts growing up, so she wasn't afraid to fight this man. She was living her life with zero fear.

Becky's husband asked her to wait for the police, but something could happen in that short amount of time. Without hesitation, Becky barged into the house and the guy knew someone had entered. He was about to torture Indiniya and cut her hair off to glue it on a manikin's head. Her husband was watching the kids and supported Becky. Becky didn't need a man to fight her battles, so she wanted to do this for all the women out there. If all women were to come together, they'll cause some real reckoning.

The guy locked the door that they were in, but with built-up aggression, Becky kicked down the door. The guy ran upstairs to attack Becky, but she dodged his attacks and threw him down the stairs. He fumbled down the steps and crashed to the floor with a thump. Becky saw Indiniya being tied up against a dentist-looking chair.

Becky called her husband to make sure the guy didn't wake up while she was untying Indiniya. She released her in time before the guy awakened. Becky's husband was about to punch him in the face, but Indiniya took a steel chair and cracked it against his skull.

As they proceeded to leave, Becky had an idea. She tied the guy in the same chair he tied Indiniya in and left him there. The police were calling Becky's husband to find the location, but they hung up because they'll rather have him suffer instead of going to prison.

Once that was all said and done, they packed up their things and went back to the hotel. After that crazy experienced, they sat, prayed, and gave thanks for surviving. During the prayer, Indiniya prayed for something miraculously to happen in her life tomorrow. As she went to bed, she didn't feel like eating or drinking. Becky still hasn't told Indiniya about her audition that started at 5:00 AM.

In the morning, Becky woke her up and told her she had a surprise for her after all the courage and bravery she had shown. Indiniya was tired, but for a free surprise, she was down. Becky took Indiniya to a casting studio and Indiniya questioned why they were there. Becky said it was a surprise.

As they left the car, two people came up to Becky and recognized her. Becky turned around and it was Joey and Aqua. We'll get to Joey's and Aqua's trip soon. You won't believe what I'll tell you.

Becky didn't know that Aqua and Joey knew each other. Joey and Aqua went up to her and had a confab with them both. Joey spilled the beans to Indiniya about the casting call. He ruined the surprise for Indiniya, but as Becky looked over at her, she didn't look disappointed. Becky showed a sigh of relief.

As they got into studio seven, Becky trusted Indiniya and let her be free. Indiniya didn't feel comfortable leaving Becky yet, but Becky told her the casting shouldn't take that long. This could help her overcome what she was going through. Becky asked Joey and Aqua to look out for her because she was nervous and didn't have a lot of friends. They agreed and become friends with Indiniya. As Indiniya went on set, the casting directors took her in.

The casting directors asked her to slate her name, tell them what she does, and answer some open-ended questions. The casting directors asked Indiniya for a monologue to see if she could capture an audience. Indiniya spoke openly about what happened to her previously. Of course, the casting directors thought it was a fictional story, but the story was nonfiction. This happened to Indiniya in the last 24 hours. They loved the storytelling and all the details she put into it. She made it to the next round and the executive producer was testing her reflex skills. Becky was already a black belt in karate, so she taught Indiniya some of her moves. She was quick on her feet and had balance like no other. She passed and went to the final round with the CEO.

The creator placed them all in a trial run of the escape room and Indiniya brought the fun side out of the game. She enjoyed puzzles and she debunked what was true and what wasn't. The creator noticed how good she was at puzzles, and they needed a person like that to be on the show. After the game ended, the CEO brought Indiniya to the side to congratulate her for being selected. She waited for further instructions in the room over.

Now let's talk about this dynamic duo of Joey and Aqua. I'll explain their journeys separately, so let's talk about Joey first.

Joey felt a range of emotions after knowing that his family and Aqua threw him a surprise party. He wanted to make things work with Aqua even though Johnny was still in the picture. He knew their connection and bond were stronger. Joey was hopeful for the future, but he still wanted to go to LA. Not for the audition per se, but to have a getaway.

As he took off for his flight, he was prepared to kick back and relax. It was a smooth transition from Joey's state to Los Angeles because he didn't live too far from California. As he left the plane, he had that night to enjoy LA. Joey already experienced LA with Aqua and he didn't like going to the same place multiple times. Joey loved trying new things and traveling to newer destinations. LA only brought him joy or value if it was for an art show or networking event. Joey still wanted to enjoy himself because this was his vacation.

Joey went to the nearest bowling alley to play bowling and shoot some pool. As he pulled up to the bowling alley, it wasn't crowded at all. So, he parked the car and proceeded to walk to the front of the bowling alley. All of a sudden, a car thrust itself in front of Joey. It was Johnny and Aqua.

Aqua put a tracker on Joey's tablet when he wasn't home for the party. Aqua remembered his password and Joey previously connected his tablet with his phone. Joey didn't have anything to hide, so he would type his password right in front of Aqua.

Before Aqua could speak, Johnny rolled down the window. He told Joey that Aqua was his and he'll never have her again. He proceeded to downgrade Joey, put dirt on his name, and humiliate him. By that time, it was already getting dark, and Joey had enough. He walked up to the car, grabbed Johnny, and threw him out the window. When you have that built-up aggression inside you, you'll burst at any given second. Not to mention seeing Aqua and Johnny together after she told Joey that they'll spend more time together brought him jealousy.

Joey pulled Johnny out of the car (through the window) and proceeded to beat him down. After a few punches and stomps, he realized that he was beating him up in public. Joey threw him in the backseat and drove them to an alleyway to finish what he started. Aqua told Joey to stop since she was still in the front seat. Joey looked over at Aqua and gave her a subtle evil look with a conniving grin. After that look, Aqua looked straight and stayed silent. Someone could be so mad that you don't know what they'll do next. Being cautious and treating them with care is necessary before they attack you as well. That's why some police officers would rather speak to you when you're full of emotions. They use calmness to get your guard down and then you'll either surrender, or people will come from behind to sustain you.

They show people getting killed by police officers to get your emotions high. They know how touchy the subjects are when a police officer kills a black person and how it'll affect the black community. They're playing with people's emotions to make you hate instead of love. They know what they're doing. They use the same tactics to get the same result. How many times do we have to march, protest, and say we need to come together? We've been marching and protesting for centuries, and they keep doing the same thing. How many open conversations do we need for people to start making that change? We always say we need to come together, but we're not moving forward with that plan. So many people want to do it themselves, not ask for help, or try and save humanity by themselves. Can people put aside their differences and toxic behaviors to come together? We've been saying these things for years now, but people still don't see the bigger picture.

They show us these shootings on the news to make us feel a certain way about gun violence. Even though they never show us the real footage. How true can it be if we don't see the proof? How will we know if it wasn't from the same articles, titles, pictures, or videos used years ago? How can we know what's happening in another country if we don't see it for ourselves? Is what they're showing us real or fake? Open your mind and start questioning things that we automatically assume to be real.

They're trying to take away gun laws, so they can barge into your door and force you to do something you don't want to do. They see no one is taking what their offering to continue with their agendas. They can't necessarily do it now since people still have guns and other weapons in their households. If they pass to revoke gun laws, then America and the whole world would be the next dictatorship.

It's like a sticky ball. They have plans A-Z, and whatever they throw at us, they'll see how long it'll stick. Once people wake up to the truth about that current plan (sticky ball falls from the wall onto the floor) they're on to the next plan (next sticky ball). Then they'll see how long that new plan sticks due to people's ignorance and gullibility in believing anything they say. Sometimes, they go back to an old plan using a newer story to see if that sticks again. It's like they're the auto body shop instead of being the mechanic. The mechanic fixes the issue, while the auto body shop makes things look pretty.

Everything's a stage and they're performing right in front of us. It's all an illusion. Don't fear, we're always protected. Due to Universal law, they cannot force us to do anything without our will or consent. They'll be punished to the highest degree over all the misery they placed upon the people, the planet, the animals, and nature as a whole. Everyone who follows the system, who is operating as a sheep or a bot, or tries to mess with the chosen ones, you'll be dwelt with.

As they went to the back alley, Johnny punched him on the side of his face. Joey lost control of the car and it went off the cliff and proceeded down a hill. The car did multiple flips causing damage to the car and those who were inside. The car ended up in a pile of woods. There were no cars, no people, and no police officers at the scene. The people from the bowling alley did hear an erupt sound coming from the back alleyway. By the time they came outside, the fence was already broken with a pile of rubbish left behind. As they looked down in the wooded area, they didn't see a car or what caused the damage to the fence. The woods where they landed was surrounded by tall trees.

As the car was tilted over, someone proceeded to exit the car and it was Joey.

Somehow Joey was still alive. He then cracked the door open to save Aqua and in doing so, she was still pretty conscious. He performed first aid and CPR on Aqua with the tools he could gather in the woods. Aqua was alive. They hugged and began to have an open colloquy about what had happened. Before diving deep into their tete-a-tete, Johnny moaned and sighed. Johnny saw Aqua and Joey having a moment together, but Johnny told Joey, "Is that all you got?" Joey was shocked that he was still alive because he didn't hold onto any car pieces, didn't have his seatbelt on, and there weren't airbags in the backseat. Joey was furious that he was still alive and interrupted his moment with Aqua. Joey walked over to Johnny and Aqua knew what was coming next. Aqua asked Joey to stop, but it was tunnel vision for Joey. He didn't hear any noises as he had his eyes set on Johnny. Joey went up to him and started beating him with the tools he found. He didn't stop and after five minutes, Joey killed Johnny.

With tears in her eyes, Aqua cried out because that was the father of Elias. Joey told Aqua to pick herself up and help him bury Johnny. They found a specific spot where they could bury him. After they buried Johnny, Aqua decided to become that toxic figure she once was. She had to have that evil intent to cover up the evidence. They decided to grab their stuff and leave the scene.

Now how did Aqua get to this point?

Aqua was tepid over the fact that Johnny was going to LA with her. She wanted to spend time with Joey exclusively. Once Johnny confirmed he was going, she knew it'll cause problems. Johnny drove his car to California since it was pretty close.

Joey wanted to take a plane to physically removed himself from his hometown. That's why he didn't drive his car because it reminded him of his hometown, and he'll be tempted to drive back.

Aqua thought if Johnny dropped her off at the bowling alley, he'll go back to the hotel and drop off his items. Since Aqua was tracking Joey, she knew he was going to the bowling alley. She thought by the time they got there, he'll be inside, but that wasn't the case. Then the rest followed as such.

Once they left the crime scene, Aqua played some music on her phone and started to slow dance with Joey. Their relationship had the Bonnie and Clyde effect.

They wanted to go bowling since they had never gone in the first place, but the bowling alley was closed. They started to become hungry, so they searched for the nearest restaurant. They found a restaurant that was a couple of miles away. After traveling through the woods for a couple of miles, they found the restaurant.

It was a diner that consistently stayed open for 24 hours per day. Joey ordered chicken and waffles while Aqua got some pancakes and fruit. They were so hungry that during their meal they didn't speak to one another. They finished eating and then called a taxi. The taxi driver asked why they smelt so bad, and Joey looked at him with a sinister look. Aqua communicated to Joey with extrasensory perception to stop. The taxi driver decided to shut his mouth and just drive to the destination. Once at the hotel, they unpacked their things and went straight to bed.

Sunday came around and it was time for their audition. Joey got up first because he knew he had his audition, but Aqua did as well. Joey asked why she was up so early, and she asked the same thing about him. They never told each other they had an audition in Los Angeles and that was the reason why they traveled to LA. This was a funny moment for them both and that made Joey more interested in the possibility of doing the show with Aqua. They both got ready for the event, and they wore the same colors and aesthetics.

Once they arrived, Joey noticed Becky who treated him, and he went right over. Aqua knew Becky as well, but she didn't want to bring up

Johnny's name. They had their interaction with Becky, and they went inside with Indiniya

As they waited for their turn, they talked to their new friend Indiniya. It was Indiniya's turn to go and when she came back, she told them that they needed to tell a story. The casting directors didn't believe in Indiniya's truthful story, so how would they believe in Aqua's and Joey's story?

It was Joey's turn soon after, but Aqua decided to walk into the room with him. After going through what they've experienced, they needed to stick together. The casting directors wondered why Aqua came in and asked her to wait her turn. Aqua said, "No." The casting directors were about to throw her out but decided to let them both perform together for the heck of it.

They told the story about what had happened yesterday, and the casting directors saw the chemistry they had with one another. They did need romance in the show, so they thought this was perfect. They issued a bypass for them to go to the final round with the CEO.

The CEO not only saw how much they worked together as a couple but as a unit as well. Even if they weren't a couple, the CEO was going to make them be in a relationship on the show.

After a few discussions with the casting directors and executive producer, they decided to hire both of them for the show.

After all the trials and tribulations, Joey and Aqua achieved what they set out to do; rekindle their relationship and spend more time with one another through this show. Now that Johnny was out of the picture, they had no distractions. The creator brought them to the other room to wait for further instructions.

Now with all seven cast members, all in the same area, the CEO, executive producer, and casting directors all gathered around to congratulate them on being hired. A few didn't know what to expect, some were nervous, some didn't care, and a few were excited.

The casting directors handed them some papers for them to sign. Aqua and Joey automatically signed while the rest were going to look it over. The executive producer was telling them that they came so far, and might as well sign the papers. Once the executive producer said that statement, Apollo and Bastet signed as well. The last three people who didn't sign yet were Indigo, Indiniya, and Aleemic.

Aqua and Joey influenced Indiniya to sign, so they could hang out with each other and make her mom proud. Indiniya fell for the trick of having other people make decisions in her life. People can easily peer-pressure you into doing something in an instant. Don't let anyone control your life. Take control over your life because you're all you have.

In the beginning, while the casting directors were passing out the papers, the executive producer gave a different set of papers for Indigo and Aleemic. Since Indigo and Aleemic had high IQs, they didn't want them to question anything about the show. They knew the others wouldn't read the fine print, so they just gave them the basic versions. For Indigo and Aleemic, they gave them similar paperwork, but used advanced wordplay and didn't state the truth about the show. You'll see why throughout this story.

Before you sign anything read the fine print because you never know what they might hide inside those long documents. The creator thanked everyone for signing and told them to call their parents. With excitement, they all called their family members and told them they made it on the show.

The casting directors and the CEO brought them on a tour of the building without showing them any of the escape rooms. They showed them where they would eat, sleep, play, and where they'll do their confessionals. During the tour, the executive producer started the process of creating the first game. Indiniya was skeptical because she had a feeling that caused her attention to be elsewhere. Once again, Joey and Aqua told her to continue with the show.

After the tour, they told them to eat some food and get some rest because the first day of the first episode was completed. They had an all-day audition, so they decided to get some rest and start fresh in the morning. They didn't tell them that the show already started from the beginning of the auditions. As they went to bed, that concluded the first episode of the series called: DAY ONE EPISODE ONE. I'll let you ponder on why I capitalized the days and episodes.

DAY TWO EPISODE TWO. The casting directors woke them up and brought them to their first escape room. It was a room filled with VR headsets and headphones. One of the casting directors said, "Welcome to the future." The room looked mystical and futuristic. It looked just like the room where they controlled The Hunger Games arenas.

As the executive producer registered and locked each of the cast members into the system, the casting directors locked their headphones and headsets in place. Once they put the equipment on, they noticed how real it all felt. There was a giant screen in the room to let the executive producer see and hear what they see and hear.

People are so attached to living in an artificial world like the metaverse that they'll give up living their actual lives.

Once everyone was ready to play, the executive producer said, "The purge has begun! May the odds be ever in your favor." It was surely enough time to play the game because they weren't prepared for what was going to happen next.

They told the cast members that they were able to eat, sleep, and do other things while participating in this game. This will transform into their actual physical selves as well. If they went to sleep in the virtual world, then they'll feel rested in their physical bodies. This made them feel more comfortable playing the game and it was an interesting concept. Instead of using their actual hands to pick something up, the system automatically knows their next move. This seems creepy and scary, but at the moment, it felt cool and exciting. The executive producer hooked them up to the system where they wouldn't have control over their physical bodies. They'll only have control over their virtual bodies. This sounds like they were being plugged into the matrix.

The show televised them operating physically and virtually while going through each escape room. It was interesting because it looked so real. They could be themselves and look the same.

After being situated, the CEO and casting directors left. All the casting directors stayed in their cars while the CEO left the studio. The casting directors came back inside to help format the show with the executive producer. The executive producer went to the bathroom while the casting directors were in the room. The casting directors knew that some of the cast members were either the chosen ones or had the potential of becoming one. They wanted to stop them in their tracks, so they advanced them to the final round. They had a bigger agenda in place and the cast members were locked and loaded to participate in their experiment. The casting directors all whispered, "It's time to play our game." Then they laughed right after. The executive producer came back and confirmed everything was set to play the game. Let the apocalyptic events occur.

Chapter Four

APOCALYPTIC EVENTS

As the games transpired, the cast members were getting used to their 'new world'. When they were in this virtual world, Aleemic was quick to say that people need to vibrate in the 5D instead of the 3D. Apollo gave Aleemic a weird glance and asked, "Where all the virtual ladies at?" Aleemic could sense the vibe of the group and decided to speak his truth later on in the show.

They all were walking together to see how this world works and operates. They were amazed by how close to reality it all seemed even though they still had headsets and headphones on. Although they had complete control over their virtual bodies, they lost the ability to control or feel their physical bodies. Furthermore, placing them in a trancelike state.

The setting of the area was just like modern California. The sun was bright, and they felt the heat on their skin. The sky rained a beautiful spectrum of rainbows that looked gorgeous. They couldn't tell the difference between what was real and what was virtual reality.

The birds were chirping and Indiniya was amazed at how lifelike the animals were. Even though most birds are drones by the CIA to watch you. Wonder why birds always sit on telephone wires? It's because they're charging. Plus, their bird poop is a tracking device. This is why it's so liquidly to stick onto the car, and then solid to hold the tracker together.

Indiniya had a connection with animals and so did Bastet.

They saw people in self-driving cars, a utopia of newer technology that was sweeping across the nation. They also saw people who were familiar and people who were strangers. It was a blend between real life and virtual, so people from the dead can come in and surprise anyone.

Apollo was asking what they had to do, where to go, and what was happening. Over the intercom the executive producer told the cast members they had 45 minutes to explore the 'outside world' and then they'll enter their first room. Indigo thought it'll be a good idea to sit down and get to know one another. Everyone thought it was a good idea and proceeded to go into a vacant mall plaza.

Apollo saw manikins that still had clothes on them but realized they weren't designer brands. By that time, Indiniya told all of them to gather around.

Indiniya thought she could find a setting on her headset to change her outfit. Indiniya started to hit herself on the head to see if this was all real or not. It was indeed real since Indiniya was in pain right after. Since it felt so real, they were all flabbergasted. They decided to sit down and wondered what could this be? By that time, the timer already hit the 30-minute mark, so they sat down and introduced themselves.

Joey thought this mall was an escape room because the game has already begun. Maybe this was all a trick for them to do something that correlates with the timer. Bastet and Indigo both agreed, and they started to question if the timer was real or not.

They knew they already started filming, but they were unsure when the game started. The executive producer told them it'll start once the timer ends, but was that a lie or was that the truth?

Everyone started to question everything about this reality. They searched all around the vacant mall for clues or anything that'll give them any guidance. It was difficult to find any valuable clues or evidence in this mall.

Aqua stumbled upon this object that was under the manikin that Apollo was viewing. Apollo left the manikin alone after noticing those clothes weren't designer. Aqua pushed the manikin over and saw a note. The note stated, "Get to know each other because time is of the essence, and you'll need it." The messenger called themselves The Riddler.

Once she received this message, it was only ten minutes left. There were seven of them in total, so they'll need to introduce themselves before the timer runs out. Aqua yelled and told everyone to hurry up and gather around. The first person who came was Joey because Aqua was the person he cared for the most. Aqua wanted to scream just to make the show have some drama before heading into a commercial break.

Once everyone gathered around, it was seven minutes left and they all needed to get to know one another. Everyone had to take one minute to talk about themselves. Everyone gave their opening introduction about themselves right before the timer ended.

The Riddler was the executive producer and the casting directors that implemented different clues and hidden messages throughout the show.

Each show and movie have subliminal messages, hidden codes, and information you have to hear and see in full context. Remember the Riddler said they'll need to get to know one another. The Riddler didn't want just a pity quick explanation about themselves. The executive producer wanted them to explain their past and karmic debt that they haven't embraced yet. The only way to overcome their apocalyptic internal issues is to do their shadow and inner work. The executive producer made sure to have them face their demons since they didn't pass the first step. They'll have to be punished for not following the commands which will lead to hindrance for their future.

The executive producer came back on the intercom and told the cast members it was time to go to their first escape room. The cast members thought they passed since they were heading to the next room. That wasn't the mindset of the executive producer.

The executive producer transported the cast members to the next room through the multiverse. Aleemic thought it was weird how they had all this control over this Universe but quickly remembered that this was for the show. Aleemic could've thought about it more but instead allowed these things to happen. Question everything and nothing's as it seems.

The first room they entered was this door that was a portal. Any door, window, or entering is a portal. That's why people close their doors, lock their windows, and so on because of this. Anything that has a hiatus is either a good portal or a bad portal.

The door was an entrance that led them outside, but they thought it was a room. They noticed a dome around them, so they perceived it as being a never-ending room. Was that the case? The casting directors knew it was another location within Los Angeles.

The earth is surrounded by an earth dome. The sky isn't what you think. Most people think it's blue, but it's multicolor. Is the moon real? If you knew how recent the moon came into the atmosphere, you'll be surprised. The moon is there to be a portal for fallen angels to come down and mess with people. Hence, people stay awake during witch hours because they're body-snatching people.

They use different tactics to keep the dying sheep asleep while they blindly accept everything as they appear. People don't question anything and think what they've been taught is the only truth out there.

As the castmates were looking around, they saw people in a panic. They were running to stock up on food, water, and toilet paper. They didn't know what was happening and the executive producer appeared and said, "Welcome to the economic and financial crash; good luck!"

At first, they didn't think anything of it. They thought that this wasn't their home and wasn't a real experience. The executive producer noticed they weren't taking it seriously and weren't interacting with this newer system, so they'll have to be punished.

He commanded the casting directors to go over to their physical bodies and steal their wallets, phones, and other valuable items they've brought with them. Apollo had the most valuable items there, so they went after him first. None of the cast members felt or heard them stealing any of their stuff.

The creators of the room had control over the food shelves and erased all the material the cast members needed to survive. The cast members only had what they found in the mall.

What they don't do in this newer world, will affect their actual real lives. Just like with the social credit score where if you don't participate, follow their guidelines, or speak out on some truth, then you won't be able to access an ATM for example. This is how the government takes more control over your money, rights, and your whole life. They'll slowly condition you in giving up your power constantly instead of controlling your own life. Some people need a government to tell them what to do because they don't take ownership of their own life. That's how brain control and manipulation work. The way to control someone's mind, body, and soul is by the mind. Wonder why it's called government? They govern people's minds.

It's like angel numbers; every number, sign, word, practically everything has a hidden meaning. You can go through each word and break it down to find the true meaning. I'll give you an example. Belief means being in a lie, fear means false evidence appearing real, and impossible means I'm possible. Many words have hidden codes within the actual word, but you get the point.

Since the cast members didn't care as much, the executive producer made this room last for three days. Show-wise, it was for a day, but for the cast members, they felt like it was for three days.

Since they didn't stock up or prepared beforehand, they were going to pay. When people don't prepare for something even though they see it getting to that point, they were too ignorant to believe it. Once it happens, they start to scramble in buying materials that'll only last them for a few weeks. People eat so much and at high rates that if they stocked up on some food in a crisis, they'll end up eating all their resources within a couple of weeks. Then what? They'll begin to starve, commit crimes, or go to a FEMA or concentration camp because they didn't plan accordingly. That's why it's important to see where the world is heading to do the necessary steps to survive. Only the strongest will survive. When people no longer have access to food (their pleasure), then they'll start to act wild.

A day had passed, and they continued to walk around and explore the area. They didn't have a timer to let them know when the room ended. They decided to wait it out, but as time went by, it became harder for them to wait it out. They started to eat and drink the remaining resources they had in one day. Aleemic and Indigo told them they should save some of the food until the room was over. The stores were practically empty only leaving unhealthy foods, paper, and some toys. They needed to feed seven people in total. With barely any food left, Aleemic and Indigo were worried. The rest of them continued to eat and drink their resources while an apocalypse was taking place. Some of them didn't care because they thought this was all staged. They thought they'll be done filming by the end of today.

That night as they were sleeping, people were rioting because they were out of a job, couldn't make money, and couldn't provide for their families anymore. All the money they saved in the bank was useless because paper money turned into digital money. Thus, wiping out their bank accounts.

With limited resources available, everyone started to break into their neighbor's houses for food and started to kill people over the resources. This was the start of the purge. People weren't prepared or weren't expecting it to happen. Indiniya was concerned about what was taking place, but everyone all started to comfort her. Most of them still thought it was fake, but was it? Will they ever get control over their physical bodies again? With multiple thoughts running through their minds, they all went to sleep. That was the completion of DAY TWO EPISODE TWO. Will they survive or die throughout the process? We shall see.

DAY THREE EPISODE THREE. The cast members all woke up thinking they'll be in a different escape room than before, but it was the same room with a few changes. To them, it felt like it a day had passed, but the executive producer made the environment, and the people feel like they've been in this economic and financial collapse for weeks.

When they went outside, they smelt something horrendous. They saw and smelt dead people on the side of the roads. "This couldn't be happening," said Bastet. "This has to be a scare tactic for the show," said, Joey. Aleemic being the conscious one in the group thought otherwise. Maybe this was all a test to see what was real and what was fake.

As they went back inside, Aleemic started to comment on some conscious information to try and awaken the viewers and his fellow cast members. The casting directors saw Aleemic as a threat and they wanted to do something to him to keep him shut. The executive producer was angry that they weren't succeeding or progressing in the game. They'll have to endure another punishment.

The executive producer came on the intercom and announced that one of the group members had to kill someone. The executive producer didn't say one of the cast members needed to die, but someone had to kill someone. No one else was in the vacant mall, so they looked outside, but couldn't find anyone. Aleemic said he had an off-grid private island that they could find, and all the cast members agreed. The casting directors had enough of his ideas and him waking people up.

As the cast members started to walk to the door, the casting directors placed a timer of five minutes up above. They told them if they didn't kill someone in five minutes, then all of them will die.

The cast members didn't take it seriously because they remembered it was a show. Would they actually die or just leave the show? Bastet asked that question.

While they contemplated, they remembered why they were on this show. They wanted to share a message and speak the truth to the viewers. The timer was ticking, and they didn't know what to do. The timer ended and they didn't kill anyone.

The door was unlocked all this time to find someone else, but the casting directors steered their minds elsewhere. They failed the mission again, and now they had to endure another punishment.

Since the casting directors told them if they didn't kill someone when the timer ended, they'll all die. The casting directors placed another five-minute timer up above. Once the cast members noticed, the mall started to slowly collapse and if they didn't kill someone within five minutes, then they'll be crushed by the building. Indiniya knew they'll feel pain due to her hitting herself in the face. They needed to do something. They went to every exit of the mall and all the doors and windows were now locked. Time was running out and the building began to shrink.

The executive producer announced that the person who does the killing will receive their valuables back and the remaining cast members will regain some resources within the show for their survival. They showed them their physical bodies and all their items were hidden in a bag away from them. Aleemic told the group that he didn't care about materialistic items, and he wanted everyone else to keep their stuff. Aleemic said he'll be the sacrifice for the group. He wanted to die on his terms and him being the chosen one, he wanted to return home to see if this was all real or not. With him saying all of this, they started to realize maybe this was real.

Apollo had the most valuable items, so Apollo was too ignorant and grabbed his lucky bow and arrow (that he found in the mall) and shot Aleemic in the face. Aleemic could've easily stopped it by his mind, but since he was caught off guard, the arrow pierced threw his brain leaving blood to gush out.

The remaining men were shocked, and all the women started to cry. The casting directors saw the arrow that pierced Aleemic had killed him. The building stopped shrinking. The casting directors said, "Now was that so hard?" Apollo just wanted his valuables back, and they showed them returning the items to Apollo's physical body. They also gave their virtual bodies some resources and materials to survive. Right after they cut the screen, they took the valuables from Apollo's physical body back and proceeded to the room. This room was war-based.

The rest of the day no one talked or spoke to one another. They just interacted with the new material that they had. Were these shiny objects worth a life? Just like celebrities who sacrifice their friends and family just to have clout and shiny objects, was that worth it? People would rather receive clout, attention, being known, and have something go viral instead of becoming wealthy. If someone was to offer another person money or have something that'll make them go viral; some people would have a hard time choosing.

Since Aleemic wasn't in the show anymore, we'll take this time out to speak about Aleemic. Aleemic was a powerful character in his own right. The messiah, the power giver, and the light barrier. Aleemic spend his time on earth achieving everything he wanted to achieve and was happy with the life he lived. He was ready to leave this planet with no regrets. The Universe always spoke through Aleemic whenever he gives a message. Everything he's done for his businesses came from a higher power and had a higher purpose in life. Aleemic was on the board of directors in the spiritual realm and was an important figure. The CIA was always after Aleemic and they disgraced him when he spoke out on the truth. Aleemic knew this was going to happen, but he would never expect it to be on a TV show. How would his family react? Is his family even still alive? Before the cast members could even question some of these things, the lights went out and it was time for bed. That was the end of DAY THREE EPISODE THREE.

DAY FOUR EPISODE FOUR. The cast members woke up still grieving about what had happened last night. They checked to see if Aleemic would've woken up or not, but he didn't.

They went to the front door, and it was now unlocked, so they went outside. Aqua suggested that they may have entered a new escape room due to how the environment looked. The only thing that stayed the same was the shelves that weren't stocked with any items. It was all controlled by the puppet masters. Not only was it an economic meltdown, but also a food shortage.

The deep state is currently orchestrating a food shortage by wildfires, killing crops, and firing farmers. When they mess with people's food, just wait and see the whole country burn down to the ground. They'll trigger the world to the brink of famine and bring scarcity of food that'll kill millions. I'm talking about riots, break-ins, etc. The IMF, the BIS, World Bank, the UN, the Rockefeller Foundation, the World Economic Forum,

Bank of America, and even the president is all precognition of a major food crisis in the near term. It's not a coincidence that the policies of these very institutions and the actions of puppet politicians that work with them are causing the crisis they're now predicting. There's no coincidence in the Universe. Therefore, it's easy to forecast a disaster when they created it.

"They now have the technology to hack humanity and let everyone think and feel what they want. Tyrants always wanted to do that, but now for the first time, they can do so. They'll eradicate faith in God, end-all free will, and make sure that humans think exactly what they want them to think." This quote came from an Israeli professor named Yuval Noah Harari who's being pushed to the forefront by the World Economic Forum. They want to create chaos to make people turn their backs on the government. Once this happens, they'll develop and start a one-world government. Which will lead to multiple acts being placed.

The one-world religion, cashless society, one-world currency, one-world military, the end of national sovereignty, the end of all privately owned property, the end of the family unit, depopulation, control of population growth, and population density. They need to attack the physical because they live only through the first three dimensions which are so dense. That's why they cannot pass above the 3rd density. The list keeps going.

Mandatory multiple vaccines, universal basic income (austerity), and microchipped society for purchasing, travel, tracking, and controlling. Implementation of a world social credit system (like China has), trillions of appliances hooked into the 5G monitoring system (internet of things), and government-raised children. The list continues.

Government-owned and controlled schools, colleges, and universities. The end of private transportation, owning cars, etc. All businesses owned by the government/corporations, the restriction of nonessential air travel, and human beings concentrated into human settlement zones and cities. The end of irrigation and immigration, the end of private farms and grazing livestock (which is happening right now), the end of single-family homes, restricted land use that serves human needs, the ban of natural nonsynthetic drugs, naturopathic medicine, and the end of fossil fuels.

This will usher in their new world order, UN Agenda 21/2030 mission and goals. Who would willingly allow themselves to live in this type of world right? You'll be surprised at how many people would say yes, I can't believe it, no way. Some of them are the ones who'll be in this reality. You'll be flabbergasted on who'll make it, who didn't, and those who died or vanished throughout the process and transformation.

They were too egotistical to realize that people will start to wake up and their plans will crumble. They won't vanish without a fight. The beast is most powerful when it's dying. They want to control and take out as many people as they can until they get wiped out. It'll only work for those who survived and haven't died throughout the process. Those souls who were captured will stay on the old earth. Everyone else who has risen above the lies and did the proper work on themselves will be experiencing the new earth of peace, love, freedom, and light. On the planet, there's already a massive split between the 3D and the 5D. Which one will you be in?

They ate most of their resources yesterday and they'll need to now start fasting to save the rest of their food. They saw a plane that appeared to be flying right towards them. It was a couple of miles away, but it got closer and closer. Aqua stated that they'll need to do something. Apollo (being as brave as he is) didn't think anything of it. He said they'll survive because it was fake. As it came closer, they started to run away. Bastet had to push Apollo out the way because he wasn't moving. Good thing they ran away because the plane crashed right into the vacant mall they used as their housing grounds.

Joey was amazed by how interesting and the realness of the show was. Indigo wondered if this regular TV show was just a show or if it was something bigger?

The building caught on fire, and they saw three people come out of the plane alive. They didn't know how many people were in the plane, but the ones that were alive walked through the fire in slow motion. Aqua stated that this must be a TV show. Everyone laughed, but Indigo questioned if this was an escape room show or a terror show instead. Why, would they leave Aleemic's avatar instead of vanishing his avatar if this was virtual reality?

As they came out of the plane, it was two females and one guy. The woman kissed the guy, the guy kissed the other woman, and then both women kissed each other. Apollo yelled out, "Hey, can I get some too! Just with the two women, you know what I'm saying?" The group laughed, but the three survivors weren't laughing. How were they surviving that long in the fire? This might be fake after all.

The three survivors looked like they were activating something. They were fire benders just like Avatar. They then shot a fireball in their direction. They moved away from it in time, but Indiniya stayed and stared at the fireball. Bastet pushed her out of the way, and they all started to run. Indigo thought this might've been an action-packed escape room in seeing if the cast could survive or not.

They all moved out the way and proceeded to find cover. They found an empty condo that looked like Apollo's last Airbnb he rented. They looked out the window and saw the three fire benders coming their way. All of a sudden people started to walk outside to notice what was happening. Remember the executive producer controls what they see, hear, and more.

The fire benders stopped and ran after the remaining people outside. The cast members took a breather and tried to process what just happened.

Bastet brought some of their resources with her, but most of their materials were now in the midst of the fire. With limited resources left, they decided to save them for later just in case. Before they could debrief there was a public service announcement from one of the casting directors. This is what she stated: "PSA, PSA, PSA! There's a virus plague out in the open, so be cautious going outside. You don't know who has it, so watch out for the people that are closest to you. Welcome to your next room agents." When she said the last line, she starred right at the cast members. Apollo said, "That wasn't very nice."

The public service announcement was finally over, but then there was a screen of the death total. Since the environment has been going through this transition for weeks now, the death total was currently 10,000. People started to believe the propaganda and every time they stepped outside or interacted with anyone, they wore masks, gloves, and hazardous suits. The people who were in this world followed what the public service announcement said because they were controlled by the ones who were controlling them.

The executive producers filled up the shelves once more, but with limited resources and material left. Indigo said, "We need more resources because we're running out." Once he finished that sentence, they saw people walking outside their houses even though it was a state of emergency and a lockdown. People were fighting over the resources, but as they were fighting, people started to fall abruptly. Just randomly fell to the ground. The death total went from 10,000 to 27,000.

The sirens were sounding and the EMTs were all in hazardous suits going after the people who left the house. The people that were still alive outside their houses have been captured and forced an injection inside their bodies. These people either instantly died, had a slow death, or turn into something we'll discuss later on. After they have committed poison homicide due to a rushed vaccine, the death toll was at 50,000. This was all happening within the first three days of the "game."

The group needed more resources because they'd been fasting for a while now. Joey and Aqua were scared of the pandemic and they didn't have any masks to leave their new base. Bastet slapped Aqua while Apollo slapped Joey. They were telling them to remember that this was all pre-planned since this was a game. This was a plandemic that was planned and a hoax by the controllers to initiate fear and exodus. Aqua and Joey snapped out of the illusion, and they all went to the nearest store.

As they started to walk outside, they saw a United Nations truck coming their way with soldiers jumping out. It wasn't just the United Nations, but also the police department and international military. They ordered a nationwide martial law with entities who weren't even from the same country.

They started to run to the nearest supermarket and locked the door behind them. They pushed some items to the front and backdoors, covered the windows, turned off the lights, and tried to stay silent.

They overheard a breaking sound which was the soldiers trying to break their barrier. After a few pushes, they finally broke into the door. The remaining cast members were in the back trying to stay quiet. The soldiers looked around and found a door that was currently locked. One soldier kicked the door down and announced that they were there. He said, "You know you cannot be out here without your shot, right?" The soldiers were about to forcibly inject poison inside their bodies. Right before they were about to do so, something happened.

It felt like they were transferred to a new reality because the soldiers suddenly disappeared. The executive producer went on the intercom and announced to the group that they'd made it past this escape room correctly. The executive producer had a timer for this room to see if they'll survive or not. The timer sounded and they were all still alive even after the military experience.

They announced to get some rest because they'll need it. Without hesitation, they quickly went to bed in the supermarket with fear written all over their faces. Before they could get some rest, the overview screen showed the new death total of being at a whopping 85,000. This made Bastet's stomach feel queasy once again. Bastet was having trouble falling asleep, so Indigo came over to comfort her. They all were going through this traumatic experience still holding onto their past. As they went to bed, they were all silent. That was the end of the escape room called the health apocalypse. You won't expect what'll happen in the next chapter called disaster & turmoil.

Chapter Five

DISASTER & TURMOIL

With all this heartache they've faced so far, they still had their internal demons that they were facing as well. That's why these are apocalyptic events because of everything that happens internally and externally to them.

You don't know a person's full story or the reason why they act a certain way. You'll have to accept people with all their flaws, baggage, and issues they come with if you truly love them. You're not like everyone else because you are uniquely yourself. Most people follow others because they're scared to step into their true selves and do what they want to do in life. Don't fear and become your true self because that's most important.

DAY FIVE EPISODE FIVE. All the cast members woke up, but they were still sleepy. Bastet wanted more sleep, but Aqua suggested to keep moving since the military could still be around. Indiniya told Aqua that they vanished.

Most of them enjoyed being in the supermarket because they had extra supplies and it was a secure place at the time. They all decided to gather around and chat with one another to reflect on the situation. They've already lost Aleemic and he still hasn't returned, so that must be confirmation that he was gone. It was hard for them to comprehend what was truly going on. Each day seemed like a whole new escape room. The cast members collected some materials and supplies just in case they need to leave the market. They sat next to one another to discuss where they came from, who they were, and their traumas.

Joey started first by explaining how he and Aqua met, their relationship, and what they've gone through together. After he said they were in a relationship, Apollo called out, "You know I'm Mr. steal your girl, right?"

Joey had endured so much on this trip to LA that he snapped and went after Apollo. Joey came up to Apollo and slapped him across the face. Apollo picked Joey up and slammed him to the ground. They started to wrestle for a bit and all the women told them to stop. Indigo went over and broke it up. Apollo said it was just a joke, but Joey didn't feel the same. Aqua said they all needed to stick together because they need to survive till the end. They didn't know when the show will end or when it'll be the last room. They couldn't even finish getting to know one another before this fight occurred.

When all the cast members were arguing, Indigo had envisioned his dream girl. Indigo had been getting this vision throughout his dreams. He was about to tell the group when it was his turn to go, but that never happened. Indigo envisioned her being outside the door. Then they all heard a knock on the door. Aqua thought it was the military, Indiniya thought it was Aleemic, and Indigo thought it was his dream girl. He did have this vision and a voice speaking to him to come and find her outside. The closer he got to the door, the voice became stronger and louder. Apollo and Joey could finally agree on something telling Indigo to not open the door. It was tunnel noise for Indigo as his main focus switched to meeting his dream girl. All the stuff they used as a barricade; Indigo instantly threw all of it out the way by himself. When he had this feeling, he became stronger. He liked the feeling he was receiving. Bastet tried to stop him, but no one could. Once the items were out the way, Indigo opened the door.

It was a zombie and before he could gain his awareness of what was happening, the zombie slashed Bastet's stomach with its nails. Bastet screamed out with the pain that rushed through her stomach. Remember Bastet's stomach was already in dying pain from earlier and now it's worse.

Indigo gained his sentient back and slammed the door right in front of the zombie's face. The fellow cast members ran to Bastet to see what had happened. As Joey and Apollo were telling Indigo why he should've listened to them, Indigo was trying to keep the door shut. Aqua and Indiniya went and gathered more supplies because they knew they'll need to leave. They were mostly focused on getting first aid materials, so they can treat Bastet. Indiniya and Aqua were about to treat Bastet, but they heard more zombies knocking on the side windows. They all agreed to move on the count of three. Indiniya asked if they'll go after three or right when they say three? Apollo said, "Come on it's gonna be three." Apollo yelled, "One, two, three!" They all ran to the back room where they were hiding before. While they were running towards the backdoor, the zombie from the front door came in and the zombies on the outside broke the windows. Indigo and Apollo were the fastest, so they were helping each other to carry Bastet. Aqua and Indiniya were carrying the supplies while Joey was carrying the remaining items.

Once they reached the back room, they remembered they barricade the backdoor as well. Joey was the only one who could declutter the items away from the door. Once he was done with that, Joey (now fueled with energy) kicked the backdoor wide open. Indigo said to Joey that he shouldn't have done that because they'll have an opening to their safehouse. So, that means they cannot come back to the supermarket because the zombies could easily enter through the backdoor.

As they proceeded to go outside, they saw zombies coming from the left side. The cast members were turning right, then once they passed the end of the building, they saw zombies coming from the right side. All they could do is run straight into the woods and hope for the best.

It was a zombie apocalypse! The health scare of the virus and the injections that people took, turned them into blood-seeking zombies. This health scare of the virus was purging humanity and depopulating the planet. This was originally planned by the dark entities and was passed down to the elite, the deep state, planned parenthood, and then delivered to the vast population.

As they were running through the woods, Indiniya was looking back too much that she tripped over a log. She cried out, "Ughhh!" The zombies heard her and started to follow the sound. Indiniya told them to leave her behind and to go without her. Indiniya felt like she was dying, but she only slipped on a log. Bastet said, "Forget her, let's keep moving."

Indigo went over and picked her up, dusted her off, and they continued through the woods. Indiniya felt connected to Indigo, so she kissed him. Aqua was cheering while Apollo said, "Eww get a room."

Indigo went back to Bastet to help carry her with Apollo. This made Indiniya feel jealous and insecure about herself. She gave Bastet an evil stare. Indigo felt the vibe from Indiniya, so he asked Joey to help Bastet while he'll carry the supplies and supported Indiniya. Once Indigo went back to Indiniya, she felt better, and they continued to walk through the woods. By that time, the zombies were dead in their tracks due to all the time they wasted. The zombies were coming left to right, side to side, and were right behind them. They started to look back and in doing so, they fell off the cliff going down a waterfall.

There were zombies at the waterfall where they fell as well. They were staring at them like they were stalking their prey. Luckily, the waterfall had enough water that they wouldn't be injured. As we stated before, Joey cannot swim, so he was freaking out. Aqua pulled him up, so he could stand since he was tall enough in doing so.

As they started to walk backward away from the zombies, Indigo said, "Ugh guys." As they turned around, they saw an alligator and different land animals coming toward them. Joey fainted and Indigo now had to carry Joey on his back. The zombies that were above the waterfall started to jump down toward them. They were all cornered with zombies behind them and animals right in front of them. Aqua cried out, "I don't wanna die."

Bastet felt an urge to activate some power within her. As she tapped more into her power, she controlled the alligator. Indiniya felt the same urge as well and she gained control over the land animals. Indiniya and Bastet had connections with the animals and in times of crisis, power comes to you when you need it the most. The alligator and most of the animals attacked the zombies and killed them off.

After seeing the zombies dying off, Aqua gained her confidence back and treated Bastet's cut. She also got Joey to finally wake up from his coma and she checked in on him. Indiniya had some of the animals stay around them for good measure. They were all shocked at what they just witnessed. Apollo asked them, "How do you do that?" They just replied with a smile. They both knew they had a special connection with animals, but nothing to this degree.

Once they were done, they let the animals free and proceeded down their route. They left the woods and found the city life once again, but the remaining zombies were there still. They saw this barn which had a ladder on the side that extended to the roof. They all climbed up the ladder, but Indiniya was still scared of heights, so she went last. Once they all made it, it was Indiniya's turn.

They were quietly cheering for her to hurry, but she was scared. She thought she was about to die again, so she cried out, "I'm gonna die!" The zombies heard her cry out, and they headed in her direction. Indigo with his mighty strength and adrenaline pumping, pulled up the ladder with Indiniya being on it. As he was pulling her up, he was losing his grip, so the fellow cast members had to help pull the ladder up with Indiniya. She made it successfully onto the roof and instantly hugged Indigo. Bastet whispered to herself, "That makes me sick." Apollo said, "Dang, we all helped you out as well." Indiniya went and hugged everyone else saying "Thank you."

The zombies gathered around the barn and even though there were a massive number of zombies present, they still couldn't reach them. Once they realized that the zombies weren't going to reach them, they decided to call it a night. The newest death total appeared, and it stated: 100,000.

Bastet was cold throughout the night, so it was difficult for her to sleep. Indigo went over to comfort her and make sure she was nice and toasty. Indiniya saw Indigo comfort and warm up Bastet and she felt that jealous feeling again. So, she started to cry out once more. Once Baset seemed to be sleeping, Indigo went over to Indiniya to comfort her and bring her warmth. Bastet looked over and saw Indigo warming her up, and Bastet whispered to herself, "What a crybaby." They all fell asleep once after.

While they were all sleeping, the entire earth had a blackout. No technology, no service, no devices, nothing worked. There was a massive boom sound that sounded like an asteroid or a solar flare that hit the earth. This caused Indigo to wake up since he could hear the slightest of noises.

Indigo got up, lowered the ladder, and quietly walked past the zombies. Indigo went to the sound of the noise which was in the woods. Once he approached the item, he noticed that something was crawling out of this massive rock. As Indigo came closer it was some alien and predator creatures coming from the rock. Indigo always felt a unique connection with extra-terrestrials and his roots with predators. It was a predator and alien invasion!

Indigo wasn't scared at all because that was like his family. The aliens and predators all touched his first eye with their lightened fingers. The rest of the cast members were all sleeping throughout this whole interaction. They were heavy sleepers while Indigo was the only light sleeper there.

Then a mixed baby of an alien and predator came into Indigo's mouth. This made Indigo freak out and the rest of the aliens and predators looked on with enjoyment. Indigo fell and choked on the creature. Then the death total came back on the screen and the new total showed 100,001. That concluded DAY FIVE EPISODE FIVE.

DAY SIX EPISODE SIX. Indiniya and Bastet were the first to wake up. Indiniya and Bastet had the best sleep because Indigo had the best healing hands worldwide. Indiniya was shocked that Indigo wasn't by her side and Bastet was shocked that he was gone. They both looked at each other and started to yell at one another asking what happened to Indigo. Bastet went over and slapped Indiniya across the face, while Indiniya punched her dead in the mouth. They started boxing while the other cast members were still sleeping. They were fighting so much, that they almost went over the edge of the barn.

The fellow cast members finally woke up and saw them fighting. They went over and broke up the fight before they went over the edge. Aqua and Joey told them they needed to get their heads in the game and try and find Indigo. They couldn't imagine where he could've gone to. They were ready to go on a manhunt to find Indigo no matter how long it takes. Just like how Becky found Indiniya, Indiniya had the same mentality. Before they could climb down from the barn, they were surprised by the executive producer.

The executive producer came on the news prompter and gave them the new death total since the last one they were asleep. It read 100,001. They asked: "Who was the extra one?" and "Where was Indigo?" The executive producer smiled and automatically switched them to a newer multiverse.

This new reality was a utopia of newer technology and a society that ran on tech. Every building, car, and item was digitally made through the power of technology. Cell phones and other technical devices are 24/7 surveillance gadgets that are tracking you and listen to everything you say, type, and/or search.

They were walking around this newer world, and they couldn't believe their eyes. They went into different shops and saw robots performing all the jobs. They didn't see any zombies anymore, just robots.

They had robotic animals and citizens due to everything being technology-based. The robots took over the entire world. The casting directors programmed the robots and turned the rest of the zombies into robots. This was more than the metaverse because not only did technology and robots took over the virtual world, but they did in the physical world as well. Everyone was out of a job, all their money was connected to the system, and if you wrongly disrespect a robot, you'll be put in jail or killed. How would they know if you disrespected a robot or not?

One cannot evolve from one's robothood until one realizes how robotized they've become.

Robots were first created to help aid human life to become easier. Humans programmed the robots with no emotion and to act through the programs. As time progressed, the robots gained emotions and feelings and were becoming intelligent. They could even give birth to a mini robotic baby as well.

The only real difference between robots and humans was that humans had a voice in their heads, while robots didn't. So, at first, no one thought too much about it as they started to come into the system. These government officials love to condition your mind slow and steady, so you'll accept these unprecedented changes.

It's now the digital age and robots are becoming superior to humans. They took over the human race and the ones who built these robots in the first place tried to escape to planet Mars. Since the whole world is a dome, they couldn't leave the atmosphere, so they decided to live underground for the rest of eternity.

Joey and Apollo started to interact with the robots to see how smart they were. They didn't know they felt emotion as well. Indiniya and Bastet wanted to see if Indigo was still alive or not. Aqua told the boys that they needed to move on because Indigo was still missing.

Indigo lived a precious life getting ready for college. He always cared for others and wanted the best for people. He still was facing some issues internally, but since he's gone, he'll have to go through them during the death process.

Joey and Apollo started teasing one of the robots by poking it. The robot faced them and pushed them to the ground. Robots were much stronger than humans and now they were smarter as well. They had the power to control humans through the microchip and nanotechnology placed in humans. Good thing none of the cast members had it because the citizens that didn't turn into robots, turned into their robot minions.

After being pushed to the ground, Joey had enough of messing with the robots. Apollo wasn't going to back down from a fight. No matter who it was or what thing it was; Apollo wasn't scared of anything. Apollo had that confidence internally that accelerated externally. Apollo was arrogant enough to punch the robot in the face. The robot ate the punch and didn't even move. The robot turned his hand into scissors and snipped Apollo's head completely off his body. Just imagine a bobblehead being completely cut off from the rest of its body. Once this happened, out of the shadows comes Indigo walking in slow motion toward the group. Indigo was still alive! Indigo came back with an alien and predator right by his side. Let's explain how it all happened.

Once the baby alien and predator went inside the mouth of Indigo, it was an awakening moment for him. The aliens and predators were smiling because they knew Indigo was transforming into them. His DNA and RNA have been unlocked and had the same powers as the aliens and predators. They wanted him to fulfill his true potential. The transformation might've seemed outlandish, but it needed to happen. After they changed the reality of this new robot world, they eliminated the aliens, predators, and Indigo from the equation. Indigo was a glitch in the videogame and somehow, they found a way back into this new Universe. The executive producer tried to take them out, but they came back with no hesitation.

Indigo's army of aliens and predators started to attack the robots. The robots were putting up a fight because they weren't going out without having a battle. The robots didn't want anyone to dethrone them from their new kingdom. Indigo's army won't stop until the beast is finished. Indigo saw the robots putting up a good fight, so he used all of his strength and power from the cosmos and wiped out the entire population of robots. This took a lot out of Indigo, and he was tired right after. After their victory, Indigo said bye to his new family and told them he'll be returning home eventually.

Indigo and the group gathered around Apollo, and they still had flowers from the supermarket, so they placed them on and around Apollo's body. Apollo didn't make it out alive because of the robot. They had a personal funeral for Apollo.

Apollo was the star of the show, and wherever he went, he brought that wow factor. No one could expect what he'll say next. Even though Apollo had a successful career, he still was reckless and wild. That was just his personality and he wanted to experience life to the fullest. No attachments, no overthinking, and no putting anyone else above or before him. He learned so much throughout the years, but he let those small toxic behaviors get the best of him. Apollo was a God, and he knew it. They all hugged one another and showed their gratitude for seeing Indigo. Indigo explained what happened and the journey coming back. Then they mourned while looking at Apollo's remains. After that, the death total appeared and totaled 176,999. They all wept while going to sleep that night. They ended DAY SIX EPISODE SIX on a sad note, but hopefully, they'll turn it around.

DAY SEVEN EPISODE SEVEN. All the cast members woke up that morning feeling way closer to one another. No one knew what to say, but you can sense the tension in their face. Against all the odds, they were all they got, and you can feel that energy within the group.

Nature had enough of these robotic remains that were still present in this reality. Nature was going to wipe out the rest of the robots and take back its true power. The destruction and chaos that these zombies and robots caused were detrimental. The backwash of it all caused dead robots, dead humans, dead animals, dead aliens, and dead predators everywhere. Nature had to wipe out the entire system to regenerate itself. So, nature gathered up all the natural disasters known to man and released them all.

Nature released firestorms, dust storms, floods, hurricanes, tornadoes, volcanos, earthquakes, tsunamis, squalls, wildfires, droughts, and sinkholes, just to name a few. Squalls were the first to appear starting with lightning. The aliens knew this was going to happen, so they built and left behind a shelter for them that'll survive all of the natural disasters. The casting directors used weather control to release their natural disasters in hopes of the cast members interacting with them. They didn't realize that nature will get involved and aliens will build a shelter for them.

Right when they got inside, the blackout happened once again. The shelter they built was huge inside and massive on the outside. It was the tallest building they had within this reality. All of them went inside and started to gather their thoughts. They tried to have a bull session, but nature was so loud that they barely heard one another. They just mostly interacted with their supplies and caught up on some sleep. The natural disasters were so bad that they couldn't even exit the shelter from the ground level. Hot lava was on the ground, so if they leave, then the lava would burn them. Hours upon hours went by as nature brought destruction to this reality. The cast members didn't hear as much noise as before. They had a barrel elevator in the middle of the shelter, so they took it up to the rooftop to see the repercussion.

As they went up, the roof opened so the barrel could fit through. Once they reached the rooftop, they saw the entire backlash of what nature did to this world. It destroyed all the remaining buildings, structures, and remains. The roof had enough space where people could walk, but you could easily fall off if you weren't careful. Even though the executive producer allowed nature to obliterate most of the current room, they could always create another one.

When the executive producer went to the bathroom, the casting directors didn't like nature destroying what they've built. This room specifically was made by the casting directors. They were so angry that the next victim they targeted was Aqua. The casting directors made a ghost figure to allure Aqua to come and follow it. As everyone else remained occupied in seeing what nature had done, Aqua looked up and saw Johnny.

Johnny was speaking to her about how bad he messed up, how much he loved her, and how he'll do better. Aqua started to talk to the ghost-like figure, but she was the only one that saw him. It appeared real just like how Indigo thought he was speaking to his dream girl. Aqua was coming closer to the edge of the roof below a pool of lava. Aqua was talking back to Johnny, so Joey finally realized where Aqua went because the last time he checked; she was right beside him.

As Joey screamed out to Aqua saying, "It's not real!" Aqua would gain her consciousness back. Joey dashed over to Aqua in hopes to hold her tight in his arms. Once Joey gained the attention of Aqua, the casting directors shot a lightning bolt right in front of Aqua. Aqua started to tumble and she fell off the roof.

Joey sprinted towards Aqua and the fellow cast members told him to wait. As Aqua was falling, Joey jumped off the rooftop and captured Aqua. Now they were both falling into a pool of lava.

They knew their time was coming to an end on the show, so they both expressed their love for one another. How could Aqua still express love for Joey, if she fell for the illusion of Johnny? Joey gave Aqua her final kiss as they both were falling. The shelter was the tallest building, so it felt like they were falling slowly to their death. They told the other cast members that they loved them and to survive the show. They were about to share their trauma, but when they were about to, they fell right into the lava.

Joey curated his paintings creatively by telling his story and everything he experienced. While most of his life he didn't have a true connection with his family, he started to see changes. They started to show him that they cared, and Joey was being noticed for everything he'd done for them. He helped Cody and Mike with their homework, supported Ashley and Michael, and became a young father to his baby girl Brenna. The only people he truly loved were Aqua and Brenna for the most part. He went through a lot, and he was still trying to find his way through all this chaos and madness. Joey loves hard and will fight for what he believes in. Hence, what he did to Johnny.

Aqua was a unique character who showed her true colors and emotions down the road. She needed some people to tell her the truth to get the gears rolling towards progression. At first, she was trying to find her way as a young mother to Brenna, but her status at school started to deteriorate. This made Aqua more insecure about herself, so she started to catfish other men while having sex with them. Not to mention her family didn't show her love and care either. Joey and Aqua were very similar and grew up practically the same. Whether it was from Vicky, Jordan, or her toxic sisters. This made Aqua's self-worth and self-confidence plummet. The only person who picked her back up was Joey.

If you're ever in a relationship, it's important to know if your partner will be there with you through the thick and thin, through your highs and lows, and will pick you up when you feel down. She didn't realize how good she had it with Joey and it started to show once she left him. Once, she started to date Johnny, she noticed the things that Johnny did was the same things she did in the past. Even though they had Elias together, it all came back to her like a repeated loop. The Universe will place you in similar scenarios if you haven't learned your lesson yet. The Universe was trying to thrust her into knowing the truth about Johnny by letting Joey do an FBI investigation. The facts were all presented to her in her face, but she didn't accept it and just let it all be.

Even though she tried to move on from Joey, she tends to always come back. Whether it was for his party, trying to hang out with him, or going to the LA trip as well. Something always gets in the way of her truthfully connecting with Joey though. Whether Joey not showing up to his party or Johnny coming to the LA trip. When the show started, she finally realized that Joey was the one for her. She still didn't truly know until she was falling to her death. Why would she follow Johnny if she had Joey that was right beside her? How did the casting directors know about Johnny? I'll leave you to speculate on these questions. Aqua had confirmation that Joey was the one when she started to fall, and Joey was still right behind her. Through thick and thin, through health and sick, through life and death. It was too late for Aqua though because her time had come.

The relationship between Joey and Aqua was interesting to write and speak on. Their dynamic between each other was uniquely special. They might be the juiciest couple in the story or characters in this novel, but that's for you to decide.

Once they died in the show, the rest of the cast members were in complete bluff of what just panned out. Indigo brought both women back inside the shelter to call it a night. The casting directors felt bad, so while they were on the roof, they planted food inside the shelter. Indigo and Indiniya didn't feel like eating, but Bastet did. The death total appeared and now it said 177,001. That was the end of the natural disasters escape room. Indiniya and Bastet both cried, and Indigo tried to comfort them both. Indigo tried to be strong for them but couldn't help but cry as well. It was a sad night for them in this escape room. That concludes DAY SEVEN EPISODE SEVEN. It also concludes the chapter called disaster and turmoil as we now enter the awakening.

Chapter Six

THE AWAKENING

With all of these external apocalyptic events that were taking place, the characters had to deal with a lot of hardship. They barely had time to digest and analyze what was taking place. They just lost four of their castmates and now there were only three left. They started to speculate if this show was even a reality TV show anymore. They started to theorize the way how the show was built. What's going on with their actual bodies? Was it supposed to be this way? Does someone suppose to leave the show in each episode? They still had a lot of built-up emotions about their past they haven't dwelt with yet. This was built-up trauma just eating themselves alive. Most of them already had trauma from their past, but the show just added more on top of it. Will they ever get to the point of blissfulness? Let's find out.

DAY EIGHT EPISODE EIGHT. Once the last cast members awakened, they were in a tightly confined box. Since this was an actual room instead of an area, they thought this was a real escape room. They spend a few hours trying to search for clues. After a few hours, the executive producer went on the teleprompter telling them they were in the next room. It's time to face their internal apocalyptic events.

Bastet didn't like enclosed spaces and as time progressed, the room got smaller and smaller. Only the people who did their shadow work got to proceed to the next round. They could either face their internal demons themselves or speak about them to the group. Bastet and Indiniya still had tension, so they didn't want to relay their traumas to one another. Everyone went to their separate corner to process everything that happened throughout their lives. Only the executive producer will know if they truly did their inner work or not. Just saying you finished doesn't mean you truly did the work. You have to be fully healed from the past, become your true authentic self in the present, and become energetic about your future. If you can pass these three steps, then you'll make it to the next round. If not, then you won't make the cut in going to the healed version of the new earth.

They had a total of 18 hours to do so. Bastet went back to sleep and decided to conduct her trauma later on. Indiniya was losing her mind at the moment because she wasn't prepared or ready to overcome her past. Indiniya was talking under her breath and was making slick comments. Bastet yelled at her saying, "Shut your mouth! I'm trying to get some sleep over here!" While Bastet turned back around, Indiniya decided to kick her in the back. Bastet had enough of Indiniya's bs, so she got up and threw her against the wall.

Indigo was trying to meditate and go through the problems that he'd experienced throughout his lifetime. He didn't have time to babysit people who were older than him. He always had to cater, hold people's hands, and show them the way to live their lives. He had enough and at a certain age and point in your life, people should've known those basic experiences or have knowledge of that information that should've been learned at a younger age. People will look at a person's age and assume you aren't experienced or mature enough. These people don't know who you truly are or know what you've experienced in the past to get you to this point. Don't allow people to make assumptions about your life or make pre-determined judgments about you. They're missing out on a blessing that's inside of you.

Indigo only yells through scream meditation, but this time he yelled at both of them. They now only had 15 hours left to go through their issues. All Indigo needed was time to himself with quietness to take this seriously. Indigo loves to socialize with people when the time was right. He doesn't need a crowd of people to make him happy because he could make himself happy by being alone. All that love, peace, and abundance that people chase after others are already inside of you. You just have to know that for yourself. That's why he loves spending time with himself by doing the things he loves. Without joy, there's no meaning in life.

Indigo finally got them to be quiet, so he could be at peace once again.

Since he was already feeling non-human just like his real family, the extraterrestrials came down and helped Indigo gain his powers back. Indigo experienced a lot throughout his journey. He learned so much throughout his life, but people still questioned if he was conscious. People tend to continuously speak to sheep, so they automatically think everyone else is a sheep. Every day he had to prove people wrong. He now knows who he truly was and where'd he come from. He wasn't of this world, this reality, this dimension, etc. That's why he was an outcast and couldn't fit in. He never fit inside their tiny boxes and was destined to do marvelous things. Now he has his spiritual team behind him and was achieving everything he once dreamt of. Indigo finally realized that everything in his life was for a higher purpose.

He accepted his flaws, his mistakes, his triggers, and the past. He now changed his old ways and healed from those experiences. He was now viewing life on a bigger scale and from a bird's eye view. He used to get triggered by some comments people made about him, but now he knows himself. He doesn't let people get under his skin because his skin is too priceless to allow people to do that to him.

After five hours went by, he was fully healed, accepted, and moved on from the past. He was now in full control over his mind, body, and soul. You can't avoid people talking about you, so be in full control over your emotions and feelings, so people won't take control or advantage of you.

There were 10 hours left on the timer and the only person who'd healed was Indigo. Indigo stayed in the room to help the others if they needed it but was just listening to music. Indiniya was still paranoid at the current moment and Bastet finally woke back up. The next person to finally take this seriously was Bastet.

Bastet was pretty much healed from a lot of her past and accepted the circumstances. She let go of her baby daddies and what they've done to her. The only thing that was holding her back was her issue with her family. The fact that her family kept this lie and was holding secrets from her for this long was devastating and hard to digest.

Bastet tried to envision what her sister may have looked like and her characteristics. After five hours of contemplating, Bastet had a vision of her sister. She remembered what Sara told her at her shop and what Victoria told her on the way to the airport. The name Sincere came up and she was starting to appear in her vision. She was about to see her sister through her vivid experience for the first time. With Sincere visiting Bastet at the hospital, it helped Bastet to envision Sincere using her third eye.

Bastet started to develop a panic disorder. This made her stomach enlarge in pain as well. Bastet's stomach was still feeling pain from the water, the zombie cut, and now from the panic disorder. It felt like a slow death that has been taking over Bastet's life. Indigo noticed that Bastet was in pain, and he went over to check on her. The more she tried to avoid seeing her sister, the more pain she was in. The casting directors helped by poisoning the food that she ate before this room started. Hence, she went right to sleep when they entered this new room.

Indigo held Bastet in his arms and Indiniya thought she was exaggerating for attention. Instead of worrying about herself, she placed drama on Bastet. Indigo heard Indiniya and it bothered him that she didn't show much sympathy for Bastet.

Bastet's whole body was in chills, and she started to become pale and numb. It was eating her from the inside out. Bastet still had five hours left and the only cure from this poison was to dive deeper and accept Sincere. She couldn't handle it and made the executive decision in her mind that she wasn't ready.

Bastet died in Indigo's arms. Her last words were "I love you" and that was it for her.

Bastet never met her sister-in-law and that haunted her for the rest of her life.

Indigo started to cry out in sheer agony for Bastet. Indigo had tapped into his emotions and felt that empathy (as an empath) for Bastet.

Indiniya didn't care and said she deserved that pain because it wasn't real. The death total randomly appeared, and it showed 177,002. Indigo asked her if it was real or fake now?

Four hours remained and Indigo wasn't pissed off toward Indiniya but was disappointed in her. He thought more highly of Indiniya, but ever since then, he thought she was better than that.

Indigo told her that she overanalyzed everything and placed solutions upon a person without letting them speak for themselves. She was quick to place judgments on people and she was fixated on that belief she told herself. No matter what you tell her, if she believes differently, it'll fly across her head.

All this time, Indiniya saw how passionate Indigo was about her. By the time she found out, it was already too late. Indigo gave Indiniya chance after chance, but he noticed that she wasn't changing. Why go back to a toxic cycle when you've healed from that situation? That'll just bring you back into the old toxic behaviors that you've once passed.

Now Indiniya was officially out of time, even though there were still three hours remaining.

Indigo got up and left the condensing building. As time started to trickle down, the condensed room started to slowly be confined. The fact that Indigo still stayed in this room just showed how much he cared for Indiniya and Bastet. Indigo was fed up and was over the disrespectful behavior of Indiniya. Indigo asked Indiniya if she wanted him to stay or not, and she said, "No. Just go." Indigo got up and left the room abruptly.

Once, he left, Indiniya started to pour down a bucket of tears. She wanted him to stay and hold onto her tight.

Most women wouldn't admit what they want until they asked you first. Or they'll try and see if you care about them or are confident enough in giving your true answer first. For example, if a woman tells you that she's going to delete your number, then asks you what would you do? If you said you'll keep her number because you saw potential, she'll agree and won't delete your number. If you said you're going to delete her number because she said she'll delete your number first. She'll deny that she was going to delete your number in the first place and then actually deletes your number.

Most women use that trick, or they'll try to make you jealous by telling you how many guys be in her DMs, texting her, or how many guys come up to her asking for her number. If you don't get jealous, then they'll come back and try to find different ways to make you jealous to see if you care. If you do show signs of jealousy, then that tells them that you care. Sure, caring is fine, but in these scenarios, you shouldn't care and have that confidence within yourself. You know your worth and you know what you bring to the table.

Without closure, Indigo was placed back inside the condensed structure. He now had to get over Indiniya and the ways she made him feel. Since he didn't leave calmly, he left with some anger inside of him.

Indiniya would try and comfort Indigo, but he had one specific mission; to heal and move forward.

Indigo was in a meditative state even though he was being distracted. It took Indigo two hours to fully detach from her. He still had love for her, but he knew what needed to be done. She would try and distract him by kissing him, trying to have sex, and talking to him. After two hours, he fully healed once more. He got up slightly, turned to her, said "I have love for you," turned back, and walked out the room.

Indiniya cried once more because she loves hard and that deteriorated her from doing her own work. She had trouble multitasking.

After 20 minutes had passed, she was ready to do the work. Since Indigo was a glitch in the system, he managed to gain an extra 20 minutes for Indiniya to do her shadow work. Now it's one hour left before the timer runs out. Not to mention the room is getting smaller and smaller. Multiple things are running through her mind at this point. The room itself wasn't her top priority, it was now herself.

Indiniya always felt unheard and mistreated because no one could understand her real intentions. Just like through texting. People can easily misread a message, type typos, or didn't explain something in full detail. You can't tell the person's body language, tone of voice, or true intentions behind a text message. Speaking on the phone to express yourself feels different.

She was awkward whenever she tried to tell people about herself. When it came to relationships, she was nervous around them most of the time. She felt weird opening up to a person as well.

After her family died and now being adopted by her sister, it all took a toll on her. She became guarded for her heart due to her past. She tends to bring up the past multiple times because that's all she ever experienced. She didn't heal from her past, so that's why she kept bringing it up. It was slowly tearing her up inside and she had a mental breakdown.

On the outside looking in, she was gold, treasure, and pleasant on the eyes. On the inside looking out, she'd been through some traumatic experiences. The only thing that was holding Indiniya back from her greatness was her past.

The past hindered Indiniya from evolving, elevating, and achieving what she desired. She tried to forget about it, run from it, and tried to hide from it, but it all kept coming back to her. Everyone she ever met triggered something in Indiniya's past that she hasn't healed from yet. She would then blame instances on the other person without looking at what she'd done. She would hold stuff against the other person if they haven't met her high standards or expectation. Indiniya was single because she's the hardest to love. She tends to find someone new to distract her from doing her work. Whenever they would bring up her issues, she would become defensive and put things off. She tries to end things fast and places the blame on them.

It was becoming too much for Indiniya that she couldn't accept and fully let go of the past. It was hard for her to be in the present without despising the past or worrying about the future. The only real connection she had was with her sister who was her new mom. Indigo saw the time was running out, so he allowed her to get one last phone call. Indiniya showed her gratitude and love for Indigo and called Becky.

While the phone was ringing, the executive producer woke back up.

The casting directors and executive producer had awakened from their nap and saw the time was running out. Also, they saw Indiniya somehow had a phone. Someone must've hijacked the system, but they couldn't think about that right now.

While the phone was ringing, the executive producer ended the call and eliminated the phone. The casting directors had enough of these silly games and decided to shrink the room completely while Indiniya's body was still there. Indigo knew her time was coming, so he felt some emotion starting to boil, but he was calm in his own right.

The buzzer sounded and Indiniya didn't face her demons yet. Even if she had more time, she already made that decision from the get-go.

The room englobed and the death total was now 177,003. Indiniya was pronounced dead.

That was the end of the day and Indigo just got some rest. He prepared his mind, body, and soul for anything that comes his way. Before going to bed, he received a download from Source stating that he was the messiah. That concluded DAY EIGHT EPISODE EIGHT, and this was the end of the awakening chapter. Indigo is now starting to feel like he's the chosen one in this show.

Chapter Seven

THE CHOSEN ONE

With all his fellow cast members gone, Indigo was the last survivor. Indigo was contemplating if this was the end of the show or not? All the hardships, heartbreaks, and obstacles to get to this point, he couldn't give up now. There's no turning back. He had overcome all the external apocalyptic events so far and now finished his internal apocalyptic events as well. Indigo learned a lot throughout this show, and now has the necessary tools to step into his Higher Self.

DAY NINE EPISODE NINE. The casting directors were surprised that Indiniya randomly had a phone. How did this phone appear in this Universe? The only person who could've done something was Indigo. That was the only person left and he had access to go inside and outside the room at any given moment. The executive producer was furious because he went against the rules of no contact with the real world. Even though it all looked real, they still viewed it as being virtual. Once they finished this dialogue, Indigo woke up.

Indigo was a glitch within their game due to his contact with aliens and predators. Indigo was walking around this world not knowing what could happen next. Indigo still had some supplies and materials that he could use to his advantage. He was the lone wolf of this town since there was no one left.

Indigo had a vision of a building that was beyond the dome of this VR world. Indigo went to the end of the dome (on its side) and started to see if he could break through. It was all pixelated and it looked like an alternate animated world. It was animated to portray it as being the VR world, but it was the real world.

Indigo used his powers to push through the spider-verse-like structure. Once he made it through, the alarm ranged in the actual world letting the executive producer and casting directors know that something happened. They were all celebrating downstairs for the success of the show, not knowing this was taking place.

Once Indigo made it through, he saw the whole world destroyed. The only structured area that was still up and running was the television set of this show.

Each complex studio was separated. He saw some cars parked in front of studio 13. The building looked so familiar to the actual building that his physical body was in, but this time it was animated.

He opened the door to studio 13 and the split between what was real and what was fake was merging. It felt like the real world and the dream world were merging. The animated world and the physical world were going in and out.

Indigo saw people having a party. The executive producer was in the kitchen cooking while the casting directors (which were five of them) were out on the floor. The casting directors and Indigo locked eyes. The casting directors bolted towards Indigo with weapons to try and kill him off. Indigo didn't know what was going on, but he had supernatural powers.

One casting director threw a knife toward Indigo. Indigo grabbed the handle and threw it right back into his skull. He was still moving, so Indigo used his claws like Wolverine and sliced his face open.

To make sure he was dead, Indigo sent him through an unknown portal using his Scarlet Witch powers.

The next casting director came at him with a sword. Indigo reversed it, grabbed the sword, and stabbed him right through the spine.

To make sure he wasn't a threat anymore, Indigo used his spiderwebs to spray him against the wall and closed his mouth shut.

The next casting director used pepper spray and a stun gun on Indigo. Indigo was having a hard time seeing, but he transferred the electric shock from the stun gun and turned it into a multitude of electricity from the Universe. He electrocuted the casting director with the power of electricity.

The last two casting directors were women, so they tried to possess Indigo by doing witchcraft and seduction. Indigo had increased intelligence and saw right past this. Plus, dark magic couldn't be done towards Indigo because he was that powerful now.

The women saw it wasn't working, so they tried to fight him. Indigo doesn't hit women, so he needed to find a way to survive.

For one of the casting directors, he used his telekinesis powers to pick stuff up and throw them at her. He hit her with a vase, and she went down with a plump.

To make sure she was dead, Indigo used his magical spells to cast from the earth, a rock that went right through her spine. He then generated fire and lava upon her by being the Human Torch. By this time, all the members of the party left the studio and went to a different studio within the set.

The only one left on the ground floor was the last woman casting director. She was crying and told Indigo that she was sorry. She used empathy and showed her emotions to Indigo. Indigo had sympathy for the woman and went over to comfort her. As Indigo went and hugged her, she used a carving knife and stabbed Indigo multiple times in the back. Indigo screeched out in pain; "Ahh!" He stepped back as he examined his stab wounds.

Indigo used some magic and accumulated the energy to fly over to her and threw her out of the building. Then he used water like Aquaman and the wind like an air bender to create a tsunami. The tsunami transferred her right to the ground.

To make sure she was dead, Indigo used his teeth like Sharkboy and bite her mouth completely off. He thought of biting her head completely off, but he opened a portal and sent her into a dark hole.

Indigo went back inside and went upstairs to the room they placed them in.

Once he opened the room, bullets started to fly in his direction. Indigo used his powers as the flash to make the bullets go in slow motion, so he could dodge them. It looked like a scene from the Matrix movie. Once the gun was out of ammunition, Indigo looked and saw the fallout of everything.

This whole time the building was in disguise and concealed from the cast members. The executive producer left to go upstairs when Indigo was fighting the casting directors. The executive producer was me, the host of this book and the illustrator of this novel. Yes, I did it.

As I went over to the side, Indigo found out this was all a simulation. There were no real escape rooms, and it was all in their heads. I went over to Indigo and tried to convince him that this was all just a prank show and everyone was in on it. Indigo wasn't buying it because he saw his fellow cast members on the ground. He saw them all dead with their headsets and headphones not connected to their bodies anymore. Indigo then came over to his body and saw himself still in this video game state. As he was studying his body, I texted one of the casting directors that he was in the room.

The casting director who was in the spiderweb had a spare knife in his pocket and began to cut his way out. Yes, the guy with the sword in his spine somehow was still alive. He didn't pull out the sword because that would make him instantly die.

With Indigo being distracted, the casting director came through the door and tried to stab him. As I looked on, Indigo heard footsteps coming his way and he did a reverse underline kick to him. Indigo screamed out with the power of his voice and pushed him through the floor. The scream was so loud that the casting director instantly died when he went underground. I luckily covered my ears, and it wasn't in my direction.

Indigo was overriding the system and that was causing the game to be destroyed. I went over to Indigo and hit him behind the head with my gun. I started to hit him repeatedly with my gun to his face. Indigo and

I are pretty similar in our own right, but he won't debunk all of my hard work.

All of a sudden, I couldn't hit Indigo anymore with my hand because it was being raised by itself. I thought to myself, what's going on? Why can't I control my body? Who's doing this? As I turned around, I saw who it was.

It was the CEO and the creator of the show, Brandon Bass. Yes, the CEO and the creator of this show was my rival, Brandon.

Brandon and I were very similar (practically the same person), but he wanted to go the safer route through this show. He was more righteous, and he calls me the savage version of himself. He was trying to control me and put me in a box. I wanted to add drama and suspense, so I admittedly abused my power in controlling the way I saw fit. Don't blame me, the most killings were done by the casting directors. Don't hate the player, hate the game.

This is the final part of the story I get to host for this book, so the last thing I'll say is, "This game isn't over. It'll haunt you forever!"

Now as the new host and illustrator, I'll relay the message about what happened next.

I used telepathy and mind control capabilities to have power over Smooth Doubleb. I have the psionic ability to get inside people's minds and control their bodies. I manipulated him into not having any power anymore. I placed him in a condensed box-like prison and shipped him away. Smooth Doubleb still had power, but not as much as before.

He and the casting directors tricked all of the cast members and got everyone killed in real life. Whatever happened in the show, essentially happened in real life as well. I watched what was taking place outside and thought we were just going through some warfare. As I watched the show, they nailed it down to a tee. There were no grey areas or any blurred lines. I couldn't believe my eyes at how they predicted what'll happen in the real world.

Before the season finale of the show, I wanted to surprise them at their party.

As I was making my way down to studio 13 (since I was in studio one), I received multiple voicemails. It was the cast members' family members telling me that they cannot get in contact with them and that they were about to die. They were dying of all the health measures, zombies, and robots. This can't be right.

As I went inside, I saw the aftermath of the party but heard people upstairs. I saw all the fellow cast members dead and saw Smooth Doubleb attacking Indigo. Now we're here.

I went to Indigo and tried to awaken him. He was out cold by all the pain he endured. I used my healing powers to heal Indigo's wounds. Once he woke back up, he thought I was going to attack him, but I wasn't, I was here to help him.

Indigo wanted to be with his family and go home, but he couldn't because they were all dead. We unplugged his headset and headphones, and his animated body merged with his physical body. He was now operating his physical body once again, but still obtaining the powers and experiences he learned along the way.

I felt so connected with Indigo that I adopted him. Indigo and I were so similar and alike. We at least had the rest of the television set and studios that were untouched, so we left and lived happier ever after. The end.

As Brandon began to close the final chapters of his book, I (Smooth Doubleb) used my powers to gain access to his book. He thought the book ended right there, but I had more to say.

I wanted to do this all by myself, but Brandon always thought I would push it beyond proportion. I practically did this all by myself while Brandon was the one to get all the praises and recognition for the story that I created. This will not end like this. Let me tell you what really happened next.

As they shipped me off in a random box to an unknown location, I still had some power. Brandon didn't take away all my power, just most of it. I also hid my other powers deep inside my soul, so he won't be able to tame me there.

I escaped the box and I telecommunicated with their pilot, and I programmed him.

I placed a tracking device in Brandon's zipper pocket, and I was surprised he didn't notice.

Indigo and Brandon were ready to leave this world behind and travel outside of this realm. They called their helicopter, and they went inside. I was watching their every move because I hacked the cameras in the helicopter. I also hacked Indigo's phone when he was going through this simulation.

They were on their way to a different world, but I programmed the pilot to make them go to Planet Nibiru. There were excited to go to Planet X and that irked my nerves.

As they were traveling, I already grabbed my private jet and started to go to the new earth. I placed the final death toll in their helicopter saying 177,010 in total. Brandon said, "Oh wow" and Indigo questioned if that was the right number or not. Indigo remembered the original number was 177,003. Then he went to the actual world and killed five casting directors. So, the real number should be 177,008. The teleprompter started to glitch and the helicopter started to shake. The teleprompter went completely blank and then stated, "The extra two are for you." I placed a target on their backs, and I was coming after them. Concerned faces were placed on both Indigo's and Brandon's faces. I made the order to have the pilot look back, smile, and say, "This game isn't over. It'll haunt you forever!" The pilot started laughing.

I didn't want to end the game until I said it was finished with my rules, regulations, and conditions. Even though Brandon and Indigo were powerful, they were too caught off guard to use them.

Brandon remembered me placing that quote before he took over as the host and illustrator of this book. Once he remembered, the helicopter started to malfunction because I just killed the pilot. I was going wherever they were going since I had a tracker on them. I have to control my jet; I'm finishing the book here.

Hey everyone, this is Brandon LeMar Bass, the author. Now you're probably saying, aren't you the creator of the show as well? No; Brandon and I are different. We are practically the same, but I'm not in this story, I'm just writing down the information.

So, the helicopter started to tumble down. What could they do? Will they survive? What would Smooth Doubleb do next? Why haven't they used their powers yet? Did Smooth Doubleb manipulate them into taking over their powers?

That was the end of DAY NINE EPISODE NINE and it was the season finale of the show. Will there be another season or was this the final season? Was this the last episode they'll ever make? That's the end of the final chapter called The Chosen One and I hoped you enjoyed it.

I know I left it off with a cliffhanger and you still have questions. This would be a great time to analyze the story and see how everything came into reality. You can discuss these questions and your theories with other book lovers to generate what you think. To catch these theories or to see how some of these events transpired, you'll have to read or listen to this book more than once. I placed multiple items throughout this book for you to question and create theories on why I placed them in the book. Every line, every message, and every word had a hidden clue to multiple theories out there. Was this a fictional book or was it a nonfictional book told in the context of a fictional book? Was this all real or fake? What about the stories and experiences of the characters? I'll let you all generate conversation about this book with one another. I also show my other books down below to help expand your consciousness as well.

The last question I pose to you is:

Are you ready to play the game, or have we been playing this game all our lives?

APPENDIX/ENDNOTES

Throughout this book, the characters were faced with multiple events that transformed their lives. Some cast members couldn't handle it while some embraced the journey. This just goes to show how important shadow work truly is. Healing from your past, cleansing your karma, and becoming your best self. If not, then the Universe will place people, things, animals, and/or places in front of you to make you finally recognize it. The thing that should be learned after reading this book was the consequences of not doing so.

As you can see, all the traumas and events they went through were based on their past experiences. It all connects with the events, and you saw how they dealt with their dark night of the soul. You may be experiencing the same traumas or experiences as the cast members, their family members, or even the side characters. What they experienced, their internal apocalyptic events, and their external apocalyptic events. I wanted to have it relatable to what people are going through behind closed doors. You may find it hard to talk about your experiences and you're not alone. We all go through stuff in life, and we shouldn't allow it to hinder us. Instead, we should deal with our demons, be at peace with our past, and move on.

Your experiences and traumas (especially from childhood or from your past lives) will change the course of your life either negatively or positively. Don't allow them to be a major factor in your life. Don't allow them to clog up your mind. If Indigo could do it, then you can do it too. Take your time and don't be so hard on yourself. Every step you make towards healing from your past doesn't go unnoticed. That's where the concept and ideas of this book came from. Hopefully, this book taught you or made you learn about something.

What these characters go through has helped me personally deal with and overcome the own issues and triggers I was facing. While writing this book, I've healed and learned so much through the process. This has been the most spiritual I've ever felt throughout my entire journey so far.

I was called upon Spirit and Source to speak on things that needed to be spoken about. The Universe had pulled me into creating this book to make it come into reality. I felt this urge and sensation in creating this book like no other. I had my fair share of trouble while making this book as well. During the process, I received dark entities trying to steal, hinder, delete, or stop the process of this book. Even though this was happening, I still felt my kundalini energy rise whenever I was working on this book.

I barely texted, called, or talked to anyone about this book or in general. I was on airplane mode, DND, and off-grid most of the time while writing the ideas for this book. The Universe wanted me to keep this a secret until it finally comes out to fruition. I had to duck around questions about why I haven't been on social media, being distant, and why I haven't posted in a while. I've been gone for a few months and people were thinking that I died.

I put my time, effort, and money into this book, and I deeply appreciate you for reading and/or listening to this book. I curated all the knowledge I've gained over my entire spiritual awakening and then some.

All the blood, sweat, and tears shed don't come as close to the way I feel about this excerpt. This book right here will shock the entire world and it'll go down in history as one of the most must-read books of all time. I made sure to get y'all some interesting quotes, quality captions, and important messages I thought of, for you to share. This manuscript has a combination of various genres in this story. You'll have to see which lines they are and if it was fiction or nonfiction. I placed a variety of hidden/subliminal messages, light codes, and various theories that should be fully thought out. I'll leave you to decide and discuss amongst yourself while generating theories for this novel.

Forget about the five-star reviews, being named the bestselling author, and how much this book will change your life. Even though I'm so thankful for your endless support for me to accomplish these tremendous accolades. I do what I do to leave a legacy and make a mark on this earth in all the realms and dimensions. I want to share that with you by being myself. As long as you put it out there, that's all that matters. I inspire you to do the same. Leave your legacy and do the skills, missions, talents, and purposes you were called here to do. When you die, how will people remember you? Did you leave your legacy and do what you desired? Did you leave a long-lasting impression by doing what you were most passionate about? With what you're doing, does it reflect who you truly are? That's for you to decide. No one's going to tell you what to do with your life. You have to make your own decisions for your own life. Remember, this is your path and your journey, so make it yours and not somebody else. Thank you and enjoy my fellow books!

BRIEF OVERVIEW OF MY OTHER BOOKS

RAISING ENERGY BY MEDITATION, FREQUENCY, AND VIBRATION

Raising your energy, frequency, and vibration is a necessary key in activating God/Goddess mode.

Failure isn't the end; it's a necessary part of the path. Failure is always in the passenger seat in his or her life. Hope will always survive in those who continue to fight. It's all about how you deal with that failure and not downplay, doubt, or talk negatively about thyself.

You'll experience the dark depths of your soul as you heal. Many people who just awakened to their Higher Selves would think their all done. That's far from the truth and is a myth. People still have to fix the problems they have internally. It's not all about waking up to the "truth" because rabbit holes go deeper than you expect.

Politicians are put there to give you the idea that you have freedom of choice. You don't; you have no choice; you have owners who own you and everything. They control the media, so they control all the news and information you receive. Shortly, the public won't be able to reason or think for themselves. They spend so much time telling you what to think, what to believe, and what to buy. They're looking for distractions and answers in the external world. They constantly copy others, try to fit in, and become consumers who suppress their potential and creativity. Instead of praising that person who sparked their interest or ideas, they'll send hate toward that person while they try and become them. They don't care about you at all, and people are too ignorant to question it. That's why they call it the American Dream because you'll have to be asleep to believe it.

Some people are too delusional to see that they're giving away their power by believing in an unknown entity that they never met. Losing your power internally will lead to you having self-doubt. Everyone loves to say self-love, self-care, and that they're working on themselves. Nothing's wrong with that, but how can they say self-love and self-care when they negatively talk about themselves. They still get nervous, have anxiety, and make negative comments about themselves, but then say loving yourself is important. It's condescending and they're lying to themselves.

People get offended when people express their true selves because they cannot look at themselves in the mirror. They feel weird when they do it, they don't truly love themselves, and they still have that self-doubt lurking through the shadows. They don't accept it and would rather point fingers at innocent people.

Is this okay with the Universe? Is it okay with Mother Gaia? Is it okay with Mother Nature? These are the questions one should be asking. Nobody in history has ever gotten their freedom by appealing to the moral sense of the people who were oppressing them.

The placebo effect is one of the least understood phenomena in modern science, yet it's something that prevails time and time again. It's literal proof that humans can heal and create outcomes solely based on belief and expectation. Creating your own reality is real.

War is a place where young people who don't know each other and don't hate each other, kill each other. This decision was made by old people who know each other and hate each other but don't kill each other.

The system will collapse faster if we refuse to buy what they're selling, their ideas, their version of history, and their notions of inevitability. They need us more than we need them. We are the majority, not the minority.

They make us pay for the water we drink, the food that we eat, the wars they need, and the crimes they commit. They make us dedicate the most important part of our life to them, but they give us wages and allow us to purchase their items to make them richer. They call it freedom and living the American dream, but I call it indoctrination, slavery, and a nightmare.

Another world isn't only possible, but she's also on her way. On a quiet day, you can hear her breathing.

The ether is the ever-present field that connects all things. Every inch of the ether consists of an infinite amount of free energy. This is the elite's greatest secret. If science were to reveal that the ether exists, it'll destroy the entire foundation of mainstream atomism and particle science. Denying the ether would be like a fish denying that it's surrounded by water.

Work for a cause, not for applause. Live life to express, not to impress. Don't strive to make your presence noticed, just make your absence felt. Let go of your ego and don't be triggered or defensive when people talk about you. Don't allow them to steal your energy. It's the way people say things, that's the difference between advice and bringing someone down. Surround yourself with people who treat you well. You can sense and know higher truth. Pay close attention to when your ears start to ring. Your ears ring when you're increasing in vibration, tuning into higher frequencies, integrating spiritual downloads, receiving insight from your Ascended Masters, or perceiving higher dimensions of reality. Both or one ear may ring simultaneously. This is normal to experience as you progress on your ascension journey.

Small minds cannot comprehend big spirits. To be great, you have to be willing to be mocked, hated, and misunderstood to stay strong.

There are multiple chakras, densities, dimensions, realities, galaxies, universes, and so forth. Don't believe everything they tell you. It's good to gain information from someone else, but when the answers come from the inside of you, that's next level mastery.

Imagine the best-case scenario for every situation. Your mind will begin to attract solutions. The more you know yourself, the more clarity you gain. Self-knowledge has no end. You don't come to an achievement, and you don't conclude because it's an endless river.

There are laws of the Universe and the Kybalion principles that represents life itself.

Observe whatever arises in your mind without attachment. Simply recognize that it's not you. The eyes are useless when the mind is blind. Your mind wants you to engage with it telling you that you're close and think more about it to find the truth. We may know a critical truth already, but why don't we understand that 90% of humanity is still blind? We should be using this information to wake them up!

Affirmation:

Nothing to get, nothing to understand, I'm already it.

Anything that enters your senses can make you trapped here for a certain period. These dark entities and their minions are against you. All their weapons are used to manipulate one's mind to keep them distracted and intentionally not ready. Know the truth, know the end or where things are heading, and don't get distracted or taken advantage of by the different roads that we take to get there. Don't believe in the system, stop listening to the media or news on social media, and know-how to recognize mind-controlled thoughts. The news broadcasting channels are brainwashing people. Know what controls the opposition and understand that everything that's happening right now is about pushing the transition and relying on narratives.

You don't want to put yourself in a position where you have to lie to someone you care about. Sometimes it's better to create a little distance. Having someone be your hero and come to your rescue is a good feeling but rescuing yourself is priceless.

We're now and always had been free. The days of darkness weren't for us; they were for them, and those days are now over. An incredible burst of peace is upon us and now we rebuild this world in our benevolent unified image. No one remembers the person who played it safe. We celebrate the people who were brave in their endeavors, who were brave in their dreams, who were brave in going after the life they truly want, and brave enough to put out the message in their hearts.

As you grow spiritually, people will inevitably fall from your life because you've risen to a new level of understanding. Let them go! Eventually, like-minded people with a similar frequency to yours will take their place.

Changing for the Better:

Change these patterns: change what you focus on and what things mean. Find the power of meaning, and what you do is controlled by what you feel. Don't have the mindset of, "Oh I might do this." When you say go, that means go now. Do that every day, so when tough things come up, you can do them with confidence when your brain responds. Before you work on your head, you have to do something to make your body strong because we all respond to challenges.

Your opinions aren't facts. They're programmed ideas from our past. They're expected visions of our future. Facts are what's happening right now, in your world, in your life, and your reality. Disregard your thoughts and listen to your feelings. They're smarter than you think. Thoughts become things. Change your focus and change your life. The essence of the Universe has three words: patience, faith, and the journey toward the unknown destiny.

Whatever happens over the next three-six months is going to determine what happens collectively over the next five years. Based on our vibration determines which collective consciousness we shift into.

When you make your thought and your emotion one, you'll manifest instantly. When you can marry your thought and emotion into one single potent force, that's when you have the power to speak to the world. You must speak to the divine matrix field in the language of meaning that the field recognizes. The field doesn't recognize our voice, it recognizes the power of our heart. In our hearts, we have a feeling that creates electrical and magnetic waves which is the language that the field recognizes. So, when you create the feeling in your heart as if your prayer is already answered. That creates the electrical and magnetic waves that bring that answer to you.

Ask without hidden motives, be surrounded by your answer, and be enveloped by what you desire that your gladness be full. I'm not saying speak a word, I'm saying be surrounded, to feel as if your answer has already happened. If you want the perfect relationship in your life, if you want the healing in the body of your loved ones, feel the feeling of what it's like as if that has already happened. Be enveloped by what you desire because that's when your thought/brain and emotion/heart become one. Ask without the judgment of the right or the wrong and the good or the bad. Ask without the ego and instead ask from the heart. You must make your future dream a present fact by assuming the feeling of your wishes being fulfilled comes from the place where it already happened. When you put those together, something happens in our hearts, not in our minds.

There's an electromagnetic force field around the earth's dome, and it's now cracked since you're witnessing ships and other celestial bodies enter the atmosphere.

Homework:

Continuously work on yourself, accepting yourself, forgiving yourself, and knowing yourself.

Self-Healing:

I'm sorry, please forgive me, thank you, I love you. I'm love and I'm the truth.

Don't chase because you're searching for something that could lead you to be taken advantage of and or used.

The more fearful you are, the more you produce food for them (adrenochrome). They want you to tune into a reality that's artificial to take away your power.

Life's about moving on, accepting changes, and looking forward to what makes you stronger and more complete.

Clairvoyance shows clear seeing, receiving guidance, and information through your physical sight or your "mind's eye." Also known as the first eye or the third eye which most people call it. Which is also attached to the pineal gland. We only see 1% of what we see out of our two eyes. We only see 5% of the electromagnetic spectrum. Claircognizance clears thinking and receives information through your thoughts of knowing what's true and right. Clairsentience clears feelings and receives information through your body and/or feelings. Clairaudience clears hearing and receives information through auditory means.

Divine union and solidarity are a much more sacred dance than we are told. It begins with how we think about each other. The Universe is listening to our every thought. When we first align with divinity through mutual appreciation, we allow the Universe in which the mind and ego often close the door. Appreciation above all else opens all of our channels. Pure love is the willingness to give without the thought of receiving anything in return. How do you tell someone you love them? You don't; you show them to the point they just know.

One should be most interested in consistency, stability, respect, and loyalty. Surround yourself with people who illuminate your path, push you to dig deeper, makes you happy, makes you laugh, pray for you, and support you even through the tough times. Those types of people are your people. Walk away from anything that gives you bad vibes. Don't explain, justify, or wait. Do what feels right to you and that's enough. When you cannot control what's happening, challenge yourself to control the way you respond to what's happening. That's where your power is!

The prettiest smiles hide the deepest secrets. The prettiest eyes have cried the most tears. The kindest hearts have felt the most pain. Sometimes being kind is more important than being right. Sometimes people don't need a brilliant mind that speaks, but a human heart that listens and understands. Soft and kind-hearted people aren't fools. They know what people did to them, but they forgive again and again because they have beautiful hearts.

Sometimes, no matter how nice you are, how kind you are, how caring you are, or how loving you are, it's still not enough for some people. Sometimes life doesn't give you what you want, not because you don't deserve it, but because you deserve so much more.

People say they want to unlock their DNA, RNA, superpowers, go to the 5th Dimension, etc. The real question should be which 5D are you going to? The healed version of the 5D, or the unhealed version of the 5D. To go to the healed version of the 5D, you must unlock your truest potential. Can you be selfish enough to love yourself unconditionally? It all starts with you. You're the co-creator of your own reality. It's all about ascending, mental health, and euphoria. Self-love, self-acceptance, and being selfish (in a good way) for your well-being.

GRANDMA GOT RAN OVER BY SANTA

https://venngage.net/ps/LllY6Iotp04/grandma-got-ran-over-by-santa

The story begins during the Age of Aquarius. This takes place before the robot apocalypse story happens. There was this girl who was singing in the woods, "Da da da." She was holding a basket full of apples. She was visiting her grandmother who was a werewolf because of her favorite TV show.

So, this girl (who was in Egypt) saw a man who had a basket full of pears. They both said "Hi" and they talked for a while. They exchanged one pear for one apple. As soon as she walked past, the guy asked her, "Hey, where you headed to?" She stated that "I'm delivering apples to my grandma." He said, "How interesting, would she enjoy pears as well?" She continues to say, "I could use some more." He stated that he shall come with.

They both went inside and saw that grandma was a werewolf. The kids were bamboozled, so they ran off looking for shelter, but it was a full moon that night. You know what that means ... Vampires and werewolves come out to play.

The vampires and werewolves came out for a classic showdown. The kids were watching from the top of a tree. Grandma was held without prejudice by the vampires.

As the kids looked on, a massive natural disaster rushed through Egypt. This disaster broke the tree that the kids were staying at. Now, the kids are legitimately in the middle of the battle between the werewolves and vampires. The grandma almost had a heart attack after seeing her granddaughter. She couldn't look at the turmoil of the events that transpired, so she started to cry.

Then, the wolves howled, and the vampires were ready for anything that could happen.

The moon was shining bright like the Anunnaki returned. The kids had the antidote for grandma to turn her back into a human. Since the vampires were part human as well, they decided to help the kids in this scenario but had to deal with the werewolves first. The werewolves and vampires went at it for an epic battle.

Since it was in the forest, more werewolves came, and now they were about to attack the kids. Since there were new wolves on the scene, they thought the kids were vampires since they were close to them. When the wolves tried to attack the kids, the kids built up so much energy that they had superpowers. They were fighting off the werewolves and it was an ultimate triple threat match.

Once the kids fought off the wolves, they rescued grandma.

Before they could give her the antidote, the vampires took it and ran away. The kids and grandma were running after them, but grandma was an older wolf, so it was hard for her to catch up.

Then, suddenly, grandma turned into her higher self.

She dashed to the vampires tearing them up into pieces.

After 15 minutes, the kids caught up to grandma. The kids and grandma had a decision to make. Either grandma can be grandma human or grandma wolf.

Grandma telecommunicated with the kids. You would think grandma would say "I'll be a human" because she's getting older, but it was a tough decision. Especially, after she had that moment with her higher self.

Grandma was thinking of staying a werewolf, and the kids loved it! They could easily make a movie, video game, and a book about this ;). Right before they were ready to call the producers, it was the night before Christmas. Santa was out and about, then suddenly, GRANDMA GOT RAN OVER BY A REINDEER.

Yes, the legendary story has come true. It's not just a cartoon story because it happened in real life. Santa thought it was a bump, so he continued to eat cookies and milk, then took a nap.

The kids called 911 and told them that grandma got run over by Santa. The 911 operator was laughing because they can't be serious. So, the 911 operator hung up.

The kids finally realized that grandma is a werewolf, so they might need to call a vet. All the veterinarian stores were closed since it was Christmas. What will the kids do next? Remember Santa is long gone delivering gifts.

The kids looked up at the full moon and wished upon a little star for answers. The moon reminded them that they had superpowers and so does grandma. Grandma was powerful even though she got hit by a reindeer.

Since the kids were young, they didn't know how to use their powers all too well. Since grandma was older, it took a toll on her whenever she used her powers. What could grandma do?

Suddenly, Santa with his magical powers realized what he has done. It must've been a Christmas miracle.

Santa came back and checked on grandma, but she was injured severely. Santa used his magical powers to heal grandma and she was healed.

Santa asked if she wanted to stay being a werewolf or to turn back into a human being. With that incident that transpired, she chose to be human and watch her kids run freely.

A year goes by, and everything has been going well.

Then, a zombie apocalypse occurred because the mainstream medical industry was poisoning the people. This caused a major outbreak, and a lot of people were dying. The government officials didn't care about the people, so they ordered all the robots to be cast down onto the earth. There was a lot of turmoil and sorrow on the planet. It was a ROBOT ZOMBIE APOCALYPSE. Can grandma and the kids be the last to survive? Find out next time on Brandon Bass's "How to Overcome Apocalyptic Events." THE END!

WINNING WITH WOMEN

So, you want to learn how to win with women huh? Well, you came to the right place. I won't give any quick fixes, scams, and all that internet BS. I'll tell you straight up from real experiences and studying other people.

Before we jump in, I have to say this. To win with women or men, whatever you like nowadays, focus on thyself first. Now I know what you're saying, "I get that every day," but it's the truth. When you think about it if you don't focus on yourself and gain confidence, how can you approach a woman? If you don't focus on yourself and build a relationship/connection with yourself, how can you do that with another woman? The more you focus on thyself, the more you attract. Have you ever experienced where you're not looking for a relationship or you just got into a relationship and just want to focus on yourself and/or them? Then, suddenly, all these women are trying to talk to you, or all these men just randomly slide into your DMs.

Let's talk about the connection between the Law of Attraction and semen retention. While you attract and manifest your divine partner, you'll have many distractions. You'll have to see people for who they truly are through your first eye. There are energy vampires who want to suck your light away and those who just want your physical body. These beings are also called energetic parasites. Parasites are those people or things that implant themselves in your energy field to take your energy. They find your weak points and use them to suck your energy. They can be manipulative or abusive people that have an addiction or have hate inside them. They implant triggers that can be used to drain you. Never let anything or anyone drain your positive energy.

Practice:

The way to stop them is by deactivating the triggers. When you no longer respond to the triggers, they'll try to intensify them, until they finally give up. When someone tries to trigger you by insulting you, or by doing or saying something that irritates you; take a deep breath and do your best to distance yourself from that person. If they trigger you, that means you still have lessons to learn with them. Remember that if you're easily offended, you're easily manipulated.

Trauma is specifically an event that overwhelms the central nervous system, altering the way we process and recall memories. It's the current imprint of that pain, horror, and fear living inside people.

Anger is a mask that people wear to hide their real emotions. It covers up their true feelings of fear, jealousy, frustration, or powerlessness. It's dealing with the situation when you haven't processed the real feelings behind it.

Please don't just go after physically attractive people and that's it. When they get old and wrinkly, would physical attraction even matter by then? That's why a lot of elderly men want younger women, and some younger women accept it because they can be their sugar daddies. The only elderly people who stay with their significant other are those who were married for a long time or bring mental stimulation to their brains (meaning soul or spirit connection).

Base it on the five factors: mentally, emotionally, spiritually, physically, and financially. Make sure you have a mental connection with the person first because that's where the connection is. Make sure you both emotionally connect because that's where the love is. If you're spiritual, make sure they're at least pretty spiritual because you don't want to be dating any sheep. Make sure you're physically attracted to them because you want to make sure you like what you see when you wake up or go to bed each night. Lastly, make sure you the person is financially driven or just strives for better. Financially don't always have to be dependent on money, but their drive, their hunger for success, and their passion could be a part of finances as well.

To get laid:

Look presentable, be confident about yourself, and don't overthink the ting. Don't go to the club only focused on the genital area, trying to have an end goal, and overthinking about talking to people. Go in there and get to know people because they'll see right through your end goal tactics with no confidence. Strike up a regular natter. If you get rejected, they wilding cause you to know your worth so move on. Don't focus on needing to get her number.

Affirmation:

I'm special, loved, worthy, and not rejected. I'll make today count, and I do matter on this earth. I'll do incredible things on this planet, I will be successful, and there's no reason to doubt myself because I am amazing!

Scenario One:

If you meet a person and you'll see them for the majority of the time, then get to know them first without having an end goal. People should be honored in receiving your phone number so treat yourself, your image, and your brand as such (royalty). Not everyone's deserving of you or your number. You don't want to randomly pass out your number to anybody. If everything checks off, move to step three.

Scenario Two:

If you meet a person over the internet or from a friend, you have a lot of time to get to know them. I know you probably want their number right out the gate but get to know them and conversant with them from the app you found them. You don't want to go into their DM's asking for their name, and then your next text is "What's your number?" That might look weird and creepy if that person hasn't gotten the chance to know you before giving you, their number. You know how women are when it comes to passing out their phone numbers. So, you'll have to play the game until they give you, their number. That only depends on step three though.

Step One:

If it's in person with a very quick interaction (ex. they just walked by), compliment them. If you're still interested, then move on to step number two.

Step Two:

If it's in person and you have a few minutes with them, generate a conversation based on that compliment or get to know them in general. If you're still interested, then move on to step three.

Step Three:

If their personality adds up and you feel the vibes, then ask them for their number. Don't outright ask them for their number before getting the chance to know them first. What if they were a secret agent? Also, forget to ask for social media, just get the number instead.

Tip #1:

Don't believe in having "a person." Everybody's going to check some boxes and everybody's going to not check some. The question is, how many do you need to be checked to then say, "I can work with the rest"? Some boxes are bigger, and some boxes are smaller.

There'll be a lot of people who make promises, tell you what you want to hear, and people who'll say y'all are destined to be together. Don't make promises that you can't keep. So many people make promises but end up breaking them and then feel bad for breaking them. People could also misunderstand you when you talk about your future when they think you're talking about a future with them.

If people just keep saying they love you early on and are highly physical, then you must watch out for those types of people. They'll use spirituality to manipulate you into thinking y'all are meant to be together for eternity. The only problem with them is that they like to use magic, witchcraft, and other dark spells.

Whatever you put out into the Universe will come back. So, if you cast a spell on someone, watch your karmic debt add up.

Semen retention is necessary for these types of moments because if you're not aware, you'll lose your sexual energy. Sexual energy and your semen are so divine and powerful that people will try to attack you in the physical realm. They're just purely 3rd-dimensional physical beings. Hence, demons are in the 3D and the sexual dark entities are in the 4D. The 4D is the dream world, darkness, fallen angels from the moon, and witch hours. Thus, some people experience wet dreams or tend to release their seeds during the night.

Succubus, incubus, and jezebel roam around at nighttime trying to suck your energy dry. That's why they want you to work so hard as a slave throughout the day, so when you get home, you'll be lazy enough to only watch the tell-lie-vision. Therefore, they promote sex in movies, TV shows, or doing hidden black magic for you to have a sexual urge. Savor pleasure, but don't try to take captive.

I would explain how to pick up women throughout this book "How to Overcome Apocalyptic Events" through some of the experiences of the main characters.

MY AUTOBIOGRAPHY

In my volume one autobiography, I'll be explaining my life from ages 0 to 25 while touching on some of my past lives as well. Volume two will be an introduction to my life from ages 26 to 50. Volume three will be from ages 51 to 75, and so on.

I have experienced a lot throughout my life and have overcome a lot. Being the chosen one comes with challenges and adversity. It's all about how you react. See the mainstream media always want you to react. That's why they hit people with sentimental, madness, and other emotions on the news for you to react. Once you give in to your emotions, you'll then react in a certain way. Don't let people get a reaction or a rise out of you. Think before you speak, think before you type, and have a balance between logic and your emotions. You can't be more of one side than the other.

Being too emotional will make you attached to certain things, and it'll bring you comfort. Once it leaves, you're heartbroken which equals sadness, which includes emotions. That's why it's so important to detox, disconnect, and not be overly attached to anyone or anything. It's a short-term pleasure instead of a long-term gain.

With that being said, you can't be too logical with everything as well. Being too premonition about everything will make you live in your head, constantly overthinking, and it'll bring traumatic reexperiences to your life. Life shouldn't be filled with stress, anxiety, depression, etc. Life should be fun, enjoyable, and living in the moment. That's why when you live in the present moment, you'll lose that nostalgic sentiment of overthinking any situation. Release and let go to flourish for a healthy balance between the two.

In conjunction with the book itself, "How to Overcome an Apocalyptic Events" some of the main characters' issues and problems could be similar to anyone's struggles throughout life itself. You'll be amazed at how similar it'll become…

ABOUT THE AUTHOR

Author Brandon LeMar Bass is a world-renowned best-selling author of multiple books. He's a worldwide inspirational guide who helps people. He raises the frequency, vibration, and magnetic energy of the planet and whoever he comes across. This is including you!

With his five-star rating, Brandon gives counseling advice on various topics through consultations. Brandon loves to reconnect people with their Higher Selves and become their greatest version! He's a true visionary, an innovator, a revolutionary, and a trendsetter.

As fitness mogul Brandon said: "Always remember, nothing can dim the light that shines from within. Seize the day and don't let anyone dim your sparkle! You're a uniquely beautiful being of light. Listen to your inner wisdom and don't worry if you encounter obstacles. As long as you listen to your intuition and remain faithful to your inner truth, you'll have nothing to worry about!"

What does he offer?

1On1 Sessions is where you can get in contact with him and schedule an appointment regarding specific or multiple topics!
https://calendly.com/brandonbass

Brandon runs his own successful multi black-owned businesses including content creation through YouTube (brandonbass99) https://linktr.ee/DoubleBYouTube #1 podcast in spirituality (Chilling With DoubleB) https://linktr.ee/DoubleBPodcast EYE AM CHOSEN clothing https://linktr.ee/EYEAMCHOSEN BLB Productions https://linktr.ee/blbproductions and his websites including https://linktr.ee/brandonbasswebsites

Brandon is a male high fashion model and an actor who goes by the musical artist name of Smooth Doubleb (Hot 100s Best New Artist) https://linktr.ee/DoubleBB

Some topics he covers (but aren't limited to) are spiritual teacher, mental health coach, therapist, holistic doctor, intuitive reader, and much more!

Brandon took the time, effort, and diligence to produce this book. If you could share this book with your friends, family, and your neighbors, he'll appreciate it.

Ready for more? Sign up for a meeting or consultation, and share this book via his link https://linktr.ee/smoothdoubleb

Visit Brandon on his social media platforms and connect with him!

Social media: https://linktr.ee/BrandonB

Services: https://linktr.ee/BrandonBass

QUOTE FROM A CLIENT

"Brandon has helped me grow spiritually, mentally, physically, emotionally, and financially. I simply contacted him to schedule a meeting and he was very responsive. His consultation sessions are so in-depth, and he was Intune with what I was going through. He just had that inner knowing about me and others. Once he taps into your frequency, then he'll begin to notice things that happened in your life. He also helped me heal my body with his hands after going through an abusive relationship. He created a safe space for me to express myself with zero judgment. I cried at the session, and he provided me with the comfort I deeply needed. This made me have a deeper connection with Brandon and he's been my spiritual teacher and therapist ever since. Brandon's heart is beautiful, just like his soul. When you look into his eyes, you can tell he's one of a kind. With all the vast options and services, he provides, you'll get all the clarity you need from any given topic. He developed and skilled his psychic and medium powers that'll help anyone on any path their traveling. I just love Brandon and what he puts out into the Universe. Whether that might be music, videos, podcasts, clothing, and of course his services. He's been there for me when I needed him the most and he never left my side. He's a real spiritualist who wouldn't judge your path and will shed light on your darkest of moments. He has motivated me to be open in relationships now, advancing my career and talents, and also reconnecting with my Higher Self. Thank you, Brandon, and I appreciate all you do for me and the planet!"

One of Brandon's clients. The name will be unknown for their privacy.

END COVER PAGE

This book is intended for anyone who's in a collapsing system because of their government officials. Anyone who's looking for answers, questioning reality, and/or having a spiritual awakening; this book is for you. This will help your ascension process and give you the necessary tools to help create your reality. You're the co-creator of your own reality, and it's time to reclaim your power. These characters in this book are relatable, so, it'll help your progression. What these characters go through and the issues they face are what people are going through right now. You're not in solitude, and you're enough. You're more than superfluous, and you have to feel that in your soul, spirit, heart, and mind to generate that energy from yourself. It's okay to be solivagant because that time alone is necessary.

This book is about a group of real people, real feelings, real emotions, going through multiple apocalyptic events that are occurring. We go through each character's past lives, childhood traumas, and what they experience before the events occur. You'll see that based on their childhood, karmic debt, and traumatic experiences affect their life decisions. Their decision-making is crucial during apocalyptic events because it's life or death. This book is more than apocalyptic events on a physical plane, but also from an internal plane as well. This book tells real stories and real problems of what people go through on a day-to-day basis. Connect deeply with the characters since most people have convergence dilemmas. This will make you feel for the characters and what they must go through internally and externally. On top of that, the characters must go through their disarray to survive. The main characters will have to team up because of what takes place throughout the story. Will jealousy and envy get in the way? Find out and see in How to Overcome Apocalyptic Events!

Brought to you by Brandon LeMar Bass (Author and Concept), Smooth DoubleB (Illustrator and Host), BLB Productions (Production), DoubleB Records (Press Release, Media Coverage, and Marketing), and EYE AM CHOSEN (Support and Management).

DoubleB Publishing, LLC (Publishing)

Made in United States
Orlando, FL
17 February 2023